At the Vice President's p
is approached by Matthev
who tells Mike he knows of a political scan~
to Watergate but refuses to tell Mike what it is. Super
model Johnny Jones comes home to his Greenwich Village
apartment to find a corpse strangled with a jockstrap. The
victim is Matthew Bokowski. Mike teams up with his
lover, tennis pro Jack Montgomery, and prick tease :NYPD
Lieutenant James Rocco to solve THE JOCKSTRAP
MURDER. Mike makes a play for Rocco and scores but
their sex party is shockingly interrupted. A senator, his son,
his son's lover and a blackmailing paparazzo join the trio
for the ride from New York, N.Y. to Washington, D.C.

Featuring a roll call of some of the best writers of gay erotica and mysteries today!

Derek Adams	Z. Allora	Maura Anderson
Simone Anderson	Victor J. Banis	Laura Baumbach
Helen Beattie	Ally Blue	J.P. Bowie
Barry Brennessel	Nowell Briscoe	Jade Buchanan
James Buchanan	TA Chase	Charlie Cochrane
Karenna Colcroft	Michael G. Cornelius	Jamie Craig
Ethan Day	Diana DeRicci	Vivien Dean
Taylor V. Donovan	S.J. Frost	Kimberly Gardner
Kaje Harper	Alex Ironrod	DC Juris
Jambrea Jo Jones	AC Katt	Thomas Kearnes
Sasha Keegan	Kiernan Kelly	K-lee Klein
Geoffrey Knight	Christopher Koehler	Matthew Lang
J.L. Langley	Vincent Lardo	Cameron Lawton
Anna Lee	Elizabeth Lister	Clare London
William Maltese	Z.A. Maxfield	Timothy McGivney
Kendall McKenna	AKM Miles	Robert Moore
Jet Mykles	N.J. Nielsen	Cherie Noel
Gregory L. Norris	Willa Okati	Erica Pike
Neil S. Plakcy	Rick R. Reed	AJ Rose
Rob Rosen	George Seaton	Riley Shane
Jardonn Smith	DH Starr	Richard Stevenson
Christopher Stone	Liz Strange	Marshall Thornton
Lex Valentine	Haley Walsh	Mia Watts
Lynley Wayne	Missy Welsh	Ryal Woods
Stevie Woods	Sara York	Lance Zarimba
Mark Zubro		

Check out titles, both available and forthcoming, at
www.mlrpress.com

THE JOCKSTRAP MURDER

VINCENT LARDO

mlrpress
www.mlrpress.com

Copyright 2014 by Vincent Lardo

Published by
MLR Press, LLC
3052 Gaines Waterport Rd.
Albion, NY 14411

Visit ManLoveRomance Press, LLC on the Internet:
www.mlrpress.com

Cover Art by Colin Doyle
Editing by Neil Plakcy

Print format: ISBN# 978-1-60820-917-0
ebook format also available

Issued 2014

Fashionable restaurants have long been a refuge for those who can afford to be fleeced for faux French cuisine and the privilege of seeing and being seen. These establishments, especially in New York, rise and fall with the consistency of madam's hemline. The current favorite, located on the Upper East Side a few steps off Madison Avenue, contained more seers than sights on this sweltering July afternoon.

Among those who had not fled to the Hamptons, Martha's Vineyard or Watch Hill, was Amanda Richards, self-proclaimed *First Lady of the Theater.* After perusing her menu, Amanda removed her glasses and rested her chin on the hand that held the black frames; it was a pose favored by the actress and could be seen on the playbill of her last hit, *Oh, Promise Me.* Her brown hair, parted on the left, fell in a cascade of soft waves to her shoulders. Her lips, unpainted and sensuous, smiled at her luncheon partner, Senator Sten Osgood Samuels.

Amanda was known for her liberal politics and the senator, an arch conservative, was known as a man who stood for family values and little else. But the politico was fortyish, good looking in a rugged, Midwest fashion and a widower, therefore possessing all the qualities Amanda demanded of a lover, should such an alliance follow this, their first date. If pressed on the subject, Amanda would light a cigarette, blow a stream of smoke into the air and coo, "But love, there's no such thing as a naked conservative and where it matters all men are *not* created equal."

Even on a slow day a Broadway leading lady and a Washington senator were scant competition for this afternoon's centerpiece, Jack Montgomery, the *enfant terrible* of the pro tennis circuit. The six-foot-two jock with the clean cut blond looks of Prince Charming and the temper of a spoiled two-year old was, to his delight, garnering all the attention of the star gazers. Having decided that he was more appealing in the flesh than he appeared on television, his loyal fans turned their attention to guessing who would occupy the empty chair opposite the tennis pro.

Would it be the titled lady who had rooted for Jack at Wimbledon and then tried to engage him in a private match that required balls but no net? The Hollywood producer who had offered Jack a million bucks for a five minute cameo role in the film version of last year's best-selling novel? Or would it be the CEO of the company that manufactured the tennis rackets Jack Montgomery endorsed and often flung to the ground before an audience of millions when it, not the player, failed to ace an opponent's volley?

The polite buzz along the banquettes rose by an octave when a smiling captain led Mike Gavin, the celebrity syndicated columnist, into the refrigerated room and to the chair in question.

"You're late," Jack said by way of greeting, but his boyish grin belied the rebuke.

"The town is gridlocked," Mike answered, sitting.

"From Sixty-Sixth Street? You could have walked."

"I did," Mike said.

"Cute, Gavin, cute."

"A Campari and soda, Alain." Mike addressed the captain who was still hovering about, pretending not to be listening. "And more of the same for Mr. Montgomery, whatever it may be."

"Carrot juice," Jack stated.

Mike winced. "I'd rather die young of cirrhosis."

"It's too late, Mike."

"It's never too late to die of cirrhosis," Mike countered.

"Too late to die young."

"Really? I don't think thirty – thirtyish, is so old."

"From where you're sitting you can touch forty."

"From where I'm sitting I can see Amanda Richards having lunch with Sten Samuels and that's more frightening than middle-age or cirrhosis."

The captain arrived with their drinks and looked down at them like an anxious nanny. "We'll call you when we're ready," Mike said, and Alain once again made a leisurely retreat.

"Here's to Wimbledon" Jack said, raising his glass.

"You lost, remember?"

"I was toasting the venue of our meeting."

To be precise, Mike and Jack had met, casually, in New York. It was at a fundraiser for *Sun an' Surf*, a charity that sent pre-teen boys from the proverbial sidewalks of New York to summer camp. Mike had plugged the affair as a favor to his friend, Commissioner Andrew Brandt of the NYPD who was the charity's main sponsor. Jack Montgomery was the keynote speaker and drawing card.

When Brandt introduced them, the columnist and the tennis pro held their firm handshake and mutual gaze perhaps a moment too long – or just long enough to establish them as members of the same fraternity. How? Some called it gaydar. Mike called it a hell of a lot of fun.

Mike flew to London for the matches on something of a busman's holiday and renewed the acquaintance, allowing him to report on the event more as an insider than an observer. Mike's daily dispatches won a wide audience and accolades from his colleagues, including seasoned sports writers. Romance wasn't on the agenda but who, Mike admitted as he succumbed, could resist the charms of Jack Montgomery? What Mike hadn't counted on was the affair continuing on this side of the Atlantic. Underestimating Jack's charms and overrating his resistance had conspired to allow Jack to move into Mike's East Sixty-Sixth Street co-op.

The spacious one bedroom flat in a landmark New York dwelling was Mike's sanctuary. The place where he could turn off his cell phone, unplug his land line, open a bottle of whatever appealed at the moment, put a Chris Conner ballad on the machine (retro chic vinyl only) and retreat from a world he found more venomous in its taking than it was generous in its giving. Why had he allowed this brash young man to cross the moat? Because the brashness was nothing more than a cover for Jack Montgomery's insecurity. An insecurity that came off as pompous in public and turned him into a lamb in the bedroom. In the most competitive of professions, Jack had made it to the top. He was a survivor and Mike liked that. Mike also liked tempering the anger and cradling the vulnerability. Never one to skirt an issue, Mike enjoyed having one of the most desirable jocks in the country at his beck and call and in his bed. Mike Gavin, defender of life, liberty and the pursuit of happiness, was not above the sin of pride.

"Wimbledon was fun," Mike conceded.

"Fun? Is that all you can say? Shit, Gavin, I gave up a princess for you."

"Her mother is a princess, Jack. Her father was a commoner, making her a Lady with a capital L."

"If she's a Lady, I'm the Prince of Wales."

"It's rumored that the Lady is going to be in New York next weekend."

"Too bad we'll be in Washington."

"The only place hotter than New York in July is Washington," Mike protested.

"Be a sport, Mike. AIDS research benefits from the matches and we're top heavy with celebrities opposite pros. Mike Gavin will lend the event prestige."

Mike shrugged. "Which means box office sales are slow, as they say in the trade."

"Which means everyone's in the Hamptons but they'll come out of the woodwork if they know Mike Gavin will be there, plugging them in print. We can take the Metro down instead of flying. Three relaxing hours in the club car and I've been invited – Mike, are you listening?"

"With you shouting, it's hard not to."

"Then why aren't you looking at me?"

"Sorry," Mike said. "I'm still not over the shock of seeing Amanda breaking bread with Captain America."

Jack turned to look at the couple who were seated on the opposite side of the room and now being served their lunch. "Where did he get a name like Sten?" Jack wondered aloud as their waiter withdrew, allowing Amanda to see them staring and respond with a discreet wave and smile. The senator acknowledged the two men with a patronizing nod.

Mike returned the greeting with a slight bow of his head aimed purposely at Amanda. "I guess he was named after the British assault weapon," was Mike's answer. "I know for a fact he gets more money from the National Rifle Association than any senator on the hill. But what's he doing with Amanda Richards? The guy is a con artist and poor Amanda, especially if she's smitten, won't know she's been had until she reads about it in my column."

"Mandy looks gorgeous," Jack said. Wearing a black Chanel suit and white silk blouse, with a hint of blush on her prominent cheek bones and a gold barrette in her hair, Amanda Richards would have to try very hard not to look gorgeous and she'd still fail.

'If she heard you call her Mandy," Mike cautioned, "she would remove a piece of your anatomy and as a result you would be able to compete in the women's finals at Forest Hills next week."

"Speaking of tennis…" Jack tried again but was interrupted by Alain who approached their table and began, with determination, to recite the day's specials. His captive audience listened politely and then ordered their lunch without consulting the menu, a sign of their regular patronage.

"I'll be there," Mike announced, picking up his glass and sipping the last of his Campari.

The win was too easy. Jack had learned to beware opponents who looked painfully beatable because looks can be painfully deceiving. He immediately went on the offensive. "You were going to come all along but like watching me beg."

The accusation wasn't entirely untrue but Mike answered with a more concrete reason for his decision to brave Washington in July. "I had no intention of coming until I got a call from the White House. The Vice President invited me to dinner Saturday night."

"He invited all of us to dinner," Jack boasted.

"All? Us? What are you talking about?"

"Look Mike," Jack began, "don't blow your top and remember it's for a worthy cause."

"Can the rhetoric, Montgomery, and spit it out."

"I signed you up as my opponent in the opening match."

Mike stared at his tablemate as if looking for signs of insanity in the brilliant blue eyes. "You're kidding?" It was more a plea than a question.

Jack shook his head as he inched his chair away from the table as if preparing to flee should violence erupt but all Mike could manage was, "Jesus H. Christ, Montgomery!"

Mike Gavin, like most Homo sapiens, had often speculated as to what he would do if he were cast in the role of Faust. Anything he wanted, no restrictions in the fine print, in return for selling his soul to the guy with the horns, tail and basket full of goodies. The fact that he never came up with anything worth the forfeit was a testimony to his charmed life.

A crown of golden brown hair that showed no signs of abdicating, a classically handsome face and square jaw that bespoke honesty and forbearance had helped Mike earn a good living as a male model that paid his way through the Columbia School of Journalism. A good inch over six feet, lean and trim, he was still the perfect mold for a size forty-long suit of clothes. His green eyes had once looked upon the world with affection but years of reporting on the foibles and fancies of modern man had seasoned the sublime with a dash of amusement and a good dose of cynicism.

He began his career as a cub reporter for the *Morning News* in the crime division, chasing ambulances, police cars and fire engines. When the paper's society editor dropped dead from too many martini lunches, Mike got the job because no one else wanted it. The 'society' Mike touted could be found in the pages of the Social Register, Who's Who and telephone directories in every city, town and village of the U.S of A.

In a year, *Mike Gavin's New York* column was the pride of the *Morning News* and read in kitchens, subways, board rooms and the Oval Office. He was loved, hated, feared and respected, everything a working journalist should be. When the column went into syndication, Mike's income soared. He rejected television offers, mostly as anchor on news shows, because he believed television news was more entertaining than informative, upholding the political beliefs of the sponsor rather than the constitution of the United States.

So, how could Mephistopheles tempt Mike Gavin? Under a cloudless sky, a relentless sun and before a thousand mortals in the flesh and countless others in front of television screens, Mike would gladly barter his soul in return for beating the bejesus out of Jack Montgomery on the tennis court.

TWO

Mephistopheles did not appear with contract and ball point pen and Mike Gavin was routed, humiliatingly, by Jack Montgomery.

A more than competent player, Mike entered the match with a congenial competitive spirit he felt the occasion warranted, but Junior had Daddy by the short hairs before a room full of company and he wasn't going to let go until Daddy yelled OUCH! Jack's opening serve emulated the legendary speeding bullet. On one of the few occasions Mike responded, Jack answered with the precision of a robot, placing the ball wherever Mike wasn't.

The louder the crowd roared, the more vicious Jack became. Fueled by adulation, buttressed by his image pulsating across cyberspace, Jack Montgomery was a man possessed. "Look world. The tennis racket is mightier than the pen."

By the grace of God, or his counterpart, the match finally ended. Mike almost walked off the court without performing the traditional handshake across the net routine but only the slightest motion of his body betrayed this intent. Smiling, sweating and swearing, Mike jogged to the net and grasped Jack's outstretched hand. The crowd applauded.

"When we get back to New York, Montgomery, pack your bags and get your ass out of my apartment."

Still holding Mike's hand, Jack waved to his fans, saying, "I'll tell the world you're a sore loser, Gavin."

Mike imitated Jack's imperious salute to the grandstand. "And I'll tell the world that Jack Montgomery has a two inch dick and a pair of balls the size of chick peas."

They walked off the court to a standing ovation, smiling and waving at the television cameras as the sportscaster proclaimed, "It was all for a good cause and these guys are buddies when they're not making like David and Goliath, though who is which is hard to say – and here comes Richard Gere and John McEnroe…"

Mike avoided Jack in the locker room which was easy to do thanks to an invasion of local reporters who were more interested in the pro than the scribe. Mike was even more irked when Jack began strutting around in the nude, as if inviting the press to bear witness to the contrary should Mike Gavin cast disparaging remarks regarding Jack's equipment that was far in excess of two inches and bounced proudly over two kiwis.

Mike showered, dressed and fled with the efficiency of a drill sergeant.

The pros had been domiciled at the Hilton so Mike had opted to stay at the Hay-Adams. He would never purposely try to hide or deny his relationship with Jack, but nor would he flaunt it. Discretion, he believed, was the better part of valor, an aphorism Mike was happy to subscribe to after his public slaughter by Jack Montgomery. Being a safe distance from his nemesis precluded a vis-à-vis confrontation which could deal a death blow to a romance that was fragile, albeit the couple involved were masculine, muscular and macho.

Mike ordered a Kir from room service, stripped down to his jockeys and fell into an easy chair, resting his long, aching legs on an ottoman. Indulgence abated the fury and the Kir put him in a contemplative mood. Was he being too hard on Jack? A pompous ass? A spoil sport? Was he looking for an excuse to get Jack out of his life? Afraid to let anyone get too close?

Recalling Jack flashing an entire press corps had Mike grinning. After the few weeks Jack had been living with him Mike had to admit, reluctantly, that the brat was irresistible. This, and the Kir, led to thoughts Mike did not want to surrender to so he gave the bulge in the jockey pouch a pat and a promise, stood up and began to dress for the main event. Donning a pair of white flannels and Polo's double breasted blue blazer he glanced in the dresser mirror and emoted, "Tennis, anyone?"

The venue for the Veep's reception was Blair House, the President's official state guest house located on Pennsylvania

Avenue, a short distance from the White House. Jack had said the dinner party was strictly for the noblesse, a word Jack had picked up in England (courtesy of the princess' daughter perhaps). Jack tended to use new words, ad nauseam, until a newer one came his way. To date, no replacement had found its way into that perfectly shaped cranium. This evening the noblesse of Washington appeared to encompass a cast of hundreds, most of whom tread the parquet warily because political gatherings were ubiquitous with land mines.

The reception rooms buzzed with a lot of very small talk. *Less Said, Soonest Mended* was Washington's eleventh commandment. The noblesse was being offered a buffet spread, mostly finger food that Mike avoided, hence the flat belly but, as one would expect at a political gala, the bar was well stocked. Mike ordered a bourbon and branch water and smiled indulgently when the bartender handed him the drink along with a sympathetic, "Nice show, Mr. Gavin." It wasn't a show and it wasn't nice but this was the town where political correctness was invented as a substitute for the truth.

There was a crowd around the Vice President so Mike delayed paying his respects and looked for a quiet corner where he could sip his drink and lick his wounds. Then he spotted Jack who was wearing white flannels and Polo's double breasted blue blazer. Great! The embarrassment of appearing to have aped Jack paled when he noted that Jack was charming Oprah Winfrey. Mike hoped, with little optimism, that Jack wasn't setting himself up for an Oprah interview. The thought had him tossing back his bourbon until the rocks chilled his teeth. He headed to the bar for a refill only to be accosted by one of the most recognizable voices in America. "Michael, love," Amanda Richards purred, turning her cheek for a peck which Mike dutifully administered. "You looked like the tail end of a dancing horse routine on that court."

"Thanks, lady."

"I'll have whatever Mr. Gavin is having," she ordered, setting up a series of whispers ("*I told you that's who he is*") from those who had paused to gaze at the actress while pretending not to notice her or Mike.

"Really," Amanda scolded, "It was all in fun and for a good cause."

"No cause is that good." Mike took their drinks from the bartender and handed one to Amanda.

"I was speaking of romance, not charity, Michael."

Seeing they had acquired an audience, Mike took Amanda's arm and led her away from the gawkers. She, to be sure, thrived on being the center of attention, be it on the stage or in a crowded room. Mike Gavin did not. As they retreated the crowd offered them the same courtesy the Red Sea had shown Moses.

They stopped before a fireplace and struck a pose under an ornate painting of George Washington. Amanda's lavender Hermes blouse hung loosely over slim hips covered in a straight, black ankle length skirt. A gold chain necklace and a pair of tiny gold earrings were all that adorned the outfit. Her brown hair glowed as did her skin that, as always, was covered with only a light dusting of powder and the slightest hint of color blended into cheeks and lips.

"Romance," Mike said, picking up the thread of their conversation, "is not exactly your long suit. Not one marriage and not one scandalous divorce. You're a disgrace to your profession."

"My actor suitors have egos the size of a hippo's behind," Amanda explained. "Coupled with mine, there isn't a house in the world big enough to contain the two of us in harmony. We would constantly be competing for space in front of the bathroom mirror. Now let's gossip like responsible adults. Who's fucking whom and why? I've been in the hinterlands with *Oh, Promise Me* for months and months."

"I hear you can run forever with that one, Amanda."

"Oh, promise me that ain't so," she laughed. "Tell me all about the adorable boy you brought home from England."

Mike noted the adorable boy was still one-on-one with Oprah as he fired away at Amanda. "I did not bring him back from England. He's twenty-four and old enough to travel on his own as well as vote, drink and consent to whatever needs consenting. Ask me no questions regarding Jack Montgomery and I'll ask you no questions about your Italian count."

"Beautiful Marcello," she sighed. "He went back to his Italian contessa. They all do, you know."

"All?" Mike questioned. "Italians in particular or men in general?"

"Italians in particular and my men in general," she conceded. "Actors, counts, politicians," she continued as if ticking off a shopping list. "I'm a romantic, not a fool. I want a human being for a mate, not a household word."

"So why were you lunching with a household word the other day?" Mike teased. He enjoyed sparring verbally with the actress because their subject matter, be it love, sex or show business, was so innocuous. All the whispers and shouting and headlines wouldn't amount to a yawn twenty-four hours after the fact. Washington gossip, though just as droll, too often had dire consequences, seasoning the pleasure with foreboding. Sten Samuels tended to bring on the latter.

"In your column you reported my lunch date with the senator and called us the odd couple. Really, Michael, how crass."

"Enlighten me," Mike baited, "and I may print a retraction."

"Well," Amanda began, "it was the strangest thing. I got a call from one of the senator's people – that's what they call secretaries in this town, people, which of course they are – he told me the senator wanted to see me regarding my position as a committee member for the Endowment."

"The National Endowment for the Arts?" Mike was nonplussed. "His only interest in the Endowment is to cut it to pennies if he can't muster the votes to kill it entirely."

"That's what I always thought," Amanda said. "But what we discussed was how the money could be distributed more equitably, to the most talented in the most need was how he put it, and what area did I think could benefit most from an increase in the Endowment."

Mike shook his head in disbelief. "Increase my eye. He's up to no good, Amanda."

"Give him a chance, Michael. Perhaps he's discovered art."

"Art to Sten Samuels is a watercolor of a flower and Whistler's Mother. And where did he ever get a name like Sten?"

With a coy smile, Amanda said, "In the crossword puzzles it's always a British gun. Do you think…"

"You have a dirty mind, Amanda."

"My press agent calls it an acerbic wit."

"Is Samuels here tonight?" Mike asked.

"No," Amanda assured him. "He and the Vice President are on opposite sides of the aisle and avoid each other in public. In private they're quite chummy."

"Politics make strange bedfellows," Mike said.

"That's what I was thinking," Amanda agreed.

"It's a figure of speech, Amanda."

"Oh?" She sounded disappointed.

"Keep me posted on your meetings with the Gun," Mike requested.

"I'll do that and even introduce you to his son." Amanda held out her hand in a welcoming gesture and Mike turned to see a boy, just out of his teen years, approaching. "The senator was kind enough to ask me to share his box for the matches this afternoon. When I got there I found this delightful young man making excuses for his father's absence. Timothy Samuels meet Mike Gavin."

Timothy Samuels was as tall as Mike with the slim, graceful body of a swimmer or runner beneath a head of brown/blond hair, blue eyes and could be labeled attractive rather than handsome. His handshake was firm, his voice surprisingly deep and his poise the result of a lifetime spent in the public eye.

"I'm an avid reader of Mike Gavin," he said, his speech a pleasant blend of Des Moines and Groton.

"I'm sure your father isn't." Mike's tone was more jocular than accusing.

"Oh, but he is," Tim insisted. "How else could he keep up with all the beautiful people like Amanda Richards?"

Amanda beamed with joy but Mike detected a nuance of contempt in the well-modulated young voice. Could it be that Amanda Richards wasn't the first of his father's lady friends the boy had been forced to squire? Was this soft-spoken preppie a bit naïve or a bitch? Mike opted to reserve judgment.

"And I admire what you did this afternoon, Mr. Gavin. I mean going up against Jack Montgomery. I'd rather oppose legalized abortion at a feminist rally."

"So would I," Mike agreed. "But I wasn't given the choice. Jack volunteered my services."

"I've heard that you two are great friends," Tim said, "and I trust Jack Montgomery is more accommodating in private than before a stadium full of adoring fans."

A bitch, Mike decided. A chip off the old block, indeed. Never make a direct statement when insinuation will suffice. Mike vented his frustration by gulping his bourbon and branch water.

Amanda, looking at Tim Samuels as if he were the prodigal son returned to home and hearth, joined the conversation by stating, "Timothy is a friend of Bradley Turner." Knowing that Bradley Turner, the novice director, was a favorite of Mike Gavin's, she seemed to imply that Mike, by de facto reasoning, would befriend Tim Samuels.

"We were at Groton together," Tim quickly clarified the connection. "I'm interested in the theater, the production end, and Brad's working on a property I think has great potential." Before Mike could reply, Tim turned to Amanda and said, "I promised friends I'd introduce you to them before they leave – that is if you don't mind…"

"I'd be delighted." Amanda prepared to play the great lady receiving the masses by bowing a farewell to Mike and taking Tim's arm. With a nod from Tim they left Mike with the distinct feeling that Tim Samuels was not in the least eager to discuss his relationship with Brad Turner. Curious?

First Samuels the elder calls Amanda Richards on what Mike felt certain was a pretext for a reason or reasons unknown. Next, he sets up a meeting with Amanda and his son. On both occasions, Mike Gavin is present. Accident or planned coincidence?

True, Sten Samuels could have had a change of heart regarding funding for the arts and he could have been legitimately unable to occupy his box at the matches today. Still, Mike found it all very disquieting, like the proverbial calm before the storm. In fact, the more he thought about it, the more bizarre it seemed.

A young man Mike recognized as one in the group watching him and Amanda and Tim Samuels chatting beneath the portrait of the founding father, broke from the others and approached Mike.

"Mr. Gavin?"

Looking at the self-stick paper tag on the man's jacket lapel that identified him as a member of the working press, Mike quickly said, "If you want to know anything about my match with Jack Montgomery, ask Jack Montgomery, if you can tear him away from Oprah. Now, excuse me."

The young man shook his head. "I just wanted to tell you how much I admire you, sir. You're the reason I decided to make the Fourth Estate my career."

Mike delayed his exit, telling himself he was a sucker and at the same time extending his hand to the reporter. His admirer shook the offered hand vigorously. "Matthew Burke," he introduced himself, pumping Mike's arm. "That's the name on my byline. On my birth certificate it's spelled Bokowski."

Matthew Bokowski had dark eyes and a small nose dotted

with freckles that reminded Mike of a minuscule ski slope. "I was hoping my star struck friend could be here tonight," Matthew went on, "I was going to smuggle him in so he could ogle all the celebrities but he couldn't make it. He's an intern at Bethesda Medical and I think he's going to make a great doctor."

The speech, clearly prepared in advance, sounded insipid when spoken aloud. An embarrassing silence followed. Mike waited until he was certain the lad had finished reciting his presentation which may have included his sexual orientation before asking, "Who are you with?" Without his reading glasses Mike couldn't make out the paper's name in small print below the reporter's name.

It was a Baltimore paper Mike had never heard of but pretended he had. "I do sports, obits, weddings and bar mitzvahs," Matthew recited his job description.

Mike responded with his stock reply. "I began chasing ambulances and police cars."

"Can I ask you something?" The young man suddenly blurted.

"You just did," Mike answered.

The mild rebuke went unnoticed, so intent was Matthew on learning what, presumably, only Mike Gavin could tell him. Resigned, Mike nodded his acquiescence.

"If you knew something," Matthew began, then paused, either for effect or in search of the right words. "...knew something that would make headlines – something bigger than Watergate – but to expose it would be unethical, what would you do?"

Here, of course, was the reason the young man had approached Mike, admiration be damned. It wasn't a new question for Mike so he gave it an old answer. "Does freedom of speech give me the right to yell FIRE in a crowded theater just for the fun of it?" Matthew's obvious disappointment prompted Mike to relent. "Look, son, you posed a theoretical question and I responded in kind. There are rules but rules can be broken if the situation warrants it. And *ethical* is as ambiguous a description as pornography. Both are often in the eye of the beholder. Can you give me a concrete example?"

"No, sir."

"Then I can't give you a more concrete answer, now if you'll excuse me, I think the Vice President is beckoning." Mike tried to make a polite retreat but the look of despair he got from Matthew Burke, nee Bokowski, said he had failed.

That look would haunt Mike Gavin for the rest of his life.

THREE

A cold autumn rain pelted the north windows in a vain attempt to rouse the occupants of the warm room from their lethargy. It was a good morning to be indoors, wrapped in a cashmere robe, sipping from a mug of steaming coffee and listening to Johnny Mathis lamenting the fact that he was *99 Miles From L.A.* The fireplace held the cold remains of last night's conflagration and in spite of Johnny's woeful lyrics, the memory of the warmth in which it had enveloped two naked bodies still glowed in their hearts if not in the hearth.

Mike sat in a cozy club chair, leafing through a magazine. Jack lay prone on a couch, his head propped up by a pillow and his robe dangerously parted to reveal a pair of legs familiar to millions, but seldom seen in repose. "I feel I've lived here all my life," Jack confided to the ceiling.

"You adapt easily," Mike said without raising his head from the magazine on his lap. "I haven't had a closet to call my own since you decided to make my home – uninvited – your New York headquarters." After six months, Mike still chose to consider this living arrangement temporary and had convinced himself that Jack's frequent trips to honor commitments was the only reason it had survived this long. The pro tennis circuit was an active and far flung enterprise, affording Mike a respite from this dicey romance.

Still addressing the ceiling, Jack replied, "I had a closet at the Waldorf bigger than our bedroom."

Our bedroom? This diverted Mike's attention from the magazine. His New York pad was his home and not to be criticized, especially by an ungrateful scamp who thought he could charm the world with a smile, a wiggle of his uptight ass and a forward thrust of his masculine *package*. Well, perhaps he could, Mike conceded with a sigh, however this did not give him the right to demean Mike's home.

The co-op was the first big investment Mike had made when the column went into syndication and he could afford to indulge himself. It was sacrosanct and not to be demeaned, even in jest. Built at the start of the last century, the duplex apartments were more commodious than most suburban houses. Several had been downsized after the market plummeted in '29 and sold to create ready cash for the owners as opposed to jumping out the window. Mike's living room (once the drawing room), bedroom (once the library) and kitchen (once the butler's pantry) was one of the few smaller flats in the prestigious dwelling.

The ceilings were high, the walls plaster, the bath lavish, the doormen polite, the concierge accommodating and the handy man actually knew how to fix a leaky faucet. If closet space was less than generous, Mike had it on good authority that the tenants of Buckingham Palace enjoyed a similar complaint.

"It's my bedroom," Mike reminded his guest, "and if you feel cramped why don't you go back to the Waldorf?"

"Because I like your coffee."

"I'm glad because it's my only culinary expertise and I thought jocks breakfasted like elephants."

"God, no, Gavin. Light and healthy is the jock recipe."

"Juice and coffee is light but surely not healthy."

"I intend to make up the deficiency at lunch. Would you believe *Chez Louis?*"

Jack was in a competitive profession and too often approached life as if an invisible net stood between him and the rest of the world. Thanks to Mike's epicurean palate and legion of famous acquaintances, Jack was never happier than when he could score points by dropping a celebrated name or place.

"Who invited you to *Chez Louis?*" Mike asked, feigning interest.

"Freddy Fine," Jack spoke the name as if it were a national treasure.

"The underwear wunderkind of Seventh Avenue," was Mike's

take on Freddy Fine.

"His money is green and my agent tells me he's ready to part with a big hunk of it for my autograph on the dotted line."

"Make sure you autograph only the dotted line." Mike referred to an incident in London when Jack invited a prince of the blood to his hotel suite where they spent the night. When reporters greeted them exiting the hotel next morning, Jack told them he was autographing tennis balls for the prince to auction at his charity bazaar. The evening papers headlined, "JACK MONTGOMERY AUTOGRAPHS PRINCE'S BALLS IN HOTEL SUITE."

With the help of pop-fashion photography Ken Wallace and model Johnny Jones, Freddy Fine had become a millionaire and a household word. In the rag trade, the trio was cynically referred to as The Holy Trinity. It began with a full page photo of Johnny Jones in Freddy's briefs with the jockey pouch *au natural*, not air brushed and castrated as all men's underwear ads appeared at the time. As photographed by Ken Wallace, Johnny's basket full of goodies was an instant hit and could currently be seen on a billboard some sixty feet high over Times Square.

Johnny was now rehearsing for an off-Broadway show, directed by Mike's friend, Bradley Turner. Mike asked "Are you going to replace Johnny Jones or let it all hang out in Freddy's boxers?"

"A new line of jeans," Jack told him as if it were already fodder for an item in *G.Q.* "Freddy thinks I have the face and body to move them."

Mike eyed the body languishing on his couch, the robe now a millimeter from indecent exposure and conceded that Jack Montgomery could not only move jeans but compel a nun to rethink her vocation. "You should be jotting this all down for your next column," he heard Jack say.

"I'm not a gossip columnist," Mike reminded him.

"You could have fooled me."

Mike tossed his magazine across the room but the missile

fell short of its target. Reaching for it, Jack rolled off the couch with a resounding thud. "When you finish lunching at *Chez Louis*, check in at the Waldorf. Your wardrobe will be waiting for you in the lobby."

"Fine way to treat a guy who just gave you a ski lodge in Aspen," Jack lectured from the floor, the blue robe now exposing more than it concealed. As if executing a graceful lob, Jack swooped up the magazine and placed it over his neatly circumcised dick. Mike laughed. The magazine cover was a full face photo of Sten Samuels whose visage was now cheek by jowl with Jack's kosher weenie.

"You bought yourself a house in Aspen and invited me there for two weeks at the tail end of the season."

"January is the height of the season," Jack amended, "and the house is next door to Bobby Redford."

"Freddy Fine, Bobby Redford – for a tennis player you talk like a hairdresser."

"My own house," Jack gushed, as he raised himself to a sitting position, thereby removing the senator from his perch. Ignoring Mike's quip Jack leaned back on the couch and began to extol the blessings that came with home ownership. "Not a place that gets disinfected when I leave, but a home that holds my gear as well as my aroma which, I've been told, ain't bad. A place to feel sad about leaving and happy to come back to." Mike knew from experience that the neophyte homesteader was apt to go on relentlessly and the theme wasn't one Mike cared to pursue.

FOUR

Jack's gift had been more than an invitation to Aspen. He had presented Mike, gift wrapped no less, with a key to the new ski lodge. Never subtle, Jack's gesture was as obvious as a ring. Mike imagined the key attached to a leash and words like rein and tether popped into his head. Hoping to avoid a confrontation, Mike diplomatically accepted the offering as part of the package for his planned two-week visit after the New Year.

Diplomacy was lost on Jack Montgomery and confrontations were anathema to the tennis star. He had responded with a loud, "It's not a fucking B and B, damn it, it's our house." With that as his curtain speech he had stormed out of the apartment with the word OUR reverberating in his wake. Mike had not seen him again for two days after the gift wrapped presentation had turned into a fracas that bordered on the comic.

The puppy had returned the night before with his tail between his legs and his blue eyes pleading forgiveness. Mike did not ask where his erstwhile roommate had been because it was none of his business. However, he did notice that Jack was clean shaven and as meticulously groomed as a child prodigy on his way to a recital. Unrequited love had not driven the athlete to a lost weekend of debauchery and despair. No doubt there were probably hundreds of palatial establishments in New York that would deem it an honor to take Jack in on a moment's notice. Mike found the thought as annoying as a speck of dirt in his eye and this annoyed him more than the thought.

Mike, too, had several nests he could bed down in on short notice including the penthouse apartment of a film star who had once played a tennis pro in a tantalizing murder mystery. Mike decided to spend the night any place but his bedroom with Jack, even if it meant crashing at the YMCA.

Mike stirred up a batch of martinis and suggested going out to dinner. Jack lit a fire but failed to lower the heat, necessitating the removal of several layers of clothing. When Freddy Fine's briefs fell to his ankles, Jack was lit from behind by the fragrant wood fire, gently palming his dick. Watching, Mike put down his martini, unzipped the paddock, freeing the stallion already unsheathed for the sport.

Dinner was forgotten. The YMCA was forgotten. The house in Aspen was not mentioned and Jack Montgomery won the match, Love-Game.

The next morning, either by design or accident, the ski lodge had surfaced. "You weren't raised in an orphanage," Mike said, hoping to circumvent yet another altercation over Jack's dream of domestic bliss.

"Worse," Jack complained. "I was raised on a cross country touring bus. You know my mother died when I was fourteen." He wiggled his toes as he spoke, staring at them. "My dad was the original merry widower who didn't stay single for long. My new stepmom was twenty-two. I think dad was afraid people would think she was my sister. About that time my gym teacher – that was their title ten years ago in Ohio and they coached everything from football to ping-pong – thought I had a better than average talent for tennis and talked my father into grooming me for the juvenile circuit.

"It didn't take much talking. I was given a private coach who perfected my serve if not my temper, and when I was the best I could be I was rewarded with a one-way ticket on the outward bound and a home life that had all the consistency of a floating crap game."

Mike knew that Jack had been playing professionally since he was a teenager and that he had a father and stepmother in Ohio. However, this was the first time he heard those facts turned into a scenario that had all the elements of a child abuse drama. Jack was either trying to arouse Mike's sympathy or rehearsing for his Oprah Winfrey one-on-one.

"You made it to the top," Mike reminded him. "Hotels with big closets and a movie star in your backyard."

"It's not enough, Mike."

"Nothing is. When you realize that and learn to live with it you'll have gone from fourteen to twenty-four in one giant step. Enjoy the moment, Jack, it's all we have."

"Is that why you won't make a commitment?"

"It's why I won't even talk about a commitment," Mike said, trying not to make it sound like a reprimand. "Contracts set limits. I prefer to soar when and where I can."

"There's plenty of room to soar in Colorado," Jack countered, placing the ball squarely in Mike's court.

Mike laughed at his ill-timed metaphor. "When you lead with your chin what else can you expect but a kick in the kimono. Don't you ever give up, Montgomery?"

"You don't get hotel rooms with big closets and movie stars in your backyard by giving up. My old coach always preached persistence is the name of the game."

"He was talking about tennis."

"He was talking about life." Jack rose with the ease and grace of a bird winging from ground to tree top. He approached Mike, placed his hands on the sitting man's shoulders and bending so that his lips grazed Mike's ear, he whispered, "Come to Aspen and we'll soar. No commitments. No rings. No strings. I promise."

Mike's hand tugged on the cord of Jack's robe but before the curtain parted the land phone in his bedroom rang. "Let the machine get it," Jack said, his strong grip holding Mike fast to the chair.

"I can't ignore it," Mike said, gently extricating himself from Jack's hold.

Mike's cell phone was his link to the *Morning News* and the myriad people, businesses and places he was wired to, literally and figuratively.

The land phone on the desk in his bedroom was black and unlisted, its number known to no more than thirteen people; his publisher, his editor and ten friends. Lucky thirteen came with the job title White House Press Secretary.

Mike picked up on the third ring and Bradley Turner's somber voice announced that this was not a social call. "Brad? What's wrong?"

"They've arrested Johnny Jones – for murder."

"What?"

"Haven't you seen a paper?"

Mike glanced at the desk clock. It was past noon. How time flies when you're having fun. The *Morning News* was probably waiting to be picked up outside his door. With a twinge of guilt he told Brad that he had been working all morning. Behind him, Jack snickered loud enough for the caller to hear. "Is Jack there?" Brad asked.

Not even murder could abate the tug of war between the tennis star and the society boy turned director with Mike Gavin being the object of the feud. The answer to Brad's query was obvious so Mike ignored it and asked, "Who's the victim?" wondering if the Holy Trinity had been reduced to a twosome.

"No one knows," Brad exclaimed. "At least that's what the papers are saying."

"Johnny must know, unless he gets off snuffing strangers." Mike was thinking that Johnny's path to stardom made him a prime target for blackmail.

"If he knows, he's not telling," Brad said. "But he couldn't have done it. He was…"

"Hold on, Brad," Mike cut in palming the phone's mouthpiece. He turned to Jack and explained, "It's Brad Turner. Johnny Jones was arrested. Murder. See if the coffee is still hot and get me a cup. If it's not, heat it." Once again talking into the phone he continued, "Brad? I'm here. Calm down and tell me everything you know. From the beginning."

He heard Brad sigh, "I am calm, Mike, and I know as much as you will when you read your paper. Johnny was at the theater all day, rehearsing, until about ten last night. I, and the rest of the cast and crew, can vouch for that. When he got home he found a body on his bed. A man. The guy was strangled with a jockstrap. A Freddy Fine jockstrap."

The headline boys will have a field day with this one, Mike was thinking as Brad described the scene. Didn't the queen of burlesque, Gypsy Rose Lee, pen a mystery called *The G-String Murders*? In this new millennium of sexual equality the murderer was giving equal time to the male fig leaf. A depraved bastard with a sense of humor.

"I assume it's only Johnny's word that the guy wearing the jockstrap a tad too high was dead when Johnny arrived home."

"Of course," Brad cried, "which makes the time of death paramount."

"Which makes the time of death Johnny's one-way ticket to freedom or the electric chair."

"That's ghoulish, Mike."

"Sorry. It's a throwback to my crime reporting days." A steaming mug of black coffee was placed under Mike's nose. The aroma brought on a moment's craving for a cigarette, a vice Mike had given up years ago. "What time did Johnny get to the theater and did he leave and come back before you broke for the night?" He blew on his coffee to cool it, took a sip and scalded his tongue.

"We began at noon," Brad said, "and worked through till ten. Johnny is not a quick study. Sure he left and came back. We broke for supper but I can't say exactly when or what time everyone returned. Christ, I've got the entire cast and crew to worry about."

"Who called the police? Johnny?"

"Right. They took him in for questioning. They didn't exactly arrest him, Mike. Not yet, anyway."

"Have you talked to him?"

"No. Either he's not in the Grove Street apartment or he's turned off his cell."

"Any comment from Freddy Fine or his PR people?"

"No," Brad told him. "Too soon, I imagine. It happened late last night so Freddy's team must be meeting as we speak. I haven't looked at the television but they couldn't add anything to what the morning papers are saying which is everything I told you. Mike, can you help?"

"Me? I'm a writer, not a lawyer."

"It's my first show, Mike, and the angels put up the money because I got Johnny Jones to make his debut as an actor. He's the drawing card and now he's a murder suspect. Two weeks into rehearsals and I'll be posting a closing notice."

"I estimate, conservatively speaking, that there are ten thousand handsome actors in this town who would be happy to step in for Johnny Jones."

"How many stand sixty feet tall in their underpants over Times Square?" Brad countered.

"Are you and Johnny doing naughty things off stage?"

"Mike," Brad moaned, "to fuck Johnny Jones you have to take a number, like in a bakery and wait till you're called. I'd be too old to get it up before I reached the hot cross buns."

"Tell me, Mr. Director, does Johnny Jones take down his pants at any time during the run of this drama?"

"No," Brad answered with a good dollop of indignation.

"Then I'll see what I can find out."

"I love you, Mike."

"For my body, my mind or my influence?"

"Ciao, Michael."

"Goodbye, Bradley."

"The rich kid in trouble?" Jack asked, hopefully.

"Nothing compared to Johnny Jones' problem. Don't ever discover a corpse, Jack, it's a hard thing to explain away."

"Thanks for the tip. No one knows who the dead guy is?"

"The murderer does and I'm sure the police will too before very long. I think you had better call Burger King for a lunch reservation. Freddy Fine is now in a deep pow-wow with his lawyers. Watching a boy fry in his Freddy Fine jockeys is not good for business."

"Did you ever screw Bradley Turner?"

"No," Mike said. He wasn't lying nor was he telling the truth. He had met Bradley Turner at the Palm Beach home of an icon of New York High Society. The lady was hot for Mike, Mike was hot for her son and her son was hot for his pal, Bradley Turner. This *ménage a quatre* came to a climax (pun intended) in Palm Beach when Madam connected with a polo playing prince while Sonny, Bradley and Mike cavorted lewdly in the family Jacuzzi.

"I think you did," Jack said.

"And I think you had better dress for your lunch at Burger King."

FIVE

Mike had acquired a part-time personal chauffeur one snowy New Year's Eve. The driving service he subscribed to, bereft of cars and drivers that stormy night, had sent their most prestigious client a staff mechanic, piloting his own ancient Chevrolet. Since that night, Frank Evans, an opinionated black man of indeterminate age, appeared outside Mike's apartment building on East Sixty-Sixth Street whenever the columnist dialed WEDRIVE and expressed a need.

When Mike's driver preference became known, those who could afford the luxury insisted on Evans when using the service, elevating the former mechanic to a position on par with his celebrated passengers. It was understood that Frank was available on a first-come-first-serve basis and Mr. Gavin, regardless of when he called, always came first.

Besides being opinionated, Frank Evans was shrewd, vocal and a compulsive gambler. The numbers racket, New York's most venerable vice, provided his daily fix. Since meeting Mike, Frank's passion for playing the street addresses of the millionaires Mike often visited socially and in the line of duty, had paid off in the form of a new Lincoln Town Car. Mike thought the whole thing pure nonsense and refused to believe the new Lincoln was the result of placing a huge sum on the Park Avenue address of Brooke Astor.

The cataclysmic match between Jack Montgomery and Mike Gavin last July had sparked a rift between Mike and the driver that still nettled months after the fact. Frank had bet a huge sum on Mike Gavin to win. Incredulous, Mike asked Frank why he had made such a foolish wager.

"Because," came the reply, "the odds were five hundred to one against you and seeing how you and whitey are so tight, I figured he would throw the match to make you look good."

Mike lectured to the driver, "Jack Montgomery throws tennis

rackets, punches and wild parties, but he wouldn't throw a match if his life depended on it." Frank wasn't interested in Jack's virtues and continued to hold Mike responsible for the loss of one thousand dollars.

"If you learned a lesson," Mike lectured, pouring salt into the wound, "it was worth the dough."

Frank wasn't interested in atonement, either.

"Give up gambling," Mike advised, not for the first time.

"I will, when you give up white boys."

By the time Mike showered, shaved, dressed and exited his front door a smartly attired doorman held open, Frank Evans was waiting for him at the curb. Mike got into the shiny Lincoln next to the driver and announced their destination.

"The Jockstrap Murder," Frank exclaimed.

So, Mike thought, the city editor boys had a christening. "I've seen this Jones boy in the magazines," Frank continued, turning into Second Avenue with the daring of a Kamikaze pilot. When Mike opened his eyes again the Lincoln had miraculously melded with the cars, cabs, buses and trucks moving briskly south. "He's a pretty boy, in case you haven't noticed."

Mike refused to take the bait so Frank asked, "Are we going to investigate this one?"

"The police will do that, Watson. I think there might be a human interest angle in it and that's all I'm after."

Frank nodded. "You figure the weapon makes it a crime of passion?"

"Depends on who tied the knot."

"Not the pretty boy?"

"I've got five hundred that says he didn't do it."

Frank hesitated, then insisted, "You know something I don't."

"Only what I read in the *Morning News* and heard on the telly as I dressed which wasn't more than what the paper said."

"Bull," Frank shouted. "You talked to your friend, Bradley Turner. Him and Jones are putting on a show."

"You know more than the papers are telling," Mike said.

"To keep your chin above the shit in this town you gotta know when the Pope takes a dump."

"Okay," Mike said, "I'll tell you Bradley told me Jones was with him at the theater, rehearsing, from noon to ten last night."

"When did the guy get wasted?"

"I don't know," Mike answered.

"Swear?"

"Swear."

"You're on for half a grand."

Six

The city planning commission, acting on an impulse that would gladden the heart of the Marquis de Sade, had selected the most confusing and congested area of Manhattan to erect the NYPD headquarters. The city's judicial complex, City Hall, Chinatown, Little Italy and the northern fringe of the financial district comprised the maze surrounding One Police Plaza. As if offering an escape from the madness, the Brooklyn Bridge rose majestically above this homage to multiculturalism.

Artificially ventilated and equipped with more scientific paraphernalia than a Jules Verne novel, One Police Plaza housed the imposing office of the guy in charge, namely, the Commissioner of the NYPD, Andrew Brandt. In this environment the tall, blond, blue-eyed top cop resembled a Viking transported to the lush tropics.

A veteran of the old Seventeenth Precinct on the Upper East Side, he now reigned from a throne he found more ostentatious than regal. Like a rich guy trying to divert attention from his elitist surroundings, Brandt pointed to a window and said, "A view of the Brooklyn Bridge. The only one that's not falling down."

"Posh digs," Mike said, looking at everything in the office but the view. "Must run the taxpayers a bloody fortune."

"Which is no reason to give you privileged information."

"Privileged? I just want some facts."

"Read your newspaper," Brandt advised.

"I need more detailed facts."

"What we need is seldom what we get."

Mike and the commissioner were old sparring partners, going back to the days when Mike was covering the crime beat and Brandt was then a lieutenant on his way up. "After you called I checked with our people in the West Village. They told me the suspect looks like a Botticelli angel. How's that for police jargon?

It must come from working in Greenwich Village. Affectation is catching, like a dose of the clap."

"Sentence them to ten years of *Miami Vice* reruns."

"What's your interest in this, Mike? Besides the Botticelli angel."

"My, my but you have a nasty mind, Commissioner. I'm just doing my job. Looking for a newsworthy angle, not a fuckable angel."

"Quit the fag talk, Gavin. Reporters don't get detailed facts on a crime investigation in progress from me. Why should you?" Brandt had risen from the ranks but had yet to mellow from straight talk to political evasiveness. Mike respected him for just that reason. A diamond in the rough was, nonetheless, a diamond.

"I could say you should confide in me for sentimental reasons, Andy, but you're not a sentimental guy, so let's say it's because you asked me to chair the *Sun an' Surf* ball in April."

"What's that got to do with a murder in Greenwich Village and a suspect who looks like Botticelli?"

Mike laughed. "A Botticelli angel, Andy, and you know my readers and rich friends will fill your tin cups with enough gold to send your lads on the grand tour, let alone to a fresh air camp for two weeks." Mike put his hand on his forehead. "I could come down with scarlet fever…"

"That's blackmail."

"Hardly," Mike said. "It's give-and-take, mankind's favorite diversion. The idea is to give as little as possible and take as much as you can get."

"You got balls, Gavin."

"And you've got a lot of little boys who want to get out of town next summer."

Brandt was going to give Mike what he wanted or he would have told Mike to save himself the trip when he called. However, Andrew Brandt didn't think anyone, including Mike Gavin, should be spoon fed what others hungered for. Mike respected this rationale but refused to kowtow to it. Hence, the game of give-and-take which wasted precious time but saved face. The routing also gave the pair a chance to flex their muscles and test the power of their respective positions. The bout usually ended in a draw but proved that the police and the press needed each other to function at their peak.

Brandt began shuffling through the stacks of paper on his desk. The commissioner, like Jack Montgomery, thrived on clutter. Mike was anal in his quest for neatness and organization and often wondered if those who could only function amid clutter were more or less neurotic than those who insisted on order before they could draw a relaxed breath. Frank Evans would say the odds were perfectly even.

"I got these from a fax machine," Brandt said, waving a sheaf of papers. "You feed it into one end and it comes out the other end. Science imitating life."

"Without the indigestion," Mike added.

"A jockstrap," Brandt moaned. "Just when you think you've heard it all you get hit with something like this." He shook his head. "Johnny Jones would you believe is Giancarlo Labella, from the Bronx."

"Giancarlo The Pretty," Mike said. "An apt name."

"A model, like you used to be," Brandt said as he continued reading from his faxed information. "Poses with his wee-wee hanging out."

"His wee-wee," Mike noted, "is covered by Freddy Fine's top-of-the-line and I heard it ain't so wee."

"No fag talk, please," Brandt again cautioned. "Yeah, he's employed by *Freddy Fine Enterprises*. Sixteen bucks for B.V.D's. My sainted mother would drop dead at the cash register."

"Freddy moved the item ten million times last year," Mike informed the agitated cop. "Multiply that by sixteen bucks, check your bank balance and weep."

Brandt whistled his surprise. "Does Freddy get to keep it all?"

"A good chunk," Mike said.

"What does Labella get?"

"Not enough, I'm sure."

"Is that why he's play acting?" Brandt was again consulting his notes. "He was rehearsing at a theater on West Forty-Second from noon till ten PM. All present; actors, crew, director will vouch for that."

Brandt had, so far, told Mike only what was already common knowledge. The last bit of fact opened the way for Mike to pose the first two questions he had come to One Police Plaza to have answered. "Time of death?"

"Nothing official, yet."

"How about unofficial?"

"Lieutenant Rocco estimates at least eight hours before he examined the body. Rigor mortis had set in. I know Rocco. He's on the case."

Mike played along. "So, what time did he examine the body?"

"About midnight."

"That puts time of death early that afternoon," Mike said. "Giancarlo Labella has a Botticelli angel watching over him. He was at the theater."

"Keep your eye on the guy with the air-tight alibi," was Brandt's comment.

"And the victim is…?"

"He was stripped of all I.D."

"But they left his fingerprints, I assume," Mike said.

"Johnny says he doesn't know him," Brandt went on, paying no mind to Mike's assertion. "So, what was the guy doing in Johnny's apartment and who let him in? Johnny says he lives alone but with this crowd the guy paying the rent doesn't always have his name on the lease."

From this, Mike surmised that Johnny's former occupation

was known to the police but Andy Brandt wasn't going to tip his hand with that bit of news. And what had Rocco seen in Johnny's apartment to suggest the boy didn't live alone? To a professional observer like Mike Gavin, Brandt's silence on these points spoke volumes.

"The victim's name?" Mike tried again.

"Matthew Bokowski."

SEVEN

"You knew the time of death," Frank accused as soon as Mike reported what he had learned from Andrew Brandt, "which eliminates the pretty boy and I'm out half a grand." Venting his fury, Frank careened past a First Avenue bus only to jam on his brakes behind a taxi that had stopped to discharge a passenger.

Mike tightened his seatbelt. "I didn't know the time of death when we made the bet and I resent being called a liar."

"And I resent being taken for five big ones."

"Relax," Mike said as Frank raced past an amber light. "Johnny's not in the clear. Not yet."

"What else did The Man tell you?"

"Never trust the guy with the air-tight alibi."

"The Man said that?"

"He did," Mike assured him.

Frank made no reply as they crawled past the emergency entrance to Bellevue Hospital, the facility's beckoning sign being a more potent restraint to drivers than a traffic cop.

"You want to call off the bet?" Mike asked.

As if the mere suggestion of calling off the bet posed a threat to his status as a gambler junkie, Frank Evans stated firmly, "The bet stands."

Frank stopped for a red light and glancing out the car window Mike found himself staring at the city morgue, conveniently nestled between Bellevue and New York University hospitals. The unfortunate Matthew Bokowski was now lying someplace within the morbid confines of that repository, awaiting the medical examiner's scrutiny. Mike recalled a pair of dark eyes, a tilted nose and an eager smile. "I do sports, obits, weddings and bar mitzvahs," those smiling lips had said to Mike.

If Mike had not dismissed the boy so abruptly, would Matthew

Burke's byline still be heading sports, obits, weddings and bar mitzvahs? And who would write Matthew Burke's obituary?

Mike had not recognized the name immediately but when Andy Brandt began to elaborate it struck him, like a poke in the ribs, that he had actually met the victim of the Jockstrap Murder.

"Reporter," Brandt had said. "Some rag in Baltimore. Writes under the name Matthew Burke."

After that all Mike wanted to do was get out of Brandt's office and get back uptown. He was sitting on something hot and experience had taught him to keep calm, keep cool and keep his mouth shut if he wanted his exclusive to remain exclusive. Confiding in Frank Evans would be tantamount to confiding in all the folks Frank chauffeured around town.

He had no qualms about not sharing with the police because he knew damn well the police were withholding from him. The time would come for the game of give-and-take but that was a long way off. Now he had to cogitate, digest all he had learned and call his editor at the *News* and tell him to hold tomorrow's headline and lead until countdown time. By then Mike would have composed his story.

"You want to double it?" Frank, too, had been cogitating.

"A thousand?"

"Unless you want to call it off," Frank offered. "No skin off my nose either way."

"Now you sound like you know something I don't."

"Only what The Man told you," Frank assured him. "Only what The Man told you." He brought the Lincoln to a stop in front of a blue canopy on East Sixty-Sixth Street. The doorman moved briskly to open the car door for Mike.

"A thousand," Mike agreed.

"A thousand." Frank sealed the wager.

EIGHT

The sky had cleared long enough to allow the sun to shine down on Mike's meeting with Andy Brandt. An hour later, as he and Frank made their way back uptown, it had retreated far to the west. A gray November twilight hung over Manhattan like a shroud heralding the demise of the waning year. Prior to its death knell the city would stuff turkeys, trim trees, mix eggnogs and sing carols before succumbing, like a contrite whore, to the winter solstice. It wasn't Mike's favorite time of year, but then neither was his birthday and Valentine's Day which, like killing two birds with one stone, fell on the same day.

Jack was home recovering from his solitary lunch at *Chez Louis*. As predicted, Freddy Fine had not kept his date with Jack but the underwear king had taken the time to call the restaurant to tender his regrets. Quoting Alain, Jack said, "Mr. Fine has been detained but insists that Mr. Montgomery dine without him."

"Detained by a murder investigation," Mike added. "Freddy wants to keep you happy in case he loses Johnny to Sing-Sing. If you start hanging around Times Square in your underpants, Montgomery, you can pack your bags right now."

"What did Andrew Brandt have to say?" Jack asked.

The question bothered Mike. He had not told Jack where he was going when he left the apartment but Jack had obviously overheard Mike's call to the commissioner. Jack had taken over Mike's closets and now he was zeroing in on his movements. Mike averted a direct response that might prove more caustic than informative by heading for the kitchen to empty an ice tray. It was half past cocktail time. Jack followed and extracted a Bass from the refrigerator, looking at the bottle like Hamlet contemplating Yorick's skull.

Mike silently counted to ten, backwards, as he returned to the living room to pour himself a bourbon and branch water at the dry bar. Sitting in his favorite chair, one item not yet usurped by

Jack, he took his cell phone out of his jacket pocket and called his editor. This done, he took a long swig of the amber fire water and told Jack what he had learned from Andy Brandt.

"You know the poor bastard?" Jack said, awed by the fact.

"I talked to him for a few minutes." Here, Mike reprised his encounter with Matthew Bokowski.

"The night of the Vice President's party. You never said anything to me about it."

"Why should I?" Mike said. "He was a kid being polite."

"Polite, my ass. That business about Watergate. He knew something and what he knew got him killed."

Mike was thinking the same thing but wouldn't concede the point at this moment. It was still early days. Egging Jack on, he said, "That's pure speculation. What could a cub reporter from Baltimore know to get himself on a Washington hit list, and why in Johnny Jones' apartment?"

"Johnny swears he doesn't know the guy," Jack said, sounding like a defense attorney.

Mike took another swig. "Johnny did an interview with *GQ* and swore he was a heterosexual but there has to be a connection between Johnny and the victim. Bokowski didn't wander into Johnny's apartment by accident, nor did he break in."

"So who let him in?" Jack said.

"Maybe Johnny himself. No one knows what time Bokowski showed up at the Grove Street apartment. Johnny got to the theater at noon. He could have opened the door to Bokowski before he left for rehearsals. Maybe Bokowski had a key. Anything's possible."

Or, Mike was thinking, Johnny's phantom roommate could have opened the door to Matthew Bokowski. Mike was sure that the cop, Rocco, had found something to indicate Johnny Jones didn't live alone. Brandt didn't say Johnny Jones lives alone. He said Johnny Jones SAYS he lives alone which means the police don't believe him.

"Maybe that's why his pockets were emptied," Jack speculated. "To remove the key."

"Why not take only the key?" Mike countered. "No, I think the murderer wanted to put as much space as possible between himself and the scene of the crime before the police could identify the victim. Emptying Bokowski's pockets was a play for time, nothing more."

"Time to get back to Washington," Jack said, as if it were a fact.

Mike nodded. "He mentioned Watergate but that doesn't necessarily mean he was talking about a Washington scandal. The word Watergate has gone from noun to adjective and describes a crime, not a place. Johnny's past and the murder weapon reek of sex."

"How about this?" Jack said. "One of Johnny's old customers is a politico. Bokowski got wind of it and made threatening noises, like Woodward and Bernstein, which is why he used the term Watergate. A meeting is convened at Johnny's flat and Bokowski is silenced."

"Leaving Johnny as suspect number one, ready to spill his guts out to save his own ass? It won't wash, Jack."

Jack waved his bottle of Bass at Mike and lectured, "That's what they want you to think. In fact, the whole set-up was designed to draw that conclusion. The murder weapon makes the motive kinky sex with the victim getting more than he bargained for. Johnny is the decoy, the sitting duck, but he's made of Teflon. Everything washes off and the bigshot goes unnoticed. If it wasn't for your chance talk with Bokowski it would have worked."

Mike was listening attentively. Jack's mind was as agile as his right arm. What a shame he didn't flaunt it the way he did his physical charms. Could Mike teach this young man to strike a delicate balance? Brainy by day, brawny by night? Mike recoiled from the corny pun and abandoned the idea. Jack Montgomery was meant to be enjoyed, like a rare vintage, and if it brought on a hangover one could always help himself to a hair of the dog.

"And Johnny agreed to this?" Mike wasn't buying Jack's scenario.

"Maybe he had no choice. In this league they play hardball."

Mike mused aloud. "Would someone kill to put the lid on a sex scandal?"

"That depends on who got caught dipping his wick in the wrong orifice."

"You do know how to turn a phrase, Montgomery."

"So, what's your lead?" Jack asked and not waiting for an answer suggested, "What about a front page photo of the Watergate complex wrapped in a Freddy Fine jockstrap?"

Mike laughed at the image it evoked and wondered if one of the tabloids would run it or some version of Jack's brainstorm. Mike's lead and copy were by now written in his mind if not on his laptop. "I'm going to tell my readers I spoke to Matthew Bokowski but I'm not going to say what Bokowski and I discussed. If the murderer wants to know he'll have to contact me and ask."

"Are you going to give him your private number or your cell phone?"

"Neither. He can get me via the *Morning News* or my web site."

"That could be dangerous," Jack said, more thrilled than concerned.

Mike acknowledged this with a nod and headed to his bedroom where his laptop sat on his desk along with his land phone, a reading lamp and an ashtray that was now a caddy for paper clips.

NINE

Mike's column appeared every Saturday on the op-ed page of the *Morning News*. The Jockstrap Murder was a breaking news story and Mike's copy, with his prestigious byline, would appear on page one of tomorrow's edition. Buoyed by his scoop, he wrote with all the enthusiasm, speed (and joy) of his days covering the crime beat. A weekly column is a slow and meticulous creation. News break copy is akin to shooting from the hip. Mike Gavin was blessed with the talent to do both to Pulitzer Prize acclaim.

Barring the outbreak of World War III, the *Morning News* headline in tomorrow's early edition would shout, **MIKE GAVIN SPOKE TO THE JOCKSTRAP VICTIM.** Following would be a clever amalgam of fact and insinuation with the accent on Blair House as the venue of Mike's meeting with Matthew Bokowski. All carefully worded to leave the reader believing Mike Gavin knew more than he was presently able to impart to his readers.

Before electronically submitting the story, Mike would check with Andy Brandt to make certain Matthew Bokowski's next of kin had been informed of the murder and that the police were ready to release the victim's I.D. to the press. Mike took advantage of his relationship with the commissioner, but never abused it.

Mike worked at his desk as Jack made himself scarce, but not invisible. As it grew dark Jack lit lamps, served snacks (mini pretzels and pistachio nuts, shelled) and removed serving saucers all on tip toe.

Mike keyed in the word WRAP as the cascade of the shower, like a distant waterfall, broke a solid hour of silence. Then the aroma of steam, talc and Lagerfeld blended to the sight of damp, naked flesh moving across the room followed by the unmistakable sound of ice cubes being pried from their mold and finally, as if in reward for a job well done, a bourbon on the rocks appeared before Mike's weary eyes.

"You're a witch." Mike toasted the naked Adonis.

Jack looked down at his cock that appeared to be reaching for his navel and objected, "I think this makes me a warlock."

Mike fisted the rigid flesh. "I think this makes you king of the mountain."

TEN

They dined at a First Avenue restaurant known for its steaks and chops. The waiter never once referred to them by name but, in the inimitable way of professional caterers, he left no doubt that he knew who he was serving.

"After lunch at *Chez Louis* you're going to put away that steak," Mike noted.

"Sex makes me ravenous," Jack told him.

"Before or after?"

"Before, after and during," Jack said, cutting into his steak and drawing blood. "Why do you always wear a rubber?"

The question stunned Mike. Lifting a piece of lamb chop to his mouth, his fork hovering between plate and lips, he stared at Jack before exploding. "Jesus, Jack. We're not alone."

Was Jack Montgomery naïve or brazen beyond belief? That he was able to pose a question like that, in a public place, while slicing into a steak and looking like Oliver Twist confronting Mr. Bumble, amazed Mike. Making statements that could not be faulted for accuracy but best not articulated in public was one of Jack's most salient traits. Unfortunately, there were others. It was the embarrassing utterance of a child who has not yet learned the rules of the game.

Jack had been raised by a series of tennis coaches who taught him to win games, not kudos from *Miss Manners*. It was just the thing a clever interviewer would focus on and use to his (or her) advantage.

When Mike got the tender morsel into his mouth he had difficulty chewing.

"No one can hear us," Jack said with a shrug.

"This crowd reads lips," Mike answered. They had been given a corner table but this afforded scant privacy in a room that was little more than a store-front with tables set along three of its walls and a row down the center to form the letter E. Looking about, Mike caught the eyes of two elderly women seated together who waved as if he were an old friend.

"You're a prude," Jack pouted.

'There's a time and place for everything and this is neither for what you have in mind."

"It makes me feel you don't trust me," Jack said, refusing to drop the subject. "Like I was a one night stand or a quickie. Don't know who was here before me so I better put on a raincoat." He methodically sliced himself another piece of filet mignon, rare.

"Can it, Jack," Mike ordered.

"Don't worry, I'm not going to mention the unmentionable."

"The word," Mike said, "is condom."

Jack signaled the waiter, indicating their empty wine glasses. Hurrying to please, he poured from the bottle of vintage Bordeaux Mike had ordered to accompany their meal.

"Named after its inventor, Dr. Condom. Did you know that? I think he got the idea from watching his butcher making sausages."

Mike ate in silence until the waiter was out of hearing range then said, "Now it's going to be all over town that Mike Gavin and Jack Montgomery discussed condoms – their origin and uses – over their evening meal."

Undaunted, Jack went right on. "Hotel maids used to put a piece of chocolate on your pillow when they turned down the bed. Now they leave a condom, wrapped in gold foil." Jack went to work on his baked potato.

"Sensible idea," Mike said.

"Is that why?"

"Is that why what?"

"Why you use them," Jack prodded.

"It's not a question of trust or distrust, Jack. With what's being passed on out there it's meant to show concern for someone you care about."

Looking pleased, Jack said, "I know. I said it to irk you and listen to you preach from your soap box. You do it so well. Thanks, Mike."

"You're welcome."

After a moment's pause Jack leaned across the table and whispered, "Why ribbed rubbers?"

"Shut the fuck up, Montgomery."

ELEVEN

The elderly ladies made a wide sweep of the room in order to pass Mike's table on their way to the front door. Impossible to avoid their stare, Mike smiled politely.

"We read you every week, Mr. Gavin," one of them said in passing.

"How nice," Mike answered. Being wedged into the corner by his table he was unable to rise but he made an abortive effort in that direction. Jack winked at the septuagenarians who fled, giggling.

"That wasn't necessary," Mike scolded.

"They enjoyed it," Jack said, his blue eyes on Mike as he thought a moment before asking, "Do people ever ask you for your autograph?"

Mike shook his head. "No. But given half a chance they bemoan their pet peeves, praise their political affiliations and offer advice on how to avoid World War III."

"Or where to draw the line between news and ethics," Jack added.

"Matthew Bokowski," Mike said. They had not talked about the murder since Mike had filed his copy with the *Morning News* but that WRAP didn't expurgate it from his conscience. Jack too, it seemed, was still struggling with the riddle of Matthew Bokowski. Holding his wine glass by its stem and gazing at the burgundy hue through the crystal, Mike appeared to be giving the matter a great deal of thought. "There's nothing unethical about reporting a sex scandal. Louella and Hedda did it for decades and spewed an army of imitators. Getting hit with a mud ball has always been the price of fame. Ethical implies something more – more what?"

"Is that all Bokowski said, Mike? Just walked up to you and asked you where public access infringed on the ethical?"

"That's it," Mike assured him.

"And you think he was gay?"

"I'm not sure. Just a guess. Remember, we only talked for a few minutes."

"He died with a jockstrap tied around his neck in Johnny Jones' apartment. The question of his sex preference is bound to arise." Not bothering to signal the waiter again, Jack refilled their glasses, emptying the bottle.

Diners began leaving the restaurant until there were but two other tables still occupied. The three waiters had gathered at the service end of the bar, eager to count the night's take as the bartender washed glasses. A bus boy diligently cleared and reset tables as they were vacated.

Mike reached for his glass but balked before picking it up. "A friend. Bokowski mentioned a friend. I forgot all about that." He shifted his position in the tight space as if he were about to push himself free of the restraining table and make for the door.

"What did he say about a friend?"

Mike tried to recall a conversation he had had with a stranger some four months ago. A conversation not unlike many Mike Gavin had been forced to abide since attaining fame as a widely read syndicated columnist. There are those who think it their civic duty to stop, detain and lecture anyone who has access to an audience. However, none of those numerous encounters had ended with the lecturer being strangled with a jockstrap.

Could Mike have prevented the murder? Was it linked to a political cover-up or kinky sex?

Matthew Bokowski was fated to keep a rendezvous with someone in Johnny Jones' apartment. A rendezvous that had all the trappings of a sex tryst and none of a political scandal. Mike thought about the ads in some of the more esoteric gay periodicals: STUD SELLS HIS SWEATY JOCKSTRAP, BRIEFS, PHOTOS. Had Matthew come to New York to make a purchase, in person? But Johnny Jones was no longer in that business. He had made it big. Sixty feet high big over Times

Square. His renewal contract with *Freddy Fine Enterprises* would be for millions plus the right to freelance, and spell that Hollywood. Also, he was currently in rehearsal for an off-Broadway show.

The fact that Mike had treated the victim like a persistent horsefly at the seashore still nettled. Had Mike taken the boy seriously would he now be enjoying a glass of wine with his star struck...

"STAR STRUCK," Mike shouted, startling himself as well as his table- mate and the waiters at the bar.

"Star struck? What the hell does that mean?"

"Bokowski's friend," Mike began to explain his outburst. "*I was hoping to bring my star struck friend so he could ogle all the celebrities.* Those were his exact words or close to them. He wanted to bring his star struck friend to the Veep's party so he could stare at you and Amanda and Oprah. Sneak him in, I guess"

"So why didn't he?"

Their waiter appeared, collected the empty bottle of wine and asked, with little enthusiasm, if they wanted coffee. "Just a check," Jack told him. The man departed with a slight bow and a grateful smile.

"I don't know," Mike was saying. "I don't know why his friend wasn't there."

"Stopped at the gate," Jack guessed. "Security was tight."

Mike shook his head. "I think I would have remembered that."

TWELVE

Something disturbed Mike's sleep that night. A sound? A dream? He opened his eyes. It took a few moments for them to adjust to the dark. He was relieved to find himself in his bedroom, Jack next to him in the fetal position he swore he never assumed. The bedroom windows shined like black glass, catching the reflected illumination of mid-town Manhattan. He slid his arm around Jack's waist, stroking a belly as flat and firm as polished granite. Jack mumbled, uncoiled and rolled on his back.

"Bokowski's star struck friend is an intern at Bethesda Medical," Mike whispered in Jack's ear. Jack began to snore.

"An intern at Bethesda Medical," Mike repeated, his fingers tracing a narrow line of soft blond hair until it fanned out into a bed of moss encircling a sapling birch.

Too excited to sleep, Mike nibbled on Jack's ear as he repeated, as if it were a mantra, the profession of Matthew Bokowski's friend. Whatever psychological mechanism had awakened Mike with this information had, for reasons that would astound Freud, also aroused his passion. He pressed his erection against Jack's naked hip as his hand cajoled Jack's flaccid, but far from inconsequential, dick to a similar state.

"An intern at Bethesda Medical," Mike said as he rubbed and stroked.

The snoring subsided to heavy breathing. "Am I in a hospital or a massage parlor?" Jack mumbled.

"A parlor and it's gonna cost you a hundred."

"I can do it myself for free." Jack was now wide awake.

"Put your trust in the kindness of a strange hand."

"Hummm. Nice."

"It gets better."

"Why does Bethesda Medical turn you on?"

"Later. First I want to have my way with you."

"You've got the magic touch, Gavin."

"Your snipped totem pole inspires it."

Jack arched his lithe frame in counterpoint to the stroking hand, increasing the friction of his thigh against Mike's belly. Turning his head, Jack's mouth sought Mike's, the tip of his tongue visible between his parted lips. They kissed, their bodies moving in unison, striving to reach the height but reluctant to abandon the thrill of the climb.

When it was time, they took themselves in hand, pacing to reach the summit in harmony. When they got there, the release was long, slow, deliberate – and unbelievably satisfying.

THIRTEEN

"We should shower."

"I'm too comfortable to move."

"We're glued to each other."

Jack laughed. "Like Siamese twins. Do we need a surgeon?"

"Soap and water will do."

They lay nestled in each other's arms, Mike stroking the blond head resting on his chest. "Don't ever leave me," Jack implored.

"I'm right here," Mike said, purposely misinterpreting the plea. "You're the traveling tennis star, letting it all hang out in men-only locker rooms across the country." His hand moved up and down Jack's spine, occasionally straying to the compact, muscled ass beneath it. When he explored Jack like this, Mike marveled at the perfection of the athlete's body.

"I'm afraid, Mike."

Mike knew what was coming. In fact he was beginning to wonder if Jack needed the help of a competent psychiatrist.

"I don't want to get sick," Jack said.

Jack was obsessed with the subject and he usually verbalized his anxiety soon after they were intimate. "We've both been tested. Negative. We don't bareback and AIDS, thankfully, is no longer a death sentence."

"Negative now. But what if you cheated on me and…" Jack shuddered.

"Swear you never will."

This was the terror of the pro tennis circuit. They should see him now.

A boy. Just a boy. Swear to me that there is no bogeyman and I won't be afraid of the dark. Swear to me that you'll be faithful and I won't be afraid of AIDS.

Sorry. There is a bogeyman and he's a virus. All the vows of fidelity won't vanquish the killer or still the fear. *Oh, Promise Me*, Amanda's last hit was, paradoxically, a comedy rife with infidelities.

Promises were easy to make in the serene afterglow of spent passion. Bonded, in spirit (and fact), by love's sweet potion. But, as Mike just said, a little soap and water can break the bond and expose the doubt. For always, there would be doubt. Jack on the road; Mike in town. The possibilities were endless. "Vows don't mean a thing," Mike said. "It's what you feel that matters and what we feel too often depends on what's available when the need arises."

"That's demeaning."

"It's the truth. I have no intention of cheating on you and I'm sure you're happy with me. Fidelity doesn't need a marriage certificate. I promise nothing and demand nothing except that, if you stray or if I do, we fess up before we tumble into the sack together. That's the only vow we have to commit to. We must."

How many minds were thinking these thoughts? How many tongues uttering these sentiments? How many lovers fearing the embrace they cherished? The dream turned nightmare. The nightmare turned real.

Jack nodded, his lips grazing Mike's nipple. "I love you."

Mike didn't want to lose Jack. This guy he had compared to a vintage wine had the kick of a much stronger brew. Could Mike turn the little boy into a young man without obliterating his charm? He was damn well going to try.

Jack raised his head. "Now tell me what Bethesda Medical means."

FOURTEEN

It was past noon by the time they had shaved, showered and dressed. Late to bed and late to rise was good for the libido and bad for productivity but the early morning caucus had resulted in a plan of action.

An intern at Bethesda Medical. A young man just starting out on a career after years of schooling. A young man who might know or might not know something about a Washington cover-up, if one existed, or a murder in New York. The young MD should be given the benefit of the doubt. Mike wouldn't risk ruining the Doc's reputation based on a hunch. This intern could be nothing more than an acquaintance, even a casual acquaintance, of Matthew Bokowski. Mike would have to speak to the young man before he put anything in print or passed this lead on to the police who, he was certain, would be questioning all of Bokowski's friends and relations. If the police got to Bethesda Medical before Mike, that was the Doc's problem.

Today, Jack was meeting with Freddy Fine. Tomorrow, he was booked for a tournament in McLean, Virginia. While down there he volunteered to drive to the Bethesda Medical complex and...

"And what?" Mike cut in on the proposal. "Ask if they have an intern on the staff who was a friend of the guy strangled with a jockstrap in New York a few days ago?"

Getting a story, Mike explained, was not akin to placing a tennis ball where your opponent couldn't reach it. It called for finesse, trickery and a bit of luck. Mike knew that pro athletes, like actors, often sent newspaper editors tickets to their games or shows hoping for a good mention in the press. Mike's plan was to have Jack, or his agent, invite the sports editor of Bokowski's Baltimore paper to the opening day of the McLean event and to the lockers after the games to meet the star.

With a bit of luck, the editor would send Bokowski's replacement to cover the story. When he met the replacement,

Jack would introduce the subject of Bokowski's murder. This could be done without arousing suspicion due to the publicity, especially in Baltimore, the murder had garnered. With Jack coaxing, the replacement reporter would reveal what he knew about Bokowski, including the name of a certain intern at Bethesda Medical.

Jack listened, nodding thoughtfully, as Mike spoke and waited until he had finished before asking, "What if he doesn't show? The press get a lot of passes, as I'm sure you know, and usually sell them for the price on the stub."

"This is a small town paper, Jack. My guess is they never get a bid from a player of your status and will jump at the chance to tell their readers they talked to you."

"And what if this replacement doesn't know dick about Matthew Bokowski?"

"Then," Mike instructed, "you drive to Bethesda Medical and ask if they have an intern on their staff who was a friend of the guy strangled with a jockstrap in New York a few days ago."

FIFTEEN

Less than an hour after the *Morning News* hit the streets Mike got a call from Andrew Brandt.

"You're a bastard, Gavin," were the words that greeted Mike when he picked up his private line.

"My birth certificate clearly states that I'm the legitimate offspring of Mr. and Mrs. Michael Gavin."

Brandt wasn't interested in witty repartee. "You didn't tell me you knew the victim."

Mike instantly decided to stretch the truth a bit. "I didn't know him when I talked to you. His byline name sounded familiar, but I didn't connect him to the reporter I had talked to until I got back uptown."

"I have a phone," the commissioner barked.

"I don't know anything that can help the case, Andy."

"That's not the way it reads in your rag."

Mike imagined the commissioner sitting at his desk, surrounded by a mountain of paperwork all shoved aside to accommodate the *Morning News* opened to Mike's lead piece.

"I was playing to the crowd, Andy. Grandstanding. The kid introduced himself to me back in July, we exchanged a few words and I blew it all up for the sake of good copy. I'm sure you noticed that I don't have a single Bokowski quote in the piece because he said nothing worthy of one." Lying, Mike thought, was like plunging into a pool of cold water. After the initial shock, one warmed to the occasion, went with the flow and forgot the water had ever been anything but tepid.

Andy Brandt wasn't convinced. "That's what has me worried. You wouldn't do anything stupid like holding back on us for the sake of an even better story – or would you?"

"I think this is all the story there is. A one shot deal. But a damn good shot, you've got to admit."

"Well, wise guy, the damn good shot made you a wanted man."

"Really? Who wants me?"

"Rocco. James Rocco. Lieutenant, NYPD. It's his case, remember?"

"Afraid I do."

"You should be afraid. Rocco spoke to me because I spoke to you and you spoke to the murder victim."

Mike laughed and when asked what was so funny, he said, "Back in the Roaring '30's there was a song called *I Danced with a Man, Who Danced with a Girl, Who Danced with the Prince of Wales.*"

"Leave your dancing shoes home, Gavin, but bring your boxing gloves."

"I have nothing to tell him, Andy. It's all in my copy, can't he read?"

"Mike, yesterday I gave you facts about the case no other reporter had access to, now return the favor and go see Rocco."

So, the game of gave-and-take had begun in earnest. Yesterday Mike had taken and what he took had enabled him to file a story that left the competition in the wake of his dust. Grandstanding, as Mike called it, was the nature of the newspaper business and Mike Gavin was the chairman of the board. Today he would pay for yesterday's handout.

"I told Rocco these were your people. Models, actors, directors…"

"And shit like that," Mike added to Brandt's pretentious roster.

"I didn't say it. You did." Mike could see the grin on Andrew Brandt's Nordic face. "Sixth precinct, West Village," Brandt directed.

"One of my old beats."

"And I told Rocco you're very cooperative."

"What are you running, Andy, a dating service?"

The commissioner hung up without a good-bye.

Moments later Mike's private line again pealed a summons. "Michael, love," Amanda Richards emoted, "I spoke to him, too."

"Who?"

"This Bokowski or Burke. At the Vice President's party."

"Are you sure, Amanda?" Amanda, like many in the performing arts, had a rich imagination. Every situation she encountered was fodder for a drama starring Amanda Richards. Reading Mike's copy and having been at the same party she might very well have recast the scene, usurping Mike and inserting herself into the picture. "You talked to so many people. Why should you remember this young man?"

"I'm an actress, Michael. Remembering is the discipline of the profession. I could walk on a stage tonight and recreate my first speaking role without blowing one line, and that was twenty years ago."

"Thirty, Amanda."

"My, my, aren't we keen. Now tell me you were sitting out front when the curtain went up."

"Hardly. I was tucked in with my teddy bear."

"Bastard."

Mike's legitimacy was questioned twice in the past five minutes and it's said there's never a second without a third. This was not going to be Mike Gavin's day. "I apologize, although I'm not certain for what. Now tell me what Bokowski said to you."

Forgetting her gift of total recall, she confessed, "I don't remember. His name meant nothing to me but when I saw his picture on the front page of your tabloid…"

"It's not a tabloid."

A dramatic pause told Mike he had just been reprimanded for correcting Amanda's addition. Having evened the score, she moved blithely forward. "I remembered his face because of the incident."

As Amanda spoke, Mike doodled on a yellow legal pad he kept on his desk. Triangle, square, triangle, cone, triangle, cube; he scribbled INCIDENT and broke in on her flow. "What incident?"

"Well," she began, making the most of Mike's interest, "when he introduced himself to me I saw his paper tag and knew he was press. We spoke only a few minutes before one of the security guards wearing a business suit who looked like a guest until I noticed his brown shoes with gum soles, asked to see his I.D."

"Why? His press tag was his I.D."

"I would have thought so, Michael, but that's what happened."

"Were they satisfied with what he showed them?"

"I don't know."

This was definitely not going to be Mike's day. "Why the hell not?"

"Don't scold. Especially early in the morning."

"It's past noon, Amanda."

"I work the night shift, love." Having completed her tour, Amanda was back in New York performing in a revival of Williams' *The Glass Menagerie* at Lincoln Center. The six week run had sold out the day the box office opened. "I don't know what the poor Bokowski showed the guard because Tim Samuels came along and dragged me away to meet more of his friends. That boy, Michael, is lousy with friends. Boys with toothpaste smiles and girls who talk like Katherine Hepburn. Really…"

Amanda went on and on but Mike was no longer listening. Someone had fingered Bokowski. No question about that. And, they had done so after Bokowski had talked to Mike. He could not be mistaken about the sequence of events as they unfolded that evening. He spoke to Amanda. Tim Samuels joined them. They talked until Tim departed with Amanda. A moment later Bokowski cornered Mike. Mike had excused himself as soon as he could without appearing rude and went to rescue Jack form

Oprah Winfrey or vice versa.

Later, Bokowski overtook Amanda and the security people moved in on him. Was Bokowski a mental case? A known kook? Impossible. He would never have been given clearance and then ambushed after the fact. Matthew Bokowski, or Matt Burke, was a staff reporter for a Baltimore newspaper; that was a fact. He was just doing his job so why did they hassle him?

"I do sports, obits, weddings and bar mitzvahs." Mike and Amanda weren't dead, newly married, or of the Jewish faith. Was Bokowski fingered because he had stumbled on something covert and was blabbing about it to a certain intern at Bethesda Medical? A Washington rumor is like the proverbial snowball rolling downhill. When it hits bottom it's a boulder that leaves a trail leading back to from whence it came.

Suppose Bokowski was spreading malicious gossip and those being maligned got wind of it. Seeing him talking to Mike Gavin would be reason enough to get the security man to give him a hard time and if that didn't scare him off – tie a jockstrap around his neck in Johnny Jones' apartment?

It made no sense but it was the job of an investigative reporter to clarify muddy waters and expose what lay beneath.

Sixteen

If Amanda's "incident" raised more questions than it answered, Mike's next call was so obtuse it defied even that dubious distinction.

"Mike, it's been too long," Ken Wallace's affected southern drawl was as recognizable as his shaved head, blue tinted glasses and perpetual tan that came from Liz Arden, not Helios. A member of The Holy Trinity, he was Mike's first contact with someone close to the prime suspect in The Jockstrap Murder case. Mike gripped his pencil, ready to record any confidence Wallace had to offer that was germane to the death of Matthew Bokowski. He could have saved himself the trouble.

Not long enough, Mike thought as he said, "Not since the opening of Amanda's retread."

Wallace laughed conspiratorially. "I don't think she'd like that."

"Retread. Revival. Much the same thing. Amanda would be the first to agree."

Mike began to doodle another row of neat, geometric figures as he waited for Wallace to get to the point of the call. The photographer and sometimes couturier was an intimate of the rich and famous and infamous. A self-styled arbiter of taste, fashion and haute monde. A nod or snub from Wallace could make or break a career, a reputation or a marriage. Friends called him a gossip, cad and bitch. Enemies preferred pimp, Judas and cocksucker. Friends and foes never exchanged a word because both camps were in a constant state of flux.

"When can we have a boy's lunch?" Wallace asked.

NEVER, Mike printed after the last triangle. "I'm a working boy, Ken, I usually brown bag it."

"I don't believe you," came the reply. "We have to talk."

"About what?" Mike quickly asked, thinking he was going

to get Ken Wallace's take on the murder and Johnny Jones' involvement.

"Jack Montgomery," came the unexpected answer.

"Then invite Jack to lunch."

"You know he's going to represent Freddy's new line of jeans."

"I know he's meeting with Freddy as we speak. They were to meet yesterday but Freddy canceled." Mike paused but Wallace didn't take the hint. "I don't see what any of this has to do with me."

"Well," Wallace drawled, "he is your boy."

"He's a man, Ken."

"Boy. Man. Retread. Revival." Wallace's phony laugh irritated Mike. "If he's being naughty I know a titled lady who would be happy to take him off your hands." He made the offer with the balls of a horse breeder looking to acquire a proven stud.

"Jack will love working for Freddy," Wallace went on. "A lot of moola and his pretty face popping out of magazines and billboards all over the country, courtesy of snaps by Ken Wallace. Vanity, thy name is ME."

Mike refrained from saying Jack was more interested in the exposure than the moola but the word exposure prompted him to advise, "I hope it's only his face that pops out, Ken."

"*Moi*, Mike? *Moi*? When I'm in my studio I'm all business. I make Mother Teresa look like the whore of Babylon. Ask – ask anyone who's worked with me."

The pause in the otherwise glib delivery didn't go unnoticed. Was Wallace going to say "Ask Johnny" but thought better of it? Johnny Jones was the current page one poster boy and a murder suspect, but his name had not even been mentioned by his discoverer and mentor? A guy whose mouth had often been compared, unfavorably, to the entrance to the Lincoln Tunnel. A "no comment" was indeed the most telling comment of all.

Perhaps what Wallace had to say couldn't be said over the

wires. If NASA could bug the moon, Mike's telephone would be child's play. Mike made two snap decisions. He would not force the issue at this juncture and he would lunch with the photographer. "Today is out, Ken. I'll check my schedule and get back to you later."

"It's appreciated, Mike. Love to Jack. Ta ta."

If they were being bugged the listeners would love the ta ta.

SEVENTEEN

After talking to Ken Wallace, Mike felt he had engaged in a cryptic conversation in which only the other party was privy to the code. Cryptic or crazy? Did Ken Wallace know who done it? No way. Wallace's weapon was a malicious tongue. The guy wouldn't touch a jockstrap unless the jock was wearing it. Mike wanted Jack to turn down Freddy Fine's offer but was not sanguine on that possibility.

As Mike reflected on Wallace's call he stared at the instrument he had just cradled. It was his land phone. His most private number. It was the line just used by Andrew Brandt and Amanda Richards. Ken Wallace was not one of the chosen Mike had entrusted with the number, but someone who was had betrayed his trust. He found this most disquieting, if not damn scary. He scrawled FUCK on his legal pad and tossed his pencil on top of the obscenity. Before going to see Lt. James Rocco, Mike called Milly Perez, his secretary at the paper, to see if any interesting calls had come in since his story hit the streets this morning.

"You expecting to hear from the killer?" Milly guessed what he was looking for.

"I thought he might give me a buzz. Any luck?"

"Just the usual, Mike," she said. "The best was from a guy who wanted to know the size of the jockstrap. Said his was stolen at his gym and thought the murder weapon might belong to him. I told him to call the police."

Mike hoped Lt. Rocco didn't get the call. "And keep checking my web site, Milly, for anything of interest in that area." She was a quick study and had the good sense to separate the wheat from the chaff and forward only the former. "I'm off to see a cop. Ta ta."

"Ta ta?"

EIGHTEEN

Mike opened the door of the Lincoln and saw the *Morning News* placed purposely on the front passenger seat so anyone entering the car was confronted with the bold headline, MIKE GAVIN SPOKE TO THE JOCKSTRAP VICTIM. Raising his head he confronted the accusing countenance of Frank Evans.

"I made the bet in good faith," Mike said, picking up the newspaper and tossing it, face down, on the back seat. He sat as far from the driver as the car's generous width would allow. "I didn't know I had spoken to Bokowski when we made the bet."

"For five hundred. But when we raised the ante to a thousand, after you spoke to The Man, you sure as hell knew."

"We did not raise the ante. You did."

Stopping at the corner of Sixty-Sixth and Lexington Frank asked, "Where are we going?"

"The West Village."

Frank made a sharp left onto Lexington, squeezing ahead of three cars and the Lexington Avenue bus. Mike was convinced that this corner would be his final look at the world.

"The scene of the crime?" Frank asked with great relish. The opportunity to quote pulp fiction dialogue overwhelmed his need to chastise Mike.

"No. The police station. Close but no cigar."

Frank drove with his neck thrust forward, his eyes two narrow slits, now peering toward a rapidly approaching Forty-Second Street. Mike long suspected the man needed glasses but was afraid to recommend an oculist. Frank did not like to be told what he needed.

"The bet stands," Frank proclaimed, as if Mike had suggested otherwise.

"The bet stands," Mike repeated as they raced through an

amber light.

NINETEEN

The desk sergeant squared his shoulders and ran a hand through his hair, looking as if he were trying to remember the police manual's recommended protocol for dealing with members of the press. He settled for pointing in answer to Mike's query. Following that lead Mike found his way to Lieutenant Rocco's office.

It was a sterile cell that contained a white Formica desk, a cushioned aluminum desk chair, a matching visitor's chair with its back to the wall, and no window. The white walls were bereft of even the usual police propaganda posters, the occupant's diplomas, commendations or art preferences. If the lieutenant had a wife and family they were not represented in color snaps on his desk. In their place stood a chrome bar boldly proclaiming the name and title of the room's occupant.

Also prominently displayed was a copy of today's *Morning News*, a note-pad, pencil and, breaking the monotony or a city decorator's idea of color contrast, a black telephone. There was nothing else in the claustrophobic cube except the lieutenant.

If his name didn't proclaim his ancestry, his clear, olive skin, brown eyes and dark hair, would. The ceiling's florescent light accentuated the gray threads just beginning to streak the hair he wore combed straight back and as fashionably long as regulations permitted. The silver would dominate before Rocco was forty and he would probably die at ninety with a full head of white hair. Even sitting, one was aware of the lean, tight, wiry body, as taut as a perfectly strung bow.

A prototype of the quintessential male, that was Mike's assessment of the officer. A macho guy with a sense of humor that would make a eulogist come off as a stand-up comic. However, a devastatingly handsome prototype. This last thought seemed to surface in Mike's sharp mind of its own accord. Mike struggled to suppress this observation as Rocco acknowledged his presence.

"The commissioner told me you were coming."

"I hope it's not an inconvenient time," Mike said.

"Would it make any difference to you?" The uneasy welcome turned to open hostility.

Mike was used to this, especially from public servants who resented privilege and thought everyone should be treated with equal distain. "No," Mike said, entering the room, "it wouldn't make any difference. It's my time being infringed upon. You wanted to see me, or was Andy mistaken?"

Mike dropped the commissioner's familiar name with the subtlety of a terrorist bomb. Jack would knock the chip off this tight-assed bastard's shoulder, but Mike's relationship with Andrew Brandt prohibited antagonizing the police. But he could tilt the chip precariously before his chat with Rocco ended.

Rocco nodded toward the visitor's chair. Score one for the visiting team. Mike's long legs were encased in a pair of faded jeans and above them a navy pea coat, its broad collar turned up against the November wind. He opened the coat as he sat, putting Rocco's eyes in a direct line with the crotch of Mike's blue-white denims. Rocco raised his eyes to meet Mike's and it was the latter who blushed. Score one for the home team and what was this guy all about, anyway?

Mike was feeling things he didn't want to feel for this dick in a three-buttoned banker's gray suit and rep tie, starched white shirt and, Mike suspected, meticulously ironed white boxer shorts. Who ironed them? Can it, Mike.

Rocco tapped the *Morning News* with his index finger. The nail was trimmed in military fashion, short and clean. "What did Bokowski say to you?"

"I'll level with you…"

"I wasn't expecting anything less."

Christ. The man was relentless. "Will you tell me what you know?"

Rocco smiled, his eyes scrutinizing the visitor. "You mean, you show me yours and I'll show you mine? Suppose I got more to show – I mean tell – then I'd feel cheated. You don't want to fuck the police, do you, Mr. Gavin?"

Who was writing this prick's dialogue? Elmore Leonard? Maybe Rocco had spent too many years in this coffin of an office. Or maybe it was the neighborhood. Perhaps affectation was catching, like a dose of the clap. And maybe the tingle in Mike's groin was a figment of his imagination. Mike's instinct, as exacting as a hound's sense of smell, told him that Rocco was putting on a show. A show intended for an audience of one – Mike Gavin. Why? And how far would Mike have to go to find out?

"You wouldn't feel cheated, Lieutenant. You'd be outdistanced." If Rocco wanted to play show and tell this was his chance to ante up.

"What do you want from us, Mr. Gavin?" Retreat. The score was now two to one favor of the visiting team and Mike was at bat.

"Do you know Johnny was a hustler? Before he stepped into Freddy Fine's briefs and caught the brass ring."

"We know. We also have a list of his old customers. The ones who get their name in your column. Dining, dancing, yachting, farting and going down on pretty boys while their wives get their legs waxed at Elizabeth Arden's. Poor souls, don't they know their husbands like hairy legs? You're not on the list, Mr. Gavin."

Of course, Rocco had his informants. In this part of the city they were easy prey for a cockteaser like this cop. Rocco gave a little and got as much as he could out of them. How much did he give? Ironed white boxers. Maybe even starched. And beneath them? Was that starched, too? Cut? Uncut? Can it, Gavin.

"I don't pay for it, Lieutenant."

"I didn't think you did, Mr. Gavin. No offense."

"I'll consider the source."

"What else do you want to know, Mr. Gavin?"

"Johnny was wide open for blackmail," Mike said.

"Do you really think so, Mr. Gavin? Ex-hustler makes good. I don't think Johnny would give a shit if they made a mini-series of his gutter to glory life story – as long as it starred Johnny Jones."

"Freddy Fine would care. A lot of little boys wear his brand of underwear and mama buys 'em. They don't want to give their darlings any ideas they haven't already acquired from MTV."

"You know a lot about the garment trade, Mr. Gavin."

Mike shrugged. "I used to be associated with the industry in a minor way."

Rocco leaned back in his chair, appraising Mike. The gray suit jacket, unbuttoned, parted and Mike noted that the cop's dress shirt had been tapered, or was custom made. Not a wrinkle to mar the pima cotton that stretched across his chest and flat belly. "You're too modest, Mr. Gavin. You were one of the highest paid male models in the business."

A compliment or a kick in the balls? With a guy like this, who knows? Mike decided on a polite, "Thank you. Nice of you to remember."

The response came with the speed and sting of a billy club. "How could I forget? My wife used to cut your pictures out of magazines and paste them in a scrapbook. Maybe it was a wish book, eh? Mike Gavin in his Arrow shirt, Brooks Brothers suit, Countess Mara tie; brushing his teeth, shampooing his hair, smoking his favorite brand. Back then they didn't pose live models in their skivvies, but I bet you would have made Johnny Jones look like an also ran."

This compliment from hell, delivered with unbridled contempt, startled the object of the grudge only slightly more than the orator.

Several months ago, Mike was ready to make a pact with the devil in return for beating Jack Montgomery in a tennis match. Looking at Rocco, pale and shaken after baring his soul, Mike wondered what the man would give to have the clock turned back a lousy ten seconds.

A patrol car pulled away from the building, its siren screaming. Were they closing ranks? On their way to rescue Lieutenant Rocco's pride? Sorry boys, it's too late. You would find the officer DOA. Poisoned by his own venom. Not an overdose, but ingested daily for some fifteen years and culminating in death at the sight of the cause of his addiction.

The siren's wail ebbed as Rocco regained his composure, stopping short of a blush. The sounds of a functioning police station filled the void. A ringing telephone, laughter, the tread of heavy feet and the unmistakable whir of a copy machine.

Mike felt sorry for the guy but he could afford to be magnanimous. He had found the flaw in his nemesis. The green eyed monster rearing its ugly head. A paltry prize but, what the hell, a prize nonetheless.

Mike broke the embarrassing silence with kind words. "I trust that was before you were married."

"We were courting."

Courting? Coming from anyone else, Mike would have laughed. But from James Rocco the quaint word was more apt than pretentious. Meticulously dressed, perfectly groomed, proffering flowers and candy, he went courting.

"I was a four-color snap. You were flesh and blood. I doubt there was even a contest, Lieutenant, and no one could make Johnny Jones look like an also ran."

"Johnny Jones is a scum bag."

"That's no reason to arrest him for murder."

"Do you think Bokowski was blackmailing Johnny, or did he have a hard-on for him?"

"I don't know," Mike answered.

"What do you know, Mr. Gavin?"

"That you believe Johnny has a roommate. One he's not

going public with."

"Sorry, Mr. Gavin. Now it's your turn. I gave. I told you we know Johnny was a hustler and we're checking out his old clients, including his boss, Freddy Fine, and the guy who takes the pictures, Ken Wallace. In case you're interested, Johnny's birth name is Giancarlo LaBella and Wallace was born Alvin Darling."

Mike laughed. "I knew about Johnny but Alvin Darling is pure camp."

Surprisingly, Rocco was also laughing, his brown eyes twinkling like a mischievous schoolboy's. The effect was disarming. "You didn't know?"

"I don't have your resources."

"What do you have, Mr. Gavin?"

"Please, call me Mike."

"Should I be honored?"

"No, relieved. Formality is a pain in the ass."

"I'm a very formal man, Mr. Gavin."

"Mike."

"I'm a very formal man, Mike."

"Isn't that better?"

"Better than what?"

"Mr. Gavin."

Rocco pulled a face. "Cut the bullshit and tell me what Matthew Bokowski said to you."

Mike told Rocco what he had not revealed to his readers. He never intended not to. The police had to know but he thought he could use his knowledge to bargain. Give-and-take. He didn't know he was going to square off with a pro at the game. Maybe that was Mike's problem. The cause of that vague feeling of disquiet that crept over him when he wasn't looking. He was surrounded by pros. When was amateur night and where could he buy a ticket?

Rocco listened with his hands clasped in a tight ball under his chin. When Mike finished, he quoted from memory, "If you knew something that would make headlines; something bigger than Watergate; but to expose it would be unethical, what would you do?" He shook his head as if in disbelief. "Are you telling me we're sitting on a Washington time bomb? A case for the Attorney General?"

"I'm only telling you what Bokowski said to me. I wouldn't give it more credence than it deserves. It's the type of theoretical question instructors pose to their budding journalists. For all I know, Bokowski was enrolled in a communications course and trying to get me to do his homework."

"Did he mention Johnny Jones?" Rocco questioned. "Indicate that he had connections here, in New York?"

"Negative. We talked for two or three minutes, not more, and I cut him off right after he asked that question. I wanted specifics. He refused to give any. I said I couldn't help him and excused myself."

Rocco nodded. "And four months later he turns up dead in Johnny Jones' glorified tenement."

Strange description for a mini apartment building on Grove Street, a few blocks from where they were sitting. More of Rocco's quaint jargon or the result of shrewd observation? Mike composed an ad for the Village Voice. WANTED, INVISIBLE ROOMMATE TO SHARE VILLAGE PAD IN GLORIFIED TENEMENT.

"Was he gay?" Rocco asked.

Mike pretended to think it over, playing for time. The intern at Bethesda Medical. It wasn't a trump card but it was the only card Mike had held on to and the game of give-and-take was nearing an end. "He wasn't wearing a neon sign, Lieutenant."

"I didn't think he was, Mr. Gavin."

"Mike."

"I didn't think he was, Mike, but I thought perhaps – I don't know how to put it politely."

"That it takes one to know one, perhaps?"

"Thank you, Mike."

"Any time, Lieutenant."

"I'll ask the obvious, Mr. Mike. Do you know any Washington bigshots who were customers of Johnny Jones?"

Mike smiled benevolently. "If I did I wouldn't tell you."

Rocco nodded his approval. "I admire loyalty."

Mike was beginning to appreciate Rocco's technique. Lead the guy in the hot seat to the edge of the precipice, show him the rocks below, then assure him that he would be safe providing he remained in the protective embrace of James Rocco. This cop was a student of his countryman, Machiavelli.

"Amanda told me something I think may be significant."

"Amanda?" Rocco raised an eyebrow.

"Amanda Richards. The actress."

"A very beautiful lady."

"She would agree," Mike said. "It seems Bokowski talked to her shortly after I dismissed him, but before the conversation got past a polite hello, the security people broke in and asked to see his I.D. Of course, he was wearing his press tag, prominently displayed."

"They were harassing him. Why?"

"I thought you could ask them why."

"We can try." For the first time Rocco made a note on his clean pad, in shorthand. "Do you know the name of the security firm?"

"No. But I'm sure it's common knowledge. Washington is a small town."

"Not small enough to give us a link between Johnny and Bokowski, and Johnny swears on his mother's grave that he doesn't know Bokowski."

"That sounds sincere."

"Really? Johnny's mother isn't dead."

"I take it you let Johnny go."

"No reason not to. Freddy Fine's jockstraps don't hold fingerprints."

"Thank God for small favors," Mike sighed.

"We'll follow up on everything you told us. The Washington connection interests me. I'll interrogate everyone who knew Bokowski. One of them might even tell us why Bokowski paid a visit to Johnny Jones, presumably uninvited."

Mike felt a twinge of guilt as he thought of someone who might know what Bokowski was doing in New York. The intern at Bethesda Medical. He decided to play give-and-take one more time. If Rocco told him why he suspected Johnny has a roommate, Mike would give him the intern.

"Why do you think Johnny has a roommate?"

"What makes you think I do? This is the second time you asked that."

"A hunch. Something the commissioner said."

"No comment," Rocco said.

You blew it, Lieutenant. Mike rose, his hands buried in the pockets of the pea coat. "I guess that's it. Stay in touch."

"You do the same," Rocco replied, more threatening than inviting.

At the door, Mike paused. "Does Mrs. Rocco still have the scrapbook?"

"I don't know. We respect each other's space. Why do you ask?"

"Just wondering if you ever sneak a peek at it."

"Bastard."

"Mike."

TWENTY

At this moment in his life Mike did not need James Rocco. Whether he wanted James Rocco in his life was a moot question because Mike refused even to contemplate the idea. He had enough on his plate, namely Jack Montgomery, and dessert, no matter how tempting, was to be avoided assiduously.

Matthew Bokowski had appealed to Mike for help, in a rather oblique fashion to be sure, but still a plea that Mike had not heeded. Now that young man was dead, brutally murdered, and this guy flashing a tin badge and a come-fuck-me attitude threatened to divert Mike from what he now realized was an obligation to Matthew Bokowski. Find his killer and bring the prick to justice, or what passed for justice in this era of plea bargaining and unscrupulous defense attorneys who too often seemed to abet rather than mitigate the offense.

Six months ago Mike would have welcomed this quasi erotic intrusion into his life. Enjoyed the diversion. The challenge. Happy to match wits and innuendos with this cop who protested too much. Make Rocco the pin-up boy of his JO fantasies. Drown the unrequited affair in hard liquor while listening to music to lick his wounds by. In short, all the trappings of a teenage crush minus the petting, the prom and the pimples.

Rocco's main attraction was his unavailability. The poet (Keats?) wrote, HEARD MELODIES ARE SWEET, BUT THOSE UNHEARD ARE SWEETER. Hence the allure of the prick teaser. Was Mike a threat to Mrs. Rocco's virtue or her husband's? Mike would like to find out. But not now. Definitely, not now.

Mike also did not need the pouting, little boy demeanor Jack greeted him with at the end of this most trying day. "Indigestion? Or did Freddy forget to bring the contract to *Chez Louis*?" Mike knew the reason for Jack's chagrin would have to be explored and dispelled before Jack would tell him what Freddy had to say, or not say, about Johnny Jones and Murder One.

"Asiate," Jack said, "in the Mandarin Oriental Hotel."

The thought of dining thirty-five stories above Central Park with a personality as volatile as Jack's gave Mike an attack of vertigo. Freddy was either most trusting or most stupid.

"The contract was signed in my agent's office this morning. Lunch was a goodwill gesture," Jack explained.

Mike went to the kitchen for ice. Jack followed. "Drinks to toast your new life in the fast lane, or should I say the runway?"

"Fuck you, Gavin."

I'd rather have dinner, Mike thought, but one must humor the young. First Rocco with a vendetta to settle, now Montgomery with a bug up his ass. "What are you drinking? Apple juice, mineral water or Bass?" Mike refused to keep carrot juice in the refrigerator on the grounds that the color made him nauseous early in the day.

"Whatever you're having."

Am I to be spared nothing this bloody day, Mike bemoaned. Jack never drank booze. Mike filled a small tin bucket with ice and headed for the living room and dry bar. Jack followed. Mike poured two Jack Daniel's and mineral water, one considerably weaker than the other. If life with Jack the jock was trying, life with Jack, the June centerfold of *Playgirl*, would be a nightmare.

"Did Freddy put the make on you?" Mike asked in a futile attempt to snap Jack out of his mysterious funk.

"No," Jack exclaimed, as if the slight had just occurred to him. "The bastard didn't."

"Not to worry," Mike told him. "Ken Wallace is going to do the principal photography and I'm sure he'll make up for Freddy's negligence."

"So where was Wallace today? Not one flash bulb popped all afternoon."

And that was it. Jack's plunge into Freddy Fine's jeans

hadn't drawn the attention of a presidential news conference and the star attraction was miffed. "I guess Freddy isn't up to his old drum beating self these days. Thanks to Johnny Jones the company is up to its chin in publicity and the P.R. boys are recommending a low profile until things simmer down." Mike paused before asking, "Did Freddy have any news about Johnny or was he afraid it would bruise the cuisine?"

Jack grimaced with every sip of his drink. If Mike were Jesus he would change the bourbon to water without embarrassing Jack. "Freddy was more interested in asking me what you know than in telling me what he knows," Jack said.

"For instance?"

"Your piece in the paper this morning. What did Bokowski tell you? Do you know what he was doing in Johnny's apartment and how he got in? Is there a Washington connection because you met Bokowski at the Vice President's party? Did you talk to the police? What do they think?"

"What did you tell him?"

"Dick."

"Good boy, Montgomery. You're learning. And what did he tell you?"

"Dick."

"Jack, he must have said something. His main man comes home and finds a corpse on his bed. A strange corpse. It's not something you can ignore like an ill-timed fart."

"Freddy is touting the company line," Jack said. "Johnny knows nothing. Zero, Zip, Nada. Ditto, Freddy."

"Johnny knows something," Mike insisted, getting up to build himself another drink. "He might not know Bokowski, or how he got in the apartment, but he damn well knows someone who does know. There's a link between Johnny and Bokowski. There's got to be. And Johnny knows who it is. My guess is so does Freddy.

"He asked all the right questions. How much do I know. How

close I am to the truth. The Washington connection. Freddy took the bait I laid out for the murderer who didn't call, by the way."

"Maybe I had lunch with him," Jack said.

"Freddy Fine doesn't dirty his hands and certainly not with a weapon flaunting his own logo."

"Try this," Jack said. "If Bokowski was threatening Johnny, maybe Freddy would get his hands dirty to keep his cash flow flowing. Of course, your pal Brad Turner also has a good reason to keep Johnny's chin above the shit. Opening a Broadway show minus its star is like launching a ship with a hole in the hull."

"Off-Broadway," Mike corrected, "and Brad was with Johnny at the supposed time of the murder."

"Maybe they're covering for each other."

"Maybe you should stick to carrot juice. Whoever killed Bokowski didn't do it to protect Johnny Jones but to implicate him in the crime or, at least, embarrass him. If Bokowski was killed to protect someone it wasn't Johnny but someone close to Johnny. Why else Johnny's apartment?"

Mike felt he had hit on a fact that made the victim and the murder venue plausible. Kill the threat, Bokowski, and scare the crap out of Johnny or put him out of the way for good. All to protect who? Someone close to Johnny. Freddy Fine or Ken Wallace? Why would they want to snuff the goose that laid the golden eggs? Johnny was the alchemist who spun cotton jockey shorts into gold.

But Freddy was squirming. Why? "Is Freddy's only concern getting his company's image tarnished, or is he afraid he might end up with a competitor's jockstrap around his neck?" Mike thought aloud.

Jack finally finished his drink "How would I know?"

"You were supposed to observe Freddy, not the absence of the media. You've got to stop letting your ego get in the way of your goal, Jack."

"What does that mean?"

"It means that when you go to Bethesda, you look for our intern, not popping flash bulbs."

Jack got up, took off his jacket and began undoing his tie. "I asked Freddy what he knew and he said nothing. Then he started asking the questions and didn't stop."

"You can learn more from questions than from answers."

"So, I told you all the questions," Jack said. "What did you learn?"

"That Freddy is scared – and why are you undressing?"

"I'm going to shower, then I'm cooking."

"You're what?"

"Cooking. I bought steaks and the makings for a salad. Why don't you start the salad?"

"I don't know how," Mike said.

Jack was down to his Freddy Fine briefs, his clothes in disarray on the floor. "Give it your best shot, Gavin."

"Pick up everything you just took off or you go to bed without supper."

Jack did as he was told with little enthusiasm. "Freddy wants to see you," he said, as if telling Mike to have a nice day.

"He said that?"

"That's what he said."

"Why the hell didn't you tell me before now?"

"Because you can learn more from questions than from answers."

"Fuck you, Montgomery."

"What did you do all day?" Jack asked.

"I talked to a cop named Rocco."

Jack dropped his briefs.

"Get in the shower, Jack."

As he retreated with an arm full of clothes, Jack asked, "What did the cop want? The one with the Eyetalian name."

"Same thing Freddy wanted."

"What did you tell him?"

"Dick."

"What did he tell you?"

"Dick."

TWENTY-ONE

Mike had told the police, in the person of Lt. James Rocco, what Bokowski said to him, withholding the intern connection for reasons already stated. That done, he could now pass on the same information to his readers – and the murderer, should he be interested. That said, Mike began mentally composing his column for next Saturday's edition of the *Morning News*.

It would include a full account of the Vice President's reception following the celebrity tennis matches, wherein Mike had been bamboozled by Jack. He hadn't reported it at the time because the sports pages had covered the games and Mike thought the reception too mundane to glorify in print. Or was it because he didn't want to give Jack the satisfaction of a coveted mention in *Mike Gavin's New York?* If Jack's weapon was a tennis racket, Mike's was the printed word, and did all affairs of the heart inevitably boil down to a series of hissy spats?

The venue of Bokowski's demise gave Johnny Jones a prominent role in Mike's proposed column for the coming weekend. Always looking for ways to best the competition, Mike wanted a one-on-one with Johnny but that, he knew, was improbable, if not impossible. Freddy Fine's lawyers and P.R. people would keep Johnny out of harm's way by making him inaccessible to all but the police, and even the police would have to show cause before they questioned Johnny more intensely than they already had.

But Mike could do the next best thing. Talk to Brad Turner, the director of Johnny's incipient play and Johnny's alibi for the night of the crime.

Jack had left early this morning for his gig in Virginia, leaving Mike space and time to move ahead with what he needed to do before he sat at his laptop and spewed it all out. Jack was amazingly efficient when it came to taking his show on the road, as he called the nomadic grind of the pro tennis circuit. He packed what he needed, with not so much as a pair of socks in excess. His toilet kit was sparse, but thanks to a flawless complexion and a beard that never knew a five o'clock shadow, it took very little to keep the star looking like a star. Practice makes perfect and Jack had been packing for the road since he was a teenager. His trainer cum manager would meet him in McLean with the tools of the trade and anything else Jack might need to perform to the best of his ability.

Mike wished that some of this efficiency would spill over to when Jack wasn't coming or going. There had always been someone to pick up after the child prodigy who Mike was trying to wean into a responsible adult. Mike wasn't disposed to play Daddy Dearest but then it was seldom one got the chance to do so with a guy as appealing as Jack Montgomery.

Compensation wasn't limited to the bedroom. After last night, Mike discovered, it extended to the kitchen. The dinner Jack had concocted for their evening at home bordered on the gourmet without being fussy. The steaks were top quality and Jack broiled them to medium- rare perfection; the French fries crisp on the outside and succulent within. As sous chef, Mike combined iceberg, hearts of romaine, cherry tomatoes and chives with an olive oil and red wine vinaigrette dressing for the salad.

Jack set the dining table, located at one end of the huge living room just outside the kitchen, with a damask cloth, the best china and silver Mike owned and never used, including Baccarat wine glasses and linen napkins encased in silver rings. The wine was a superb Bordeaux-St. Emilion which Mike hoped Jack had not charged at Mike's wine merchant, but of course he had.

The macho steaks and fries saved the presentation from being too precious.

"To the chef," Mike toasted with his wine.

"To good food, good grog and good company."

It was an evening of domestic harmony on a blustery fall night that had Mike looking forward to the joy of crawling beneath a downy quilt with his self-styled roommate. The only jarring note came when Jack speculated as to the possibility of there being a two-bedroom, two-bath, apartment available in the co-op Mike so loved.

This Mike deflected by asking if Jack had told his agent to send a couple of passes to the sports editor of Bokowski's Baltimore newspaper. He had. Mike then began to prompt Jack on the art of subtly pumping the reporter – if he showed up – for information that might lead to the name of Bokowski's intern friend. As it turned out all this was not necessary because the mountain would come to Mohammed. More later. Right now, the bed and downy quilt awaited.

TWENTY-TWO

Even Mike Gavin, a proud Columbia alumnus, conceded to the fact that the Yale Club (Brad Turner was an Eli) was the finest of the school clubs in New York. Twenty-two stories high and as imposing as its progenitor in New Haven, the Yale Club boasted three restaurants (one on the roof), a library, a gym, a pool (albeit a small pool), squash courts, a barber shop and many posh rooms that rivaled the accommodations of the city's better hotels.

The commodious lounge area or club room had two fireplaces and enough comfortable leather chairs and sofas to make any British gentlemen's club envious. Across the street from Grand Central Station (a block from Brooks Brothers) and the second floor bar, just off the lounge, was well staffed, well stocked and the place to see and be seen at cocktail time when business men and women down a quick one before catching their commuter train to Westchester and Connecticut.

The concierge told Mike that Mr. Turner would meet him in the men's locker room. Mike took the elevator to the fifth floor where the clerk at the reception desk told him that Mr. Turner had just come down from his squash game. Entering the men's lockers, Brad, sweating and stripping for the showers, greeted Mike with, "Perfect timing."

Brad Turner was a walking illustration of the old saw that proclaimed *all good things come in small packages*. Not more than five feet, eight, with dark hair that fell in bangs across his forehead and bright blue eyes that beamed at Mike from above a trim but muscular body. Brad Turner was the boy next door of song; rich, smart and, right now, stripped down to his jockstrap.

"I hope that's not a Freddy Fine jock," Mike said.

"I wouldn't be caught dead in a ….Sorry. That was a gross *faux pas*. No, it's just a plain old athletic support to house John Thomas and the family jewels." Brad got out of the jockstrap to reveal a pair of hefty gems and a bald headed John Thomas.

He grabbed a towel and headed for the showers. "I'll be back in minutes and we'll go to the roof for lunch."

The men's locker room was empty this early in the day. It would begin filling up around four and reach peak attendance after five. Mike sat in one of the comfortable chairs facing the TV which was thankfully turned off. Watching Brad's buttocks scudder across the empty room, Mike thought of that afternoon in Palm Beach where he, Brad and what's-his-name, had let it all hang out in a hot tub. It was a somewhat embarrassing memory but when motive and opportunity prevail it's hard not to succumb.

Motive and opportunity. The two factors a prosecuting attorney presents to a jury to build a case against the accused. Apply this line of reasoning to The Jockstrap Murder and you come up with Bokowski's intimating via a theoretical query that he knew something that would cause a stir bigger than Watergate. This conversation took place in Washington and Bokowski worked for a Baltimore newspaper. It would take the wit of a fruit fly to know Bokowski was sitting on a political time bomb.

Motive for The Jockstrap Murder? Silence Bokowski. *Cui bono?* A person or persons in the political arena, an area as big as the US of A.

Opportunity wasn't so easy. The murderer didn't happen to meet his victim in a lonely place on a foggy night. No, sir, he met him in the Greenwich Village apartment of a celebrated male model who didn't know the victim, nor did he know what the guy was doing in his apartment or how he got in the apartment. A classic locked room mystery and the police didn't have a clue – or a key.

Or did they? Johnny's roommate? That is, IF Johnny had a roommate.

TWENTY-THREE

The romance between Brad and what's-his-name didn't make it back to New York. The next time Mike saw Brad was at one of those off-off Broadway plays being performed in an unheated basement (it was mid-winter), Mike had been dragged to by Amanda who was there at the behest of the play's director with whom she was having a fling – as opposed to an affair. Flings were fun. Affairs were tedious. So states the conventional wisdom of Amanda Richards.

Brad Turner was the stage manager. Mike and Amanda were treated like royalty backstage which was on stage when the curtain was down. Amanda went off with her director and Mike took Brad for a drink at a local pub with sawdust on the floor and a sign over the bar that shouted IF YOURE (sic) GAY STAY AWAY. A glance around the crowded room informed Mike that the pub's clientele couldn't read.

Brad confessed that he was often tempted to call Mike but didn't because *"A guy like you can be very helpful to a guy who wants to make it big in the New York theater world and I'm going to make it standing on my two feet, not lying on a casting couch."*

After that, Brad Turner was Mike's fair laddie and rewarded with the number to Mike's most private land phone. That someone had abused that honor by giving the number to Ken Wallace still irked Mike. He had a strong suspicion that the culprit had given the number to Freddy Fine who passed it on to his buddy, Ken. Mike was biding his time before inciting the riot act and breaking a tennis racket over the culprit's blond head.

Brad returned looking bright eyed and bushy tailed, wrapped in a towel. "I couldn't get a partner so I played with the pro and got squashed, excuse the pun. I had to release the tension, Mike, or I'll explode. The theater's dark and we don't know when…"

"You're babbling," Mike said, moving to the bench fronting Brad's locker. "Take a few deep breaths and get dressed. We'll hash it all out over lunch and a beer."

Brad did as he was told and Mike crossed his arms over his chest and enjoyed the sight of Bradley Turner getting into his preppy motif. Blue boxers, chinos, button down white shirt (no tie needed thanks to the club's new relaxed dress rules), blazer and penny loafers.

They took the elevator to the top floor and stepped into the club's roof restaurant with its three spectacular city views, east, west and south. The captain knew them both by name but discretion being the better part of name dropping he led them silently to a table overlooking the outdoor terrace, facing east. "You said beer?" Brad asked as the captain dropped menus on the table.

Mike nodded as he picked up his menu and Brad ordered two light lagers. "The chicken salad is excellent," Brad recommended. "Not diced chicken wrapped in mayo but a nice mixed green salad topped with sliced chicken breast."

"Sold," Mike said, closing the menu he hadn't perused.

Mike began by asking Brad to go over, in detail, everything he could remember about the events that preceded Johnny finding the body in his apartment. It was the same chain of events Brad had reported to the police. Rehearsal was called for twelve noon at the theater on West Forty-Second Street. Johnny showed up on time as he always did. They worked straight through to about six then broke for dinner. Yes, Johnny left the theater as did all the cast. Brad and the stage manager ordered sandwiches and sodas from a local deli and remained in the theater.

Everyone was back in the theater by seven or a little after and rehearsal resumed till ten that night. Brad talked to Johnny for about ten minutes before Johnny left the theater. A cab took Johnny from the theater to his apartment on Grove Street which would be about a fifteen minute ride if the traffic was light.

Johnny called the police as soon as he saw the body. Rocco and his crew arrived sometime after eleven when Rocco estimated the corpse had been dead for hours. Rigor had set in. The murder took place in the early afternoon..

"Johnny was at the theater when Bokowski was murdered," Mike said. "Your main man didn't tie the love knot around Bokowski's neck."

"Johnny might not have done it personally but his bedroom is the crime scene which leaves him wide open to suspicion of aiding and abetting. It's only Johnny's word that he doesn't know the victim nor how he and the murderer got into his apartment."

"Do you believe him?" Mike asked.

Their beers arrived in smart pilsner glasses. Both men sampled the brew before Brad answered. "I believe him, Mike. Johnny is a Bronx boy, full of the old piss and vinegar, street smarts and ambition. He's a prick tease, a hustler and a con artist, but he's not a murderer nor is he an actor. Trust me with this. I saw him in Freddy's office the day after he found the body on his bed and he was in a state of shock, Mike, and it was no act. I've been trying to teach him to act for a couple of weeks now and the best he can do is recite his lines and make them sound plausible and not laughable. That corpse scared the crap out of Johnny and I'm witness to the fact. Guts and guile are Johnny's trump cards, not brute force."

"Which begs the question, why are you using a guy who can't act for your debut venture as a director? Surely not because he looks good in Freddy Fine's jockey briefs."

"The producer finds him enticing enough in Freddy's BVD's to put up the moola for my show." Here, Brad elucidated. The play, a pastiche of comedy and mystery, by Tina Baron, was performed in a few 'barns' on the strawhat circuit the previous season. The producer, Max Berger, saw it and decided the male lead was perfect for Johnny Jones, the dream boy of *Freddy Fine Enterprises*. Max contacted Tina who directed him to her agent who is Brad's agent. Seeing a chance for a package deal, the agent brought Max, Tina and Brad together and, Brad emoted, "A star was born."

"The play is an unabashed takeoff of any of Joe Orton's

prize comedies but I jumped at the chance of doing it because I'm the new kid on the block and offers are few and far between – read that nonexistent. Also, I think Hollywood has the hots for Johnny and if I can put him over in this cream-puff I could thumb a ride on his Westward-Ho wagon."

Their chicken salad a la the Yale Club arrived looking as appetizing as Brad's prediction. Digging in, Mike said, "You were in the right place at the right time and took advantage of the fact. Good for you. Your star is on the ascendant, Bradley, and I can say I knew you when."

"That said, I'll add my misgivings. Your story reads like the plot of a Hollywood musical which can be taken with that grain of salt on the screen but rejected as bullshit in real life. It's all too convenient for you, this Tina Baron and our Johnny. Excuse my English, but what the fuck is this Max Berger all about?"

Brad hailed a passing waiter and asked for refills on the beer. To Mike he said, "I'm so glad you asked because I've been wondering what Max is all about since the day I met him."

"And what's your take on him?"

Brad laughed. "He reminds me of an actor in a Hollywood musical, playing the part of a Broadway producer."

"As they say in the antiques trade, what's his provenance?" Mike asked, tossing back his beer before a new one was placed before him.

"He says he represents a small group of investors who want to put up some risk capital and get into show business. No, I never met any of the people he says he represents, nor do I believe him but in this business you don't grill an angel. You take his money and run with it, which is what I'm doing."

"You're a clever lad, Bradley. Who do you think sent Johnny this angel?"

"God, of course, in the guise of Freddy Fine. Freddy wants to make his mannequin a popular actor which will increase the popularity of the Freddy Fine logo by tenfold. He doesn't back Johnny openly for two reasons. One, it looks too gross, too manipulative. Two, if Johnny falls on his face the shame won't rub off on Freddy. Hence, Freddy digs up Max, from God knows where, and a play gets on the boards."

"Could be," Mike said, "and if what I suspect is true, this gets Freddy Fine and Co. off my list of murder suspects."

"Enlighten me," Brad responded.

"I thought the murderer did his thing in Johnny's apartment to implicate Johnny in the crime and close down the play before it even opened. If that's so, Freddy and his people are out of the running because they have a vested interest in the play's success, which leaves us up the old tainted creek without a paddle."

"You really think someone is trying to sabotage the play?"

"It figures," Mike answered. "You just told me that without Johnny there is no play, but none of this tells us what Matthew Bokowski from Baltimore was doing in Johnny's apartment, who let him in and who tied a jockstrap around his neck when he got him there."

"That you actually talked to this Bokowski is beyond amazing. It's awesome. Can you tell me what he said to you?" Brad asked.

"I'm going to tell the world with Saturday's edition of the *Morning News*, but I'll give you an exclusive right now."

Mike held back until the waiter had cleared their table, offering them coffee and dessert which they declined in favor of another beer. When the waiter was out of hearing range Mike told Brad, verbatim, what Matthew Bokowski had said to him, including Bokowski's mention of a friend who was an intern at Bethesda Medical.

"Bokowski was silenced," Brad concluded.

"By who and why in Johnny Jones' apartment?"

"Beats the shit out of me, Mike."

"There's got to be a connection between Johnny and Bokowski. Johnny may be telling the truth when he says he doesn't know Bokowski, but Johnny knows how Bokowski got in his apartment, or who let him in. There's another key to the

Grove Street flat and Johnny knows who has it. I think the police suspect Johnny has a roommate. So do I. Or a lover. You've been with him every day for the past two weeks. Is there a roommate or lover?"

Brad shook his head. "Johnny the pin-up boy is a publicity hound but he keeps a low profile when it comes to his personal life. We have a bunch of teenage girls who hang around the stage door waiting to see him coming and going. Even a few boy fans keep a vigil but no one guy or gal in particular."

Brad waited for the waiter to deposit their beers and remove the empty glasses before he continued. "A taxi picks up Johnny every night after rehearsal. A few times, when I left with Johnny, I noticed there was someone in the waiting cab. A guy, but he kept himself hidden in the back seat. Once he pulled the tip of his hat down to cover most of his face when Johnny opened the door to get in."

"What kind of a hat?"

"A baseball cap, I think. Yeah, I remember. The Orioles."

"The Baltimore Orioles," Mike said. "All roads to Baltimore."

"You want to know who I thought it was?"

"I'm all ears, Bradley."

"Being an incurable romantic, I was hoping it was an actor. Some big Broadway or Hollywood star who's married and getting it off with Johnny but is terrified of being caught in the act."

"An actor or a politician," Mike said. "Remember the Watergate reference. I think there's a Washington connection and if that's what he is he wouldn't be the first Washingtonian who liked a piece of boy ass on the side."

Brad took a slug of beer and offered, "Or an actor with political ambitions. We have precedent for that. Namely, George Murphy, Ronnie Reagan and the Terminator himself, Arnie Schwarzenegger."

Mike nodded thoughtfully as he savored his brew. This meeting with Brad Turner was proving more enlightening than Mike had hoped for. What Brad had seen wasn't proof that Johnny Jones had a lover but it announced that Johnny was seeing someone who didn't want it known that he was on intimate terms with the popular model. How far would that person go to keep his relationship with Johnny a secret? That would depend on how much he had to lose if the relationship went public.

It wasn't much to go on, but it was all Mike had and how long would it be before Lt. Rocco was wise to Johnny's phantom boyfriend? If Rocco found something in Johnny's apartment to indicate Johnny didn't live alone, did what he had seen identify Johnny's roomie? "An actor or a politician or Pete Sampras." Mike wondered aloud.

Brad sprinkled water on Mike's less than radiant spark. "It doesn't make sense."

"The victim Bokowski," Mike said as if conceding defeat.

"Of course. If Bokowski was silenced because of what he knew and if what he knew was that some VIP was rubbing dicks with Johnny Jones, HOW, I ask you, could a cub reporter from a tiny rag in Baltimore know about this when not even the great Mike Gavin is aware of it."

"Thanks for the backhanded compliment, Bradley. I try not to stick my nose into other people's bedrooms in the hope that they'll keep their sniffers out of my bunk house."

"Speaking of bedrooms, how's the blond jock? Surprised he let you off the ball-an'-chain long enough to break bread with the likes of me."

Mike wagged a finger at his lunch date. "Don't be a bitch, Bradley. It doesn't become your sexy preppy image. Jack is playing a gig in McLean, Virginia as we speak and he's going to see if he can trace that intern at Bethesda Medical that Bokowski mentioned in our brief chat."

Brad groaned in mock surprise. "You trust that arrogant pipsqueak to make discreet inquiries in an area rife with rumor and conjecture. You got large *cojones*, Michael."

"Jack may be arrogant, but I believe pipsqueak means

something small and nowhere is Jack Montgomery small."

Brad had managed to get a rise out of Mike Gavin and smiled indulgently at his triumph. Then he went in for the kill. "Remember our brief encounter that afternoon in a Palm Beach hot tub? You, me, and my pal, Randolph."

"I recall the occurrence with a sigh and a blush."

"Did you ever tell Jack about our moment in the sun?"

"No."

"Why not?"

"Less said, soonest mended."

"Remind him of what Jesus said about who may cast the first stone. And didn't Prince Perfect have himself a princess at Wimbledon?"

Mike rolled his eyes. "I keep telling everyone her mother is a princess and her pop is common folk like me and you, which makes her a Lady."

"Jack might enjoy a three-way in a hot tub," Brad insisted.

"And the pope might enjoy serving a Seder dinner in the Vatican. Let's keep Palm Beach between us, Bradley."

"Us and Randolph," Brad said. "Or have you forgotten Randy Randy as he was known at Groton?"

"The name I forgot. The rest of him is still most vivid. What ever became of Randy Randy?"

"He's engaged to marry Liz Singleton in apple blossom time."

Mike grinned. "How nice. Is Liz lovely?"

"She's worth about fifty million dollars and when granddaddy dies she'll be worth twice as much."

"She's lovely," Mike declared. "Your mention of Groton reminds me that I met a buddy of yours in Washington that ominous weekend. Tim Samuels."

"Tiny Tim," Brad exclaimed.

"Really?" Mike said.

Brad laughed. "No, no. Nothing like that. He broke his leg playing football one season and hopped around on a crutch most of one semester. Hence, Tiny Tim. Get it?"

"Yes, Bradley, I get it. His father is the senator who's so far right he's wrong. Get it?"

"Tim's okay. He was interested in the theater at one point. Came to see me a few months back but nothing came of it. Was he at the dinner where you met Bokowski?"

"He was, but I'm sure they don't know each other. Tim was a guest while Bokowski was a working member of the press and never the twain shall meet."

"Are you going to mention the intern in your column on Saturday?"

"No," Mike told him. "I have no idea what his relationship was with Bokowski so don't want to implicate him unless it becomes necessary. However, I am going to quote you, if I may."

"You know the old show biz quip. You can say what you want about me as long as you spell my name right."

TWENTY-FOUR

Mike sat at his desk, keying in his copy for Saturday's column.

Yesterday I told you I spoke to The Jockstrap Murder victim. Now I'll reveal the venue of our meeting and what he said to me.

Mike assured his readers that he had given this information to Lt. James Rocco, officer in charge of The Jockstrap Murder case, yesterday and that he would continue to cooperate with the police in any way they thought he could further their investigation.

Next he reported on his exclusive interview with Bradley Turner, giving a first-hand account of Johnny Jones' activities leading up to the discovery of the body in Johnny's bedroom.

Bradley Turner, director of the forthcoming play starring Johnny Jones, told me he believes Johnny is sincere when he says he doesn't know the victim, Matthew Bokowski, or how Bokowski and the murderer got into his apartment.

True to his word, Mike didn't mention the intern at Bethesda Medical, but he did appeal to friends and acquaintances of Matthew Bokowski to contact the police, *or this column*, if they believed they had any information that might explain how, or why, Matthew Bokowski got into Johnny Jones' New York apartment. Adding, *discretion assured and it's a reporter's Hippocratic Oath never to reveal a source.*

It was a broad hint but the murderer, if astute, would read between the lines and know Mike Gavin suspected there was a friend of the victim who could account for Bokowski's fatal New York junket. What had Bokowski said that Mike Gavin wasn't reporting? Albeit, Lt. Rocco might also pick up on this and chastise Mike for his lapse in memory. (Mike grinned sheepishly at the idea of being chastised by Lt. James Rocco.)

Mike returned to the Watergate theme for a finale and rattled the beads when he wrote that Lt. Rocco wasn't ruling out The Jockstrap Murder as a case for the Attorney General.

Was Matthew Bokowski (AKA Matthew Burke) silenced for what he knew? What's the connection between the victim and Johnny Jones? Surely there must be a connection even if Johnny doesn't know it – as yet.

Johnny says there's one key to his apartment and that key was with him in a theater on West Forty-Second Street when the killer and his victim entered (not breaking in) Johnny's Grove Street residence. When you've ruled out the impossible, look to the plausible.

During my interview with Bradley Turner, the name of playwright Joe Orton was dropped. I believe it was Orton who said, "The whole trouble with Western Society today is the lack of something worth concealing." The Jockstrap Murder will prove Joe Orton woefully wrong.

It's the job of an investigative reporter to ruffle feathers but as Mike looked over his copy he wondered if he had gone a tad too far. He had insinuated much and raised enough doubts and questions to tweak the ire of folks from Pennsylvania Avenue to Seventh Avenue. If the killer had got into Johnny's apartment with a magic key, why couldn't the prick use the same divine tool to get into Mike's apartment?

Here, right on cue, Mike heard his front door open. Someone, uninvited, was in the apartment.

"Ready or not, here comes papa!"

Mike was amused, and relieved, to hear the sonorous voice of Peter Grimes, Mike's Man Friday. The founder and sole employee of the domestic agency *Your Man Friday* had arrived to perform his weekly chores for which he charged a living wage, if one lived on champagne and caviar.

Grimes' name was operatic but his forte was strictly Broadway. A chorus boy, he had hoofed his way through a dozen musicals including the Ethel Merman classic, *Gypsy*, where he was seen as one of the newsboys in the *Baby Jane and her Newsboys* routine, and as Riff in the touring company of *West Side Story*.

Between shows he paid the rent by cleaning the apartments of many of the stars, producers and directors he toiled with on the boards. When the plague ended the careers of hundreds of male gypsies faster than bad reviews, Grimes got out of show business with his tits intact (as he liked to say) and went into service, as he labeled his new calling. His clientele was strictly A-List and he was often invited to dinner by those he condescended to service.

When the disembodied voice became a presence in Mike's bedroom it asked, "Who snuffed Bokowski in Johnny's pad?"

"Strange," Mike said, "I was going to ask you the same thing."

Grimes, who still had an athlete's physique – although Mike suspected the ex-hoofer wore a dancer's belt or male girdle to hide the handle bars – feigned astonishment and shook his head of silver hair. "I don't know nothin' 'bout birthin' babies or corpses in Johnny Jones' bed, Master Mike." He removed his camel hair polo coat and school muffler (Yale today) and proceeded to hang them neatly in the bedroom closet. "You need a bigger closet, Master, or a lover with a smaller wardrobe."

Mike ignored the comment. Now in his work clothes – designer jeans and white dress shirt with open collar to reveal a black Tee – Grimes began stripping the bed. "So you spoke to the poor guy in the jockstrap necktie. My, my, Master, you sure do get around. What did the poor soul say to you?"

"Read all about it in Saturday's *Morning News*."

"Which means he didn't tell you he knew Johnny Jones or planned to visit him." Grimes went into the bathroom to empty the hamper. "The heady aroma of Lagerfeld tells me Adonis performed his ablutions here this morning. The scent lingers like a haunting refrain, as lyricists like to say. I knew an actor who had skin like leather, thanks to all those years in the saddle, who would dab Lagerfeld on his balls after showering to please his boyfriend, who was nominated for a supporting Oscar when he portrayed a ballplayer. Now that's what I call type casting."

Emerging with an armful of laundry, Grimes dropped them on the bed and began separating shirts destined to be picked up by Mike's commercial launderer from items that didn't need ironing and could be taken to the laundry room in the basement and have done before he left. Pausing, he picked up a pair of shorts. "These are not yours."

Mike turned in his swivel chair. "They're Jack's."

"May I have them?"

"No. You may not."

"Jack Montgomery's worn knickers would command a fortune on eBay," Grimes insisted.

"You would keep them for your own depraved purposes like the dirty old man you are."

"You have a dirty mind, Master."

"And laundry in need of washing, not viewing on e-Bay."

"Color me gone," Grimes said, stuffing the sheets and washables into a laundry bag.

Mike held up a restraining hand. "What's the scuttlebutt on Johnny Jones and his connection to The Jockstrap Murder?" This wasn't the first time Mike had used Peter Grimes to learn what the gay community and Grimes' theater clients were saying about the scandal of the moment. Johnny and his employer were known in both social sets.

"Johnny's former occupation," Grimes said, hefting the loaded sack over his shoulder like a sailor toting a duffle bag. "What else? I never tattle on those I serve, hence Jack's jockeys in your hamper will not be the lead item on the six o'clock news this evening. That said, I'll tell you what I'm sure you already know. Johnny, nee Giancarlo, was a hustler who caught the eye of Ken Wallace. Ken, who pimps for Freddy Fine, introduced Johnny to Fred and the Holy Trinity was born."

"So who's Matthew Bokowski?"

Grimes lowered the laundry bag to the floor and answered, "A smart-ass reporter who was looking for an exclusive interview with Johnny, or a piece of Johnny's coveted derriere, and when he got turned down he threatened to expose Johnny as a former ten-bucks-a-blow boy, thereby getting himself lured to Johnny's apartment where he got his comeuppance."

"Forget it," Mike said. "Bokowski was a rube kid from Nowhereville. He wouldn't have the knowledge or the balls for what you're suggesting and Freddy's people wouldn't turn Johnny's pad into a murder scene. It ain't good for the underwear trade."

But, Mike was now thinking, if Peter Grimes was reporting the views of the cognoscenti they would think themselves correct when they read Mike's words, *Was Matthew Bokowski (AKA Matthew Burke) silenced for what he knew?* come Saturday morning. And was Lt. Rocco pursuing a similar course? That intern at Bethesda Medical was Mike's only hope of linking Bokowski and Johnny Jones and that hope was now riding on Jack Montgomery's charisma and wit. Mike shuddered.

Grimes once again hefted his load. "You asked, Master, and I told. Now I am off to the salt mines below stairs."

"Ten-bucks-a-blow? For a domestic engineer you seem to have more than a nodding acquaintance with Johnny's curriculum vitae."

"True, but I never sold my ass for a quick buck or a job on the Great White Way. In lieu of selling it, Master, I sat on it and look where it got me." Grimes patted the bulging bag hanging over his shoulder and made his exit singing "Rub-a-dub, dub, strange undies in the Master's tub."

Mike threw the ashtray after him, sending a stream of paper clips across the room.

Twenty-Five

Mike read his copy once more before keying in his editor's online address and pressing SEND. Both his and his editor's electronic addresses were in a secure mode and could not be accessed by anyone who didn't know their passwords, ensuring that only his editor and his secretary, Milly, would see the column before his multitude of readers.

It was midweek, leaving enough time for additions and deletions should either be necessary. In a few days Mike's conversation with Matthew Bokowski and his plea to Bokowski's friends and associates to come forward would be on newsstands from Maine to Baja. Would Lt. Rocco of the spread legs and inviting package wrapped in pressed gray flannels be among the readers? White starched boxers?

Mike felt a tingle where it matters and was saved from scratching the itch by the arrival of Peter Grimes, back from the salt mines. Having no desire to hang around the apartment and watch his Man Friday do everything but the windows, Mike washed, got into a pair of twill slacks, white cotton turtleneck sweater, topped with a black, three-quarter length car coat. Wrapping a black and white stripped muffler around his neck he bid farewell to Peter and fled.

Being a few weeks before the shortest day of the year, the sun had sunk someplace behind New Jersey shortly after four that afternoon. It was now dark and emerging from his apartment building Mike received a smart salute from his doorman and headed south on Lexington Avenue, walking toward Bloomingdale's, accompanied by Christmas shoppers on their way to Blooms and the posh Midtown shops that line Lexington and Madison Avenues.

Mike wasn't a fan of the Yule season, nor was he an Ebenezer Scrooge. The only child of a school teacher mother and bank executive father, raised In Queens, New York, and blessed with two sets of grandparents and an assortment of uncles, aunts and cousins, there were always more plums than prunes in his Christmas stocking. His problem with the-season-to-be jolly was that it accentuated the plight of the have-nots and made the tinsel look like what it was – tinsel.

From this arose Mike Gavin, columnist and investigative reporter; hope of the rooters in the bleachers and nemesis of the box seat boys who too often entered the fray with loaded dice. Hence, his current crusade to avenge the brutal death of a young man whom Mike had shunned when he should have heeded.

However, Mike had to concede that from Thanksgiving to Christmas, New York (especially the Isle of Manhattan) took on all the glitter, glamour and heady allure of fabled kingdoms from Camelot to Shangri-La. It was a time for giving and besides stuffing big birds one had to stuff envelopes for all the folks that made life a bit easier for Mike Gavin.

People passing Mike, coming and going, toting handsomely wrapped packages had Mike wondering what he should get Jack. Something for the new house in Aspen? No, Mike didn't want to think about the house in Aspen, commitments or nuclear war, seeing little difference between the three.

Like a hound following a scent, Mike walked several blocks past Bloomingdale's, turned east toward Second Avenue until alighting on a bar stool in Destry's, a pub that was so discreet its entrance was indistinguishable from its brownstone neighbors, with the exception of a framed black and white glossy head shot of Dietrich on the front door. The bartender acknowledged Mike with a nod and filled his order for Jack Daniel's on the rocks, no fruit.

Destry's clientele was varied to say the least and ran the gamut this evening from middle-age gents in suits and ties, younger guys in zip-up ski parkas, sweaters and duffel coats to a couple in jeans, hard hats and work boots. Conversations were subdued and not in competition with television, juke box or music coming from no place discernible.

The bartender was plump with rosy cheeks and an amiable

smile that displayed a set of expensive caps -- or were they now called veneers? He gave Mike time to sample his bourbon before he sidled over and said in hushed tones, "Johnny's got his butt in a sling."

"Johnny's got an alibi," Mike answered. "Tell me, Jeff, do you know Bokowski or did you recognize him as someone you had seen by his photo in the papers?"

"Negative on both counts," Jeff said, then turned to fill an order. When he came back, Mike asked, "Did Johnny have any clients with connections in Washington? Not the state."

"In here they don't pass out their calling cards or discuss their occupation with me or each other. This is Destry's, Mike, not Le Cirque."

"What about celebrities? Actors and the like."

"Mike Gavin comes in to ask questions."

Mike laughed. "Touché, Jeff, touché. Seriously, ever see Johnny with a big Hollywood or Broadway name?"

"Big is a matter of opinion. They come in but I'm not going to name names. I will tell you that I never saw one in particular leaving with Johnny when he was on the game. Why? Who do you suspect?"

"I won't name names," Mike teased.

"Christ," Jeff said, "what are we playing? Don't ask, don't tell?"

Mike shrugged. "What's happening in the pool room?"

"You shopping?"

"Window shopping, Jeff. Tis the season."

Mike pointed to his glass and Jeff poured a refill. Mike picked it up and made for the rear of the room, exited at the far end which led to a vestibule off of which were the rest rooms. Beyond an open doorway was the entrance to the pool room, Destry's alter ego.

It was crowded, noisy and equipped with a stereo system that at the moment was wailing *Love For Sale*. Really! There was a mini bar to accommodate the men, old and young, clustered cheek to jowl (or hip to crotch) as they cruised, literally and figuratively, around the room's namesake.

Four young men were playing a game of pocket pool (excuse the pun) under the scrutiny of the animated window shoppers. The players, three in jeans, one in white sailor bell bottoms, displayed their wares (rear view) as they hunched over their cue, aimed and sent the cue ball rolling across the green felt. Standing (front view) they planted their cue firmly on the parquet and assessed the audience, hoping to catch the eye of an out-of-town gent who had sent his wife to Radio City Music Hall or had left her home in Indiana. The tourists didn't haggle over cost because it was a long time since they had tasted of the forbidden fruit and longer still before they would again be offered the dessert tray.

The scene had Mike silently reciting a line from Wilde's prison *Ballad: Some love too little, some too long/ Some sell and others buy.*

Here was where Giancarlo LaBella was discovered by Ken Wallace and this quartet was hoping for a similar fate. Lots of luck, boys, Mike mused. All you'll get for your efforts is a guy on his knees, worshiping at the shrine and a sore behind, although a proficiency at pocket pool may be a positive side effect.

Mike didn't know what the going rate was, certainly more than ten-bucks-a-blow, but whatever it was he knew that if a customer wanted his boy to climax he had to pay double or even triple for the privilege of putting the stud out of action for several hours. The modus operandi was as prescribed as union rules in a closed shop.

This wasn't Mike's scene. Too commercial. Too obvious. Too cut and dried if not cut-rate. He preferred the chance encounter. The fleeting glance from across a crowded room. The foreplay of innuendos and gestures. Yes? No? Maybe? Lt. James Rocco? Yeah, like Lt. James Rocco.

As he turned to leave the amp was belting out *Hey, Big Spender*. The guy who programmed the music for Destry's pool room was as subtle as a speeding locomotive.

Mike had gone to Destry's to have a look at Johnny's roots and confirm the fact that anyone, celebrated or unknown, could have mixed and mingled in that pool room without raising an eyebrow, sex being the common denominator.

Jeff had told Mike he would never name names, so if Johnny had made a contact there who was now Johnny's phantom roommate, the guy would have no fear of being outed by the denizens of Destry's.

Who was the timid guy who picked up Johnny at the theater? Actor or politician? These days, the guy could be both. Johnny may not have known Bokowski, but he knew something he wasn't telling Lt. Rocco. Like the intern, Johnny was keeping his mouth shut. Out of loyalty, or out of fear? What was the pure and simple truth? Another Oscar Wilde quip crossed Mike's mind and made him smile: *The truth is rarely pure and never simple.*

Twenty-Six

The apartment was scrupulously clean and smelled of lemon Pledge and pine air freshener. Peter Grimes' aromatic calling cards. It was also dark and devoid of any trace of human habitation. Mike switched on lamps as he walked past them on his way to the bedroom where he hung up his topcoat and checked his land phone. It was not signaling a waiting message, nor had his cell phone summoned him even once this evening. This did not help his disposition which hovered precariously between melancholy and clinical depression.

He didn't turn on his laptop, fearing his web site and e-mail would be as mute as his phones.

He undressed and got into a comfortable robe. He perused his collection of phonograph albums displayed on the built-in shelves in the bedroom, many of which were family heirlooms handed down from parents and grandparents. All shiny black vinyl. He selected Streisand's *The Way We Were* on the grounds that if one was feeling sorry for oneself, one should have mood music to go with the mood. The apartment was wired so that the woeful lyrics could be heard from wall to wall and in all the nooks and crannies.

In the living room he took his favorite chair just as Barbra's opening words told Mike where he was headed. *"Memories..."*

When Mike Gavin was a cub reporter with the *Morning News*, covering the crime beat, Ken Mason was a rookie policeman. Both were young, handsome and ambitious. A reporter and a cop whose paths crossed because they were both involved with the pursuit of justice, albeit from different points of view.

Mike was impetuous and as cocksure of himself as the young man in the glossy ads he posed for before giving up modeling for the fourth estate. He was a born and bred New Yorker and all that implied.

Ken was as corny as his home state, encompassing every cliché of a rube in a big city, from the top of his buzz cut head to the toes of his penny loafers. He was just past the teenage awkward stage of existence when he got off the Greyhound toting a cardboard suitcase; more legs than body, more arms than torso, and both appendages often refusing to obey the commands of a very astute mind. His sad, brown eyes looked upon New York as if seeing were not akin to believing.

What was the likes of Ken Mason doing in New York? He came, as did thousands of others before him, in pursuit of a dream. Thanks to the wonder of television and a multitude of shows that extolled the guts and glory of New York's men in blue, Ken Mason, from ages six to twenty, longed to join the ranks of his beloved NYPD heroes. To this end, he attended a local community college where he majored in Criminal Justice and upon graduation his parents tearfully kissed him goodbye, stuffed his wallet with the princely sum of one thousand bucks and made him promise to shun the temptations of Sodom on the Hudson and call home weekly.

The cop and the reporter met in courtrooms, where Ken tripped over himself when walking to the witness box; in the city morgue, where Ken looked paler than the body on view; in detention halls where Ken was reprimanded for being too kind to the inmates.

Ken Mason wanted to be everything Mike Gavin was and disguised his admiration by being as rude to the reporter as he was kind to his prisoners. Mike was irked by his attraction to this pumpkin from Kansas and hid it by trading barbs with the cop whenever the occasion permitted.

"Don't trip over any clues, Mason."

"The only clue I'm looking for is how they let you in here. This is police business, Gavin."

"It's my job to be here, officer."

"Why? You could be showing your capped teeth to a camera and picking up my week's salary in an hour."

Mike was covering night court when Ken and a couple of

colleagues arrived with a trio of prostitutes working the Port of Authority bus terminal. "You have some taste in women, Mason," Mike teased Ken.

"They all have your name in their little black books. Whoever would have thought pretty boy had to pay for it?" Ken responded in kind.

Caution be damned, Mike thought, as he answered, "A pretty boy could be a customer or competition, Mason. Ever think of that?"

The hook had been baited. The minnow blushed (or did Mike imagine this?) and fled the shark's jaws.

That night, for the first time, they had a cup of coffee together and actually communicated outside the line of duty. Was Mike's boldness the impetus for this show of comradery? Mike didn't know, nor did he care. One or the other could have made the suggestion or they could have been walking in the same direction as they left the court and sauntered across a deserted Center Street an hour before dawn.

They found an all night diner and sat at the counter, ordering coffee and cinnamon Danish. They were both aware of the ease with which they had gone from working acquaintances to friends but neither mentioned the fact. "What are you doing in that uniform, Mason? You should be teaching English Lit in a fancy private prep school in New England."

"And you should be in Hollywood dazzling the world in your jockey briefs."

"Which tells me," Mike said, "you used to read all the glossy magazines, including the ads."

"Actually, only the ads," Ken admitted. "Tell me, Gavin, did they air brush your crotch or are you really flat down there?"

So, the minnow was back eyeing the bait.

As naturally as they had had their first coffee and sweet roll together, they began having dinner together as often as their jobs allowed. To Ken, dining out was eating a Salisbury steak seated at a table as opposed to a burger and fries at the counter. When Mike treated him to a steak at Vincent Sardi's, Ken was awed to be in a bistro frequented by celebrities and twice as awed by the cost of the prime filet.

Next, they began going to the movies together. Because they both often worked nights, this was usually an afternoon outing. They discovered they were partial to musicals and second rate mysteries, now known as film noir.

They talked about their work, schools they had gone to, what it was like growing up in a big city and small town. By some strange unspoken agreement, they never discussed what they did when they were not with each other. Mike feared his leisure pursuits would appear frivolous, if not shocking, to Ken, while Ken didn't want to air his mundane existence to the sophisticated Mike Gavin.

When Mike bought theater tickets he refused Ken's offer to pay his share. When Mike did it again, Ken would go only if he treated Mike to dinner. Mike agreed and suffered through meat loaf and hash browns.

This went on for a few months and Mike Gavin, whose sex life was never wanting, found himself courting and wanking while in the process. Then, one rainy afternoon, seated side-by-side in an almost empty movie house, their hands touched, hesitated for a moment, then clasped one into the other. Both breathed an audible sigh of relief.

Mike: "Your place or mine?"

Ken: "Yours. It has an elevator."

Ken Mason wasn't a virgin, nor was he a Don Juan. Like most wholesome American boys he came of age indulging in circle jerks in groups of two, three and more, depending upon the venue of the act; the boy's locker room and the wooded area behind the baseball field being the most active. Sleep overs and sharing a tent on camping trips accounted for the *pas de deux*. He suffered through innocent crushes on the star of the high school football team, his math teacher and a rotating number of television cowboys.

In college he had his first affair with a fellow student whose sex life was on par with Ken's. Their ids ran amuck and years of lost time was made up for before ego and superego brought them to their senses. Vows of eternal love were broken upon graduation. Ken headed East. His school chum went West. Both took with them the other's cell phone number and fond memories.

Mike Gavin was a motivated teacher. Ken Mason, a more than willing pupil. After doing it, repeatedly, Mike said, "I always wanted to kiss a cop."

"Really?" Ken said. "I never wanted to kiss a newspaper reporter."

And Mike Gavin fell in love.

Being lovers did not diminish their friendship. Having nothing in common made the affair wide open to discovery. Like Anna and her Siamese pupils, getting to know each other left no room for ennui, nor did they contemplate a future of perpetual togetherness. Mutual contentment was unspoken proof of their commitment even as Mike, the sophisticated cynic, waited for their ideal to go the way of mice and men. Five years later, he was still waiting.

Ken rose to the rank of sergeant. Mike Gavin became society editor of the *Morning News* with his own byline column. Given their chosen professions both were in the public eye and sensitive to scrutiny of their private lives. They maintained separate apartments and seldom mixed with the other's social milieu. If their work brought them face to face in a public setting they continued to play the roles of friendly adversaries.

There were summer weekends in the Hamptons, winter ski weekends in Vermont, vacations in Europe and the Caribbean. Apart their lives were full and productive; together they were reflective and at peace. It worked, and what works is good.

As was, and still is, Mike's style, they didn't flaunt, nor did they purposely hide their relationship to which many intimate friends were cognizant. One of them was Ken's boss, then Lt. Andrew Brandt. This came about when a police officer in a small southern town was fired after ten years of exemplary service with all accrued benefits forfeited because he marched in the Gay Day parade in the community he had sworn to defend against such usurpers of the common good.

He was quoted as saying, "The only crime I committed was living a lie all these years. I lost my job and gained my self-respect. I believe I won."

This goaded Ken to make an appointment to meet with Andy Brandt tell him that he and Mike Gavin were lovers, celebrating five years of togetherness. Brandt said, "Congratulations, now get back to work. And if you ever give that reporter classified police information I'll kick your ass from here to the Bronx and back again."

Mike went to bat for the fired officer. He used his national column to strike a blow against injustice in all its forms, shapes and guises. He visited the officer's home town where he was applauded and splattered with dung. The officer was not reinstated. Injustice survived Mike's onslaught. But if he made one reader in a million more aware and more tolerant then Mike Gavin believed he, too, had won.

However, Mike's crusade landed a salvo in his own backyard. He wrote about a cop in the Bible Belt but was thinking about a cop in New York, and himself. Addressing his readers he found himself among them. Ken's coming out to Andy Brandt was replacing the closet door with an opaque curtain. Mike Gavin thought a man should practice what he preached.

"I'm looking for a bigger apartment in my building. Two bedrooms and maybe a den we can set up as an office. Meantime, Mason, give your landlord notice and move in here."

"Okay, but I want you to know why I'm doing it."

"Because you're crazy about me?"

"No, because you have an elevator."

And Mike Gavin fell in love for the second time in his life. It just happened to be with the same guy.

Sgt. Kenneth Mason, age twenty nine, was killed in the line of duty when he tried to disarm a drug crazed man brandishing a pistol at visitors, many of them children, at the entrance to the Central Park Zoo. After firing at Mason, the man was brought down by Mason's partner, officer Dennis Peabody.

Sgt. Mason was given an honorable departmental funeral, the eulogy delivered by his superior and friend, Lt. Andrew Brandt. In attendance were Mason's parents who came to take their son home to Kansas for interment in the family plot.

The syndicated columnist, Mike Gavin, devoted a column to the brief life and times of Sgt. Kenneth Mason, ending the emotional tribute with these poignant lines from Thomas Gray's famous Elegy:

Here rests his head upon the lap of Earth

A youth to Fortune and to Fame unknown,

Large was his bounty, and his soul sincere,

He gave to Misery all he had, a tear,

He gained from heaven ('twas all he wished) a friend.

"Memories…"

TWENTY-SEVEN

"I killed Matthew Bokowski."

To say that Jack was nonplussed would be tantamount to saying the Titanic ran into an ice cube. After a decade working the pro tennis circuit, Jack was immune to the requests, offers and ravings of fans who patiently waited for him to shower, dress and emerge from the stadium after the matches with offers of marriage or more illicit forms of cohabitation; advice regarding health, love and financial investments; lucky charms; aphrodisiacs; tennis balls to be signed; hands to shake and hands trying to cop a feel.

He was prepared for any of the above when he spotted the rather good looking young man waiting for him on this cold and rainy night on day two of his three-day gig in McLean. A murder confession was not among the repartee of his adoring fans but since his association with Mike Gavin had gone public thanks to the tennis matches in Washington last July and the ramblings of sports writers, gossip columnists, TV talk show hosts and the internet, Jack's fans were now more catholic in their offerings. Aware of the kooks who stalked celebrities and the fact that he was in a dark alley illuminated by a single light bulb atop the exit he had just emerged from, Jack gave the intruder a polite smile and, without breaking his stride said, "You should talk to the police. I believe there are a couple stationed out front."

"Aren't you Mike Gavin's friend?"

Still walking, Jack answered, "You can contact Mr. Gavin via his web site or the *Morning News*."

"I read that you would be here and I thought I might get to Mr. Gavin faster by speaking to you."

"You have spoken, now if you'll excuse me…"

The man, frustrated by Jack's brush off, began to plead. "Please stop a moment and listen to me. I'm not a nut case and

I didn't mean I tied the knot about Matt's throat. I sent him to Johnny's apartment. I was the one they wanted to kill."

That got Jack's attention. He stopped trying to flee and paused long enough to confront his assailant. "Are you a doctor? An intern at Bethesda?"

The man started and tensed, looking as if he now wanted to hightail it out of the dark alley. "How did you know that?"

To add more drama to the moment, the persistent drizzle turned into a downpour. "I think we had better talk," Jack said. "I believe there's a pub just across the street." He reached for the man's elbow, urging him to follow.

"How do you know who I am?" the man insisted, not yielding to Jack's pressure on his arm.

"I'll tell you that over a drink we both need. Now move your ass before we drown in this godforsaken alleyway."

"Fuck you," the man cried.

"That's an option we can discuss when we're better acquainted."

The guy hesitated a moment, laughed, and trotted after Jack.

Jack was drenched by the time they made it to the pub that called itself a sports bar, no doubt owing to its location opposite the arena. Once inside, the other man removed his blue slicker and Jack, his hair plastered to his scalp, was amazed to find himself in the company of a sailor or, to be more precise, an ensign, no less. In the dark alley he hadn't noticed the regulation officers' cap.

Seeing Jack's reaction to his uniform, he said, "Navy Reserve. They financed my way through medical school and now it's payback time."

Of course. Bethesda Naval Hospital. Jack was surprised Mike hadn't made the connection. Some of the men at the bar who had been to the matches acknowledged Jack with thumbs up and verbal compliments on his win. There were several booths, all empty, and Jack steered the officer to one of them as he signaled the bartender and ordered two beers. "Unless you want something stronger," he said after the fact.

"Beer is fine." When they sat the ensign asked, "Did Matt give Mike Gavin my name?"

Jack picked up a paper towel and mopped the top of his head. "Only your occupation. I'm Jack Montgomery, by the way."

"Troy," the man said, offering neither his hand nor his surname, unless it was Troy.

"Makes me think of Paris," Jack said, then added, "Not the city."

"Did Mr. Gavin tell the police about me?" Troy asked, unable to suppress the dread a positive response would evoke.

Here, the bartender himself waited on the pair, staring at Jack in a manner that made one think the man was bowled over at the sight of a genuine sports figure patronizing his sports bar. In addition to the beers he presented them with several packets of mini pretzels, presumably on the house.

"Did Mr. Gavin…" Troy began again as soon as the bartender was out of earshot.

"Why didn't you go to the police when you heard what happened to Matt and who wanted to kill you?" Even as he spoke Jack knew he was asking too much too soon. In the excitement of actually talking to the guy he had come to find – and perhaps discovering his quarry was a good looking navy ensign in uniform – he forgot everything Mike had told him to do in the unlikely event this should happen. Unfortunately, he did recall two words Mike had repeated several times, namely, *be subtle*. Poor Jack had been as subtle as a brick coming down on a mosquito.

"I didn't go to the police because I don't want to end up dead or, worse, lose my commission and my internship at Bethesda. I just finished years of schooling and impressed the brass enough to get this assignment. I'm on the way to achieving everything I dreamed about since I was in grade school – and then this had to happen.

"A less selfish reason," he went on, "is patient confidentiality. The relationship between doctor and patient is as sacred as that between priest and penitent in the confessional."

Confessional? Not knowing where this was leading and not eager to find out Jack gave up trying to remember Mike's instructions and faced the ensign as he would an unexpectedly good opponent across a net. Exchange a few friendly volleys before going in for the kill. Hence, he didn't blurt out *What Happened?* Instead he reassured Troy that Mike had not revealed his relationship with Matt Bokowski, whatever that was, to the police. "He didn't tell the police about you because all Matt said at the vice president's party was that he wished his star struck friend was there to ogle all the celebrities. He said his friend was an intern at Bethesda. Mike is a pro, he wouldn't implicate anyone in a murder investigation on those few words from the victim. I came here for the matches and Mike asked me to try to contact you. He wanted to question you before he blabbed your identity to the police."

Troy was so relieved he picked up his beer and quaffed half the glass. "I love Mike Gavin," he said.

"So do I," Jack answered.

There was an awkward silence broken when Troy said, "I'm not gay."

It was Jack's turn to sample the beer, grimace, put down his glass and say, "I didn't ask."

Don't get personal, was another bit of advice Mike had given Jack in preparation for a chance meeting with the intern. *I'm fucking up by the numbers* Jack was thinking as he tried to avoid staring directly at Troy which was not easy when you're seated in a tight booth in a sports bar. But more than his failure as an astute interviewer was bugging Jack Montgomery. He found the ensign attractive to the point where he began to speculate whether it was the guy or the uniform, the singer or the song, he found so appealing. Jack suppressed a smile as he recalled a sage bon mot. To wit: *There's no such thing as a naked sailor.*

Jack was more relieved than disappointed at Troy's revelation. He wouldn't have to wrestle with the idea of a one night stand with the ensign and, should it happen, tell Mike of his indiscretion as they had agreed to do if either of them strayed. Would Mike be mad or glad if it had happened? Jack didn't want to think about that just now, nor did he want to think about how many guys he had bedded who professed not to be gay. Instead he tried to concentrate on what Troy was telling him – as he was supposed to do.

"That crazy guy," Troy was saying with more affection than ire. "He was the star fucker. That's why he volunteered to go to New York and see Johnny Jones. He thought he could wangle an interview with the underwear model."

"Volunteered?" Jack questioned. "Why don't you start from the beginning and let it all hang out – no pun intended, ensign. Just a figure of speech."

Troy shrugged off the comment. "Let's get one thing *straight*, Mr. Montgomery. No pun intended, just a figure of speech." Jack laughed. The guy was more than just a pretty face. "I'll tell you what I know because I want the bastard who did in Matt to pay with his fucking life. I can't go to the police so I'll tell what I know to Mike Gavin hoping justice will be done, but if Gavin or you quote me or implicate me in this fiasco I'll deny I ever talked to you."

"What if your testimony is essential to the case?"

Troy sighed in despair. "Do you believe Lee Harvey Oswald shot JFK?"

"Christ," Jack cried. "That's ancient history. Is this going to be another conspiracy theory? Spare me, officer."

"I'm telling you we're dealing with Washington where nothing is what it seems and no one is who they profess to be. Politicians here think they're our royalty, made for exceptions, not for laws. There's a conspiracy brewing at every lunch date, dinner date and garden party. In Washington *quid pro quo* is sacrosanct and God help the fucker who doesn't abide by it."

"Mike calls it give and take," Jack said. "The commandment by which we all live and sometimes die. Matt used the term Watergate when he talked to Mike. Is this another Watergate?"

"In Washington anything that puts a career in jeopardy is a potential Watergate and the guys in power will stop at nothing – I mean nothing – to keep a drip from becoming a cascade. Someone suspected a leak and reached for a plug by the name of Matthew Bokowski. He never knew when to keep his mouth shut. He also idolized Mike Gavin, in case you didn't know."

"Mike feels a responsibility because he gave Matt the air, paying no attention to what he was trying to tell him," Jack confided.

"And I feel responsible for sending him to New York. That's why I'm willing to let it all hang out, as you put it. It's my atonement, but I won't go public. These fuckers play hard ball and sacrificing my nuts won't bring Matt back."

True but a tad harsh, Jack thought as he asked, "You going to tell me what it's all about?"

"Do I get that guarantee?"

"Mike never reveals a source," Jack said as he pulled out his cell phone and began to text message Mike.

With the Dr. Insists U vow anonymity ASAP.

Jack stared at the narrow screen. Troy stared at Jack. Everyone at the bar stared at the tennis pro and the naval officer. In less than a minute Jack had his reply.

Granted. Kudos to U.

"You have your guarantee," Jack said, waving a hand at the bartender who immediately began pulling two fresh brews.

One could say it all started in the first grade where Matthew Bokowski met Travis (Troy) McBarb. For little Matthew it was love at first sight, an unrequited affair that continued till college did them part. Travis, called Troy by Matt because Troy was a walled city wherein dwelt Hector, his bro Paris, their dad Priam and a gal named Helen who got there by default. And it was where Achilles did in Hector to avenge the death of Achilles' lover, Patroclus.

For Matthew, all of the above residents of Troy were Travis McBarb rolled into one hunk of a guy. In his daydreams (masturbation fodder to be more precise) Travis was Paris when Matthew was Helen. Matthew was Patroclus when Travis was Achilles. Travis' Achilles slew the school bully (Hector) then hitched the bastard to his chariot (bicycle) and dragged the bleeding corpse around the schoolyard to the cheers of the student body.

With an imagination like that what else could Matthew Bokowski aspire to become but a newspaper reporter, a profession that required much improvisation to add drama to the mundane. Shortly after dubbing Travis Troy, Matthew Bokowski decided on Matt Burke for his futuristic byline signature.

With a pal like Matthew, what else could Travis McBarb want to be when he grew up but a doctor with a special interest in the human mind. i.e. psychiatry.

One might say The Jockstrap Murder had its roots in a first grade classroom inhabited by a fledging reporter and medical doctor.

As a naval hospital, Bethesda was available to navy veterans and their families. Its location made it a venue for Washington VIPs from the Pentagon to the Senate to the House and all stops between. Faces that made headlines in the daily press were commonplace at Bethesda.

For an intern going into psychiatry, Bethesda Medical was an ideal assignment. The Gulf Wars had produced an almost endemic number of service men suffering from what the government euphemistically referred to as 'mental stress.' Here Travis had the opportunity to study firsthand the ravages of war on the human mind as well as the body. However, a specialty in psychiatrics would evolve after his internship, so for the present Travis rotated his time (often gruelingly) between all medical disciplines.

This schedule was the reason Travis met his nemesis, who he called Patient X, who suffered from chronic hepatitis B, an ailment that, like a volcano, could lie dormant for long periods (smoldering within) and erupt periodically, often without warning. The disease is contagious and often sexually transmitted.

That said, we now look at some of the perks of being young, handsome, in uniform and connected in the D.C. area. Marines, to be sure, were a favorite adjutant to a political hostess's dinner table, but a gorgeous medical intern in a sailor suit soon found himself on many a madams' A list.

It was last July at one of those affairs, a sweet sixteen birthday party for a senator's daughter – that Travis locked eyes, not horns (that would come later) with Patient X, as he will be referred to from this point on. The senator, or his PR guru, had managed to nab the birthday girl's heartthrob, Johnny Jones, for the occasion. True, it was rumored that Johnny Jones would go to the opening of an envelope if asked, however it was a thrill for the giggling teenybopper guests to meet the popular male model and roar their collective approval when he told the crowd Freddy Fine's briefs were his working uniform and tonight he was going AWOL.

After whirling the birthday girl around the dance floor and placing a chaste kiss on her cheek, Johnny made his exit to applause, whistles and cat calls; the latter from the boy contingent who were probably all sporting Freddy's line beneath their tux pants. Travis wished he could escape as easily as Johnny Jones but he thought it prudent to wait at least until the senator's daughter had blown out the candles on the largest sheet cake Travis had ever seen before he fled. These social obligations, approved by his MD supervisors, gave the intern a break from his rounds and, if he could get away early, he could use the leftover time to catch up on much needed sleep.

Having danced with all the mothers, grandmothers and maiden aunts while avoiding all ladies under eighteen (noblesse oblige had its limits) and exchanging risqué stories with the gentlemen in the smoker lounge which contained a booze bar as opposed to the non-alcoholic punch being passed off on the kids who all carried flasks, Travis felt he could make his exit in good conscience.

His departure was far less noticed than Johnny's, for which Travis was grateful. In Washington, a low profile was deemed respectable when not running for office. Outside the county club the usual number of limos were lined up, their drivers chatting in groups of two and three. Familiar with the territory Travis made his way to the parking area behind the club where he had left his car thus avoiding the car jockeys who sneered at anything less than a five buck tip.

The parking lot was huge, filled with shiny prestigious foreign autos and lit with street lamps placed at intervals that did little to illuminate the vast spaces between the lamps. Approaching his car, Travis spotted two figures engaged in a passionate embrace. He paused, looking for a way to avoid passing directly in front of them when a car suddenly switched on its headlights and pulled out of the space directly opposite Travis and the lovers. The car's brights lit up the scene for just the few moments needed for Travis to find himself staring into the startled faces of Johnny Jones and Patient X, who were staring back at him.

The exiting car turned and in the restored darkness Travis ran to his car, got in and drove off.

It was a credit to the young doctor's commitment to his profession that his gut reaction to the scene in the parking lot was of a medical rather than titillating nature. Had Patient X informed Johnny Jones of his condition and did Patient X take proper precaution before his passionate embrace led to something far more intimate? Travis certainly hoped so.

Later, he wondered if it was Patient X who had arranged for Johnny's appearance at the senator's daughter's party since it was now obvious that Patient X knew Johnny Jones very well indeed. This being Washington he speculated as to what the senator promised to do for Patient X in return for delivering Johnny to the gala? Travis didn't remember seeing Patient X at the party but he could have missed him among the guests who ran the gamut from teens to seniors and not being obliged to dance with men he had entertained the female wallflowers, as was his duty, and not the male contingent.

That night, before dozing off, Travis recalled the look in Patient X's eyes as he held Travis' gaze. They were, for that moment, prey and predator. But who was the doe and who was the lion? Travis wasn't sure.

TWENTY-EIGHT

The day Jack Montgomery was bamboozling Mike Gavin on the tennis court, Travis McBarb and Matt Burke were having lunch at a McDonald's midway between their respective places of business. Matt, as usual, was treating Travis to the latest local gossip – political, sexual and miscellany – the latest, seeming to cover all categories, had it that a senator's son who had long been on the fringes of Washington's gay set was becoming more overt about his sexual preferences. And who was this brash young man? No one knew for certain but Matt had a list of possible candidates and named them for Travis.

"Why them?" Travis wanted to know.

"Elementary," Matt bragged. "There are one hundred senators. I delved into their domestic lives and learned who among them had a son or sons. I made a list of all the male offspring over six and under twenty-six. I knocked off the few that were married and/or not living in Washington. The results are my candidates."

"That's as scientific as casting a horoscope to predict the future."

"Didn't Nancy Regan use horoscopy to run this country?"

"And look where it got us," Travis said.

But Matt's big news was that his paper wanted to cover both the celebrity tennis matches hosted by Jack Montgomery and the vice president's party that evening honoring the participants. Matt volunteered to cover both assignments but his editor said he could do one, not both, and Matt chose the party over the matches. "It'll give me a chance to see the players close up and maybe talk to a few. I know Mike Gavin will be there. He's at the games as we speak and he'll show up at the party with his pal, Jack Montgomery."

Matt looked so pleased with himself, Travis thought he would take him down a peg and show him that life at the hospital wasn't as dull as watching paint dry. Knowing Matt would tell him in great detail about the names he would rub shoulders with at the party, Travis told Matt he had not only been to a party with Johnny Jones but had caught Johnny in *flagrante delicto.*

Matt paused in the act of bringing a soggy fry to his lips and stared at Travis open-mouthed. Knowing that his friend did get invited to Washington soirees coupled with the fact that Travis McBarb never lied or exaggerated a tale, Matt didn't for a moment doubt the doctor's startling disclosure. Awed, or flabbergasted might be a more apt depiction of Matt's reaction to the news, he blurted his gut reaction to the startling story – "Did you see his dick?"

Travis glanced around the eatery which, thankfully, wasn't crowded. "Good grief, Matt, is that all you think about?"

Nibbling on the fry Matt shrugged and asked, "With Johnny Jones what else can you think about?"

"You might be wondering who Johnny's partner of the moment was."

"I do wonder, Troy, but you won't tell me, will you?"

"Right. I won't."

"A Washington VIP?"

"No comment."

"A patient?"

"No comment."

"A VIP patient?" Matt concluded.

Travis looked at his watch. "Speaking of which, I must get back to them."

Like an angler fishing for trout or a reporter angling for a story, Matt refused to let go. "You're sitting on something hot, Troy."

"Yeah, I'm sitting on another Watergate," Travis answered, more in jest than in earnest. "Ask your colleagues Woodward and

Bernstein what I should do or even better, ask Mike Gavin when you see him tonight."

The rest is history.

Neither had touched their brews which had lost their foamy heads but Jack had knocked off a packet of mini pretzels as he listened to Travis' fascinating story, his mind full of questions for Travis and ideas to bounce off Mike when he got back to New York. "You did say Bethesda is available to Navy vets as well as their families."

"I didn't say," Travis answered, suspecting where this was heading and not wishing to be put in a corner where he would have to deny or confirm Jack's suspicions.

Before Jack could try again they were approached by the bartender who was waving an eight by ten glossy photo under Jack's nose. It was, not surprising, a shot of Jack in action on the courts The few framed photos mounted on the walls were of baseball and football stars of at least a decade ago so Jack assumed the guy had sent someone across the street to the arena's gift shop to buy it. "Would you mind autographing this for our collection, Jack?"

Smiling graciously, Jack took the offered photo and pen and fulfilled the bartender's request with a sweeping hand, not missing the fact this would be the only autographed photo in the *collection*. A few other customers had come in out of the rain and all eyes were now focused on the star and his drinking companion. The ensign did not like attention and said so when the bartender had retreated with his prize.

"I feel like a duck in a shooting gallery," Travis complained.

"You get used to it," Jack said, happily resigned to the fact. He took a sip of his beer, now tepid, and opened another package of mini pretzels.

Travis picked up his glass more as a means of procrastination than a need to quench a thirst if he had one.

"You were saying?" Jack prompted.

"I was saying that having a drink with you is as discreet as sipping our beer in the nude."

Jack flashed Travis a conspiratorial wink and a smile. "That can be arranged, ensign."

"Spare me," Travis pleaded, mimicking Jack's similar plea.

Jack shrugged his broad shoulders in acquiescence and returned to business. "What happened after Matt spoke to Mike at the reception last summer?"

Interning at a major hospital is a twenty-four/seven commitment. What leisure time Travis was allowed he used to catch up on much needed sleep. Contemplating clandestine love affairs, however unconventional, was not a viable option for the intern. His only thought on the subject was what would transpire the next time Patient X came in for his periodic visit and their eyes met, yet again, under the cruel light of a physical exam. After witnessing that scene in the posh country club's parking lot the doctor's command to *Bend Over* was suddenly rife with innuendo. Travis didn't see Patient X for several months and thought the incident over and forgotten. Then he got a new patient.

To be assigned a new patient wasn't unusual. However, a patient who had been put to the top of a long waiting list for immediate attention was indeed an exception to the rules, such as they were. The new patient's name was not one Travis had ever heard and the man himself, waiting for Travis in the exam room in a hospital gown, was not immediately recognizable, but in Washington the powers behind the thrones kept their names and faces in the shadow of those they served.

Travis introduced himself, then picked up the patient's chart prepared by the nurse in the assembly line tradition of modern medicine. Glancing at the man's vital signs, Travis was about to comment on the blood pressure numbers which appeared high when the patient, sitting on the examining table, folded his arms and said, "I'm here on behalf of one of your patients."

Travis started, then answered, "I don't understand."

"I didn't come for a physical. I came to talk to you."

"You could have called for an appointment outside the hospital and not infringe on patients' time."

The bogus patient looked to be about forty, give or take a few years, with dark hair fashionably cut, dark eyes, a disingenuous smile that displayed good teeth and slim physique encased in plaid boxer shorts evident from the back of the hospital gown that had come loose from its ineffectual rope belt. He rolled his eyes and said, "Obviously, doctor, I didn't want to draw attention to our meeting and thought this the best way to accomplish that goal."

"How did you get an appointment? You were never on the wait list."

The man shook his head in mock despair. "Don't play the naïve rube with me, doctor. Your patient has clout, as you damn well know and – read my lips – he'll use it to make or break you."

"Don't threaten me, mister. I can press a button and have security in here and you out of here in two minutes."

"Calm down, Travis – you don't mind if I call you Travis, do you, Travis? –I come to praise Caesar, not to bury him. Listen to me before you press a button and self-destruct."

Realizing he was talking to a shark of the political persuasion who was programmed to convert or annihilate the enemy, Travis went on the defensive. "If this is about my patient and his boyfriend tell him I couldn't care less so his secret is safe with me. And, if he hasn't done so, tell him to read the pamphlet on safe sex he was given when he was diagnosed and follow the instructions."

"Why don't you tell him yourself, isn't that your job?"

"Look," Travis said, glancing at the patient's chart. "Look, Mr. Martin, I have no intention of getting involved in a patient's love life, regardless of who the happy couple may be. Tell that to your boss."

Martin shook his head, feigning sorrow. "But you are involved,

Travis. You were either in the wrong place at the wrong time or the right place at the right time. Which will it be?"

TWENTY-NINE

"He aced you on every serve," Jack commented as Travis took a swig of his beer.

"He was tugging my short hairs with one hand and juggling my balls with the other," Travis answered.

Enviable maneuver, Jack was thinking but wisely refrained from voicing that opinion. "I take it you opted for the right place at the right time."

"I opted to keep my job as a medical intern and commissioned officer in the U.S. Navy with a rosy future. I never intended to involve Matt in the bastard's scam."

"Then why did you?" Jack asked, not too kindly.

"Murphy's law," Travis said. "Anything that can go wrong will do just that."

"You mean you fucked up."

"Not me," Travis said. "The guy who called himself Martin and Martin's contact at the hospital got their wires crossed and Matt got wasted."

Travis had agreed to meet with Patient X and Johnny Jones, ostensibly to discuss safe sex but actually to make Travis a part of their romantic deception. As a member of the club he couldn't blab what he knew for the same reason he couldn't name Patient X. The sanctity of the doctor/patient relationship.

Travis admitted that when negotiating with Martin he wasn't above the sin of greed. Play ball with these guys and who knows what doors might suddenly open to admit a good looking naval officer with a degree in medicine. This was after all, Washington, D.C. where *quid pro quo*, give and take, one hand washes the other and I'll show you mine if you show me yours was de rigueur. The only axiom Travis didn't contemplate was the one that cautioned, if you play with fire you may get burned.

Martin said Travis could meet with his patient and Johnny Jones in Johnny's apartment in New York. The hospital was out of the question and a clandestine meeting in Washington had all the privacy of a fish bowl. Travis told him an intern seldom, if ever, got a day off. A trip to New York was impossible. Martin smiled his condescending smile and said, "Trust me."

The meeting between the doctor, his patient and the patient's lover had been arranged in minute detail before Martin had consulted with Travis. That he was being coerced, or blackmailed, was obvious to Travis but his options were limited to cooperation or annihilation.

The intern schedule was posted every Monday morning. The coming Monday's schedule would show that Travis McBarb had the day off on Wednesday the fifteenth. A round-trip reservation had been made for Travis on Delta's shuttle to New York for nine that morning. Finally, Martin gave Travis Johnny Jones' New York address, verbally. There would be no paper trail connecting Martin with Travis McBarb.

The intern schedule the following Monday showed Travis McBarb had 24 hours leave on Thursday, the sixteenth. Travis was sure Martin had said Wednesday, the fifteenth. He called Delta to confirm and, as expected, was told his reservation was for the fifteenth. He couldn't appeal to his commanding officer to say a mistake had been made because he had never requested leave time. If he drew attention to his predicament he would be opening a Pandora's Box out of which would fly a few disembodied heads, including his own.

"I had no way of getting in touch with Mr. Martin, if that was his name, to tell him of the snafu. I couldn't contact Patient X without getting his private number from the hospital's confidential patient's files because I would have to give a reason for the request. And, if I didn't show up in New York on the fifteenth, Mr. Martin and Co. would think I had reneged on the deal and take their revenge before asking for an explanation. What could I do?"

THIRTY

"What he did was send Matt Burke, nee Matthew Bokowski, to New York to explain his absence," Mike completed Jack's tale of his meeting with Travis McBarb.

"How'd you guess?"

"Because Bokowski is dead, that's how."

They were seated on the couch in Mike's apartment where Mike had brewed a pot of tea while eagerly awaiting Jack's return from his tennis gig. Jack hadn't even unpacked his gear before Mike had him reporting on the meeting with the handsome ensign.

"The pieces of the puzzle are falling into place to form a picture," Mike said. "Travis had lunch with his pal and told him about seeing Johnny Jones and Patient X making out in the parking lot the night of a senator's daughter's birthday party."

"But he didn't name Patient X," Jack cut in.

"No, he didn't. That night, at the Veep's party, Matt cornered me and posed his theoretical question, hinting at a Washington scandal to equal Watergate. The cub reporter couldn't wait to spill what he knew, or what he almost knew, and wanted to impress me and maybe arouse my curiosity enough to elicit my help in exposing Johnny's D.C. boyfriend. The ploy didn't work."

"You gave him the brush off."

"Don't be crude, Jack."

"But that's what you did."

"Okay, it's what I did and it can't be undone so let's move on. This Mr. Martin gets himself on Travis' patient list and coerces Travis into doing his bidding. He wants to make sure Travis keeps his mouth shut and arranges a meeting between Travis, Johnny and Patient X in Johnny's New York apartment. The best laid plans of mice and men usually get fucked up, as the poet wrote, which is what happened to Travis' day off. He couldn't get to New York so he sent poor Matt in his place."

Jack nodded. "Matt went ape shit at the thought of meeting Johnny Jones. All he was supposed to do was explain why Travis wasn't there and then beat it."

"How much did Travis tell Matt about this meeting in New York?"

"Just that his patient had recognized him in the parking lot and wanted to explain the situation. He invited Travis to New York to meet with him and Johnny. Travis couldn't get the day of the meeting off and the rest is history."

"Not knowing the devious particulars of the meeting, Matt couldn't resist flashing his reporter credentials and thereby signed his own death warrant," Mike surmised.

"Would they have killed Travis?" Jack wondered.

"No way," Mike told him. "These are politicians looking to cover their tracks and political pros play by the rules which include blackmail, name calling, arm twisting, stealth and castration to name a few. Murder is taboo because it leaves a trail in the form of a corpse and after three days a corpse stinks and draws attention to itself as the Jockstrap Murder is now doing. Whoever met Matt at Johnny's apartment, Patient X or Mr. Martin, panicked at the sight of a reporter and silenced him with the first thing that came to hand which happened to be a Freddy Fine jockstrap. Most unprofessional, to say the least."

"If they think Travis betrayed them by sending the reporter," Jack said, "Ensign McBarb is on his way to military oblivion."

"True," Mike agreed, "but not on the heels of doing in Bokowski. The murder weapon and the Johnny Jones connection put them in the spotlight. They'll keep a low profile until the Jockstrap Murder is put on a cold case shelf. Travis can't prove a word of what he told you and they know it, so they'll deal with the ensign when it suits them. Till then, Travis McBarb will have to sweat it out."

"You'll keep them in the spotlight," Jack said, confident that

Mike could, and would, do just that.

With a nod, Mike got up and went to the dry bar, returning with a bottle of brandy, he poured a slug into his hot tea. "I feel a cold coming on," he said.

"Try antihistamine," Jack said.

Ignoring the sage advice Mike continued, "There's a huge hole in our jigsaw puzzle, Jack. A vital piece is missing. Can you guess what it is?"

Jack looked into his teacup in search of an answer and found it. "The time frame?"

"Exactly," Mike exclaimed. "Travis sees the lovers in the parking lot and tells Matt what he saw without naming his patient. Matt talks to me at the Veep's party. All this last July. Now, November, Mr. Martin comes to put pressure on Travis to keep his mouth shut. Four months between the act and the follow-up. Why?"

Jack shrugged, feigning ignorance. "I'm just a jock with more brawn than brain. You tell me."

"Something happened to Patient X to make it imperative that his affair with Johnny must never go public. Being a political animal I would guess his concern is more for his constituents than anything else. These are the people who can keep him in office or toss him out."

"You're taking it as fact that Patient X is someone who sits in the House or the Senate and will soon be campaigning to keep his job."

Mike shook his head. "I'm not assuming anything. From what we know, it's obvious that Patient X is an elected public servant, as they like to be called."

"Then what we have to do is learn whose job is up for grabs in the next national election and make a list of the *impossibles*, the *probables*, the *maybes* and the *discernibles*," Jack said. "In short, pal, we have to vacuum the closet."

"Have you ever pushed a vacuum, Jack?"

The conversation had Mike recalling the in-depth article on Senator Sten Samuels he intended to do before being waylaid by the Jockstrap Murder. This was prompted by the senator's lunch date with Amanda Richards last summer when Mike dubbed them "the odd couple" and Amanda announced that the senator expressed compassion rather than hostility to federal funding for the arts.

The essay would state the obvious; conservatives running for office had to bend slightly to the left to appear more palatable to the masses, just as liberals had to tilt to the right for the same reason. Mike's political wisdom would advocate believing nothing you read or heard from campaigning politicos and half of what you saw.

Mike knew that Samuels' term in the Senate had not yet expired so if he wasn't running for reelection was he priming the pump for the big prize? The presidency? That would certainly account for Mr. America buttering up a liberal like Amanda. And, of course, a celebrated liberal that would get the senator plenty of media attention. Last July, Samuels might have been testing the water and finding it comfortable enough to plunge in he was now making sure no scandal would deter his chances for a run for the White House.

Was Samuels Patient X? No way. On Jack's list of candidates Samuels would be written off as an *impossible*. But one never knew, did one? Was it Freud who said there's no such thing as a coincidence?

Jack's report also reminded Mike of the power enjoyed by the political elite in the U.S. of A. They could manipulate the uniform and civilian staff of a major hospital and did just that when they made a guy appear on an intern's schedule and made him disappear when he had served his purpose. They murdered Burke, nee Bokowski, and could probably do the same to Travis McBarb if he proved problematic.

This latter thought had Mike asking, "So tell me about the ensign, Jack."

"I did," Jack answered. "Everything he told me. Verbatim, as they say."

Not bothering to ask who "they" were, Mike said, "What he told you, but not what you were thinking as he talked."

Pretending he didn't know what Mike meant, Jack said, "I was thinking what a bum deal Bokowski got, thanks to the ensign."

"You described Travis as movie star handsome with a body that knows how to fill a sailor suit. I believe those were your very words, verbatim, as they say."

"Fuck off, Mike."

"I think fucking was just what you were thinking about as you ogled the ensign."

"I didn't ogle him. I looked, okay, but I didn't touch."

"Because you couldn't," Mike quickly countered. "Travis let you know he's not interested in sharing a bed with another cock. Straight as an arrow, as they say."

"You're baiting me, Mike."

And that's just what Mike was doing but his purpose was more than just to tease. He wanted to make a point so he went right on probing. "I'm showing you the reality of a discussion we had a few nights ago. What would happen if one of us hopped into bed for a quickie with a handsome face and a body that knows how to fill a sailor suit?"

Looking uncomfortable, Jack said, "I didn't hop into bed with anyone."

"Talking to Travis, did you get a little bulge in your jockeys?"

Flustered, Jack pounced, "Are you getting off on this discussion?"

Mike shook his head. "We'll do that later. Right now I want to know if you fondled your noodle last night, thinking of the guy in the sailor suit."

Jack knew when his opponent had him beat and acquiesced rather than return the volley. "Okay. I spanked the monkey thinking of the ensign."

Spanked the monkey? Good grief, that was as bad as verbatim. And how did spank the monkey ever become a pseudonym for jacking off? Mike often thought of doing a column on these meaningless idioms asking readers to explain the source of the anonym. Not willing to let go, Mike said, "So you strayed in thought, rather than in deed which, I guess, doesn't warrant a confession which we promised we would do if ever the thought became a deed. You're off the hook, Jack. We'll rack up Travis as 'wishful thinking.'"

Refusing to admit to a lapse in their relationship, even in thought, Jack went on the offensive. "Didn't you ever go solo over a 'wishful thinking' acquaintance?"

Mike's game of taunt and tell suddenly ricocheted and hit him in the balls. He retreated into his cup of laced tea, fighting off the image of Lt. James Rocco stepping into a pair of starched white boxers — or out of them — the prize always obscured because Rocco was a cock teaser in fantasy as well as in fact. This appealed to rather than repelled Mike who was always ready to go for the blue ribbon, especially when the prize was Lt. James Rocco.

It now appeared that last night Mike and Jack were both spanking the monkey (Ugh) over a wishful thought and both 'thoughts' belonged to a clan that donned uniforms. The difference being that Jack would never see his nemesis in the flesh again while Mike had committed himself to working with Rocco in pursuit of the Jockstrap Murderer. That sobering thought jolted Mike out of his reverie. What was he going to tell Rocco?

Mike now knew why Bokowski was murdered and why he was murdered in Johnny Jones' apartment. This knowledge would save the NYPD countless man hours of time and money while putting Rocco miles ahead in his pursuit of the murderer. That it would also enhance Mike's prestige as an investigative reporter who goes for the facts and gets them expeditiously, did not escape Mike's joy in besting Rocco. However, he had promised Travis McBarb he would never reveal his source and he had promised Rocco he would share information. To share with Rocco would expose the ensign. A classic case of damned if you do and damned if you don't. Mike had to devise a way to give Rocco the information he needed while protecting McBarb.

First, he had to question Johnny Jones and squeeze the truth out of him. Travis McBarb, unwittingly to be sure, had confirmed that Johnny had a lover who was politically connected. This was Johnny's phantom roommate whom Rocco suspected existed probably because the phantom had left tell-tale signs of his presence which Rocco was quick to notice when he searched Johnny's apartment. Two razors, perhaps, or two toothbrushes. Of course, Johnny could explain the double items by saying he liked to be prepared for 'sleep-over' guests when he got lucky.

The underwear model and erstwhile actor was lying through his teeth to save his ass and would continue to lie until he was confronted with the facts. Johnny knew about the meeting in his apartment but he was genuinely surprised to find a corpse there because murder wasn't on the agenda. Johnny must have soiled his Freddy Fine briefs. He wouldn't, or couldn't, contact his lover because when the shit hits the fan, Washington office holders are adept at leaving town or, if necessary, leaving the country. Poor Johnny was on his own and in need of a reassuring shoulder. Enter Mike Gavin.

How to get to Johnny to offer his condolences and help was the problem. The play was on hold so its director, Brad Turner, was incommunicado with his star. Freddy Fine's PR men and lawyers must have Johnny in protective custody. But where? Not the scene of the crime and not Fine's apartment. Both locations were too obvious. This left the third member of the Holy Trinity, Ken Wallace, who would know where Johnny was being kept out of harm's way; and didn't Ken invite Mike to a boy's lunch a few days ago? Mike had promised to check his schedule and arrange the lunch date which he had no intention of doing – until now.

"I'm going to have lunch with Ken Wallace," Mike announced.

"Better you than me," was Jack's reply.

"Is that any way to talk about your personal photographer who will make you famous with a click of his Nikon?"

"I'm already famous, in case you haven't noticed."

"I like your modesty, Jack."

"I'm not bragging. I'm complaining. It's not easy being me."

"Your conceit is exceeded only by your good looks." He kissed Jack on the lips.

"You want to fool around?" Jack asked.

"I want to spank your monkey, partner."

THIRTY-ONE

Like Julius Caesar, Ken Wallace was every woman's lover and every man's wife. Caesar, so history tells us, crossed the Tiber with an army at his back. Wallace crossed the Hudson with a camera hanging from his neck. His age at the time of the crossing is a moot question because Wallace has so often lied about his age, his place of birth, his given name, his ancestry and everything and anything that delineates the birth and rearing of the guy now known to millions as Ken Wallace.

"A fashion photographer of note took me under his wing when I was twelve. He taught me by day and buggered me by night. I was a good lay and a quick learner. So quick, I was buggering him before I was twelve and a half. In that position, excuse the pun, I was more assistant than student; a whiz in the darkroom, the bedroom and the steam room. I could manipulate a tripod and a condom with one hand; both essential to the trade. When my mentor began asking me to compose a layout, I knew it was time to move on."

Given his newly acquired expertise, it was only natural for Wallace to become a paparazzo, a trade to which he took like the proverbial duck to water. Part voyeur, part spy and all deviant, added up to what it takes to getting your rocks off by chasing "names" and taking their pic when they are most ill prepared to have their picture taken. In this manner Ken Wallace eked out a living, not much more, but in constant pursuit of "names" he learned, first hand, where the "names" resided, wined, dined, partied and fucked. Knowledge he would soon parley into becoming a "name" he named Ken Wallace.

Wallace shagged an actor whose good looks and beefcake physique had women and gay men eyeing him with impure thoughts. Producers wanted to sign him to play Tarzan swinging on vines in his leather fig leaf. But could a fig leaf hide what was rumored to be the biggest cock in captivity? It was said this potential ape man had a dong bigger than the appendages of comedian Milton Berle and the legendary Porfirio Rubirosa.

Bigger than uncle Miltie who was believed to have the biggest cock in show biz or, perhaps, in the world? Impossible. Bigger than the guy who married billionaires Doris Duke and Barbara Hutton? The five-and-dime heiress paid Porfirio two million bucks to get rid of him, the sum calculated to be two hundred thousand per inch.

They still talk about the night Berle and Rubirosa unzipped in the men's room of the old El Morocco to compare peckers and declare a winner. Porfirio pulled out ten inches, hanging. Berle took one look and said, "I'll just show him enough to win."

One particular morning Wallace waited for the actor who was his current target to emerge from his apartment on Central Park West, knowing the guy's routine was to take an early morning jog in the park before breakfast. The man looked splendid in his T-shirt and shorts which exhibited a masculine bulge cynics said was the result of a baseball installed in the pouch of his jockeys, and off he went with Wallace in hot pursuit.

The jogger was either not aware that he was being followed or didn't care if he did know. When he suddenly paused, turned and headed into a cluster of bushes, Wallace raced to the spot, got down on his belly and crawled behind the bush from which the actor's head appeared above the foliage. As suspected, the guy was taking a piss. Snap. Snap. Snap. The actor turned, spotted Wallace on his belly and pissed on the intruder. Snap. Snap. Snap. Wallace's golden shower drenched him in gilt.

Wallace became a "name" among the paparazzi and the tabloid editors. He sold the print both domestically and abroad. In Europe they ran the picture uncensored. Here, they placed a big, black dot over the spraying phallus. A very large dot, to make sure deprived readers knew what they had been deprived of. Never one to miss an opportunity to push the envelope, Wallace talked the editor of one rag, sold at the checkout counter of most supermarkets, into writing an article on how he came to take the celebrated picture. Wallace described in detail the thick six inches of uncut hose that attacked him as he was doing his job.

You might think this was enough for any guy to lick his chops over. Not Ken Wallace. He composed a dozen letters to the editor claiming to be from avid readers who wanted to know the meaning of uncut as it pertained to the male anatomy.

This elicited another article wherein Wallace discussed circumcision, before and after, naming Hollywood's most famous foreskins. To wit: Clark Gable, Burt Lancaster, Yul Brynner and Johnny Weissmuller. He even got in the tidbit that the late president Kennedy was snipped while at Choate. He dubbed the men Cavaliers and Baldies, after which he never mentioned a guy without adding the proper epithet. How did he know? Mostly, he guessed, hoping for a confrontation with a cavalier who was a baldy or vice versa, and he got it.

One afternoon at a very popular restaurant, a guy he designated as cavalier approached Wallace's table, unzipped, pulled it out and shook it in Wallace's face, shouting, "You're wrong, cock sucker."

All the money in the world couldn't buy the media space this generated for Ken Wallace.

None of this was new. A gay newspaper, many years ago, published lists of actors, politicians and sports figures who were intact or otherwise.

Due to overexposure, as it were, the actor who pissed on Wallace never made it to the silver screen. He was Wallace's first casualty, but not his last.

Having established himself as a penis maven, Wallace became a popular dinner guest. The hostesses who invited him were the kind who ask their hair dresser to dine. Hardly A list, they are to society what Andy Warhol is to Rembrandt. Wallace dissed the ladies to their faces and behind their backs.

They loved it He hired a press agent who got his name in gossip columns.

He treated the ladies to lunch and their husbands to blow jobs.

Ken Wallace was flying high; then he met Freddy Fine and soared. Fine was a Seventh Avenue men's underwear manufacturer, a business he had inherited from his father. *Fine's*

Finest was the company's logo and in over 50 years that was as innovative as it got. Freddy was an unimposing married man who personally selected his male models, posing them in their Freddy Fine finest and masturbating over the memory.

Freddy hired Ken Wallace to photograph the boys and men for the firm's ads and catalogue. Sensing Freddy's need, Ken took Freddy into the changing room with his model, had the model remove his boxers and gave the guy a blow job as voyeur Freddy watched and got himself off. This routine became standard operational procedure for Freddy Fine and Co. When Ken encouraged Fine to share the goodies, the boss was forever in awe of his photographer and signed him to an exclusive contract. Freddy and Ken became a team and it proved a marriage made in heaven.

Facilitating was another of Ken's talents. He knew how to put one in touch with Dr. Feelgoods, unscrupulous lawyers, creative accountants, businessmen in need of relaxation, housewives in need of stimulation and husbands in need of diversity.

Wallace attracted rumors (mostly generated by himself) the way navels attract lint. One of the most persistent had it that Wallace had an ongoing collection of "names" he photographed as works of art, fictional characters and historic figures, with their private parts very much on display. A famous Hollywood actor as Romeo, a queen's daughter-in-law as Lady Godiva and even a one-time presidential candidate as El Greco's nobleman with the real thing where the cod piece should be.

Many wannabes boasted they were in it and probably weren't and many superstars denied they were in it and probably were. Did it exist? When asked, Wallace always answered with a wink and a salacious grin.

Freddy owned a house in East Hampton where his wife summered. He bought a house in Fire Island Pines where Ken summered. Freddy commuted between these pricy pieces of ocean front property. It was exhausting but with Ken Wallace forever scouting for likely models, it was also most rewarding.

It was at the Pines where Ken first spotted Giancarlo LaBella strolling down Fire Island Boulevard. LaBella not only filled his swimming togs, he overflowed them. The package he displayed seemed to shout "OPEN ME FIRST." His body was pure lust, his face angelic. He could make men erect and women moist and have them believing they were having a religious experience.

Ken approached LaBella and handed him his card. Without looking at it, LaBella said. "A hundred bucks. If you want me to cum, a hundred-and-fifty." And Ken knew he had picked a winner.

Thirty-Two

"I thought a private lunch *pas de deux* would be better than being seen together at Le Cirque and having everyone wondering who was fucking who. Or should that be fucking whom?"

Wallace owned a floor-through in a townhouse on West Seventy-Eighth Street; two flights, all up, as he liked to tell visitors. Neither faux antique, white telephone modern or Victorian clutter, the décor was a blend of thrift shop trash and Salvation Army treasures. Like its owner, it was pure hackney and, like its owner, it worked.

Mike entered the apartment, assayed the décor and handed Wallace a bottle of Avieto Classico. "I brought white wine based on the educated guess that you would be serving either tuna or chicken salad avec potato salad and coleslaw. In short, the mayonnaise blue plate special."

"You didn't come for the cuisine, you came to interrogate me. If you give me your coat, I'll give you back this lovely bottle of wine which you can open in the kitchen as that's where we'll be dining. It's that-a-way," Wallace concluded, pointing.

The sophisticated fashion photographer who recently added couturier to his curriculum vitae because he was personally designing Freddy's new line of jeans, was acting like a Bronx housewife entertaining her best friend. Reruns of Lucy and Ethel? He didn't drop the phony corn pone accent because he didn't want Mike to forget that he was dealing with bald, brash, bitchy Ken Wallace, prick extraordinaire. And Mike did not forget, not for a minute. He removed his pea coat and handed it to Wallace. To tweak Wallace, Mike had worn his Levi's, albeit a pair he had tailored for a perfect fit.

Taking the coat, Wallace glanced at Mike's package and asked, "Cavalier or Baldy?"

"Ask Jack."

"Jack Montgomery, the all American boy. Never fear, I'll ask him."

"You might also ask him who strangled Matt Bokowski with Freddy Fine's jockstrap."

The kitchen table was set for two with place mats rather than a cloth. On it were two wine glasses, a corkscrew and a buffet spread. No tuna or chicken sandwiches but plates of shrimp, deviled eggs, prosciuttto wrapped around bread sticks and a salad of tomato and mozzarella cheese.

Mike was decorking the wine when Wallace joined him in the kitchen. "If I knew who strangled the reporter I would have given you an exclusive the day I called you. Reading between the lines I would say you know more about it than I do."

Strange as it might seem, Mike thought Wallace was speaking the truth. Wallace's job was to protect Johnny Jones, breadwinner of the Holy Trinity. If he knew anything about the murder that might clear Johnny, he would tell it to the police and the press. Forget exclusive. If he knew something that put Johnny in harm's way he would keep his mouth shut. If he knew nothing, he would call anyone who might elucidate him about the unfortunate event in Johnny's apartment. Thanks to his reportage, Mike seemed to know more about the murder than anyone, including the police and Johnny Jones, if one could believe Johnny.

"You called me shortly after it happened and you didn't say one word about the murder," Mike reminded him.

"Land phones have a thousand ears and cell phones are broadcasting stations. Trust me. Eavesdropping is how I get all my gossip. What's your secret?"

Wallace had kept his mouth shut because he had nothing to say and Mike had kept his mouth shut because he didn't want to affect anything Wallace might say. Two pros at the give-and-take game had outsmarted each other, as well as themselves.

"I get my gossip, hot off the press, from my cleaning person, Peter Grimes."

"That old gypsy? He's hoofed his way through more shows

than Fred and Adele and Ginger, combined. If you're missing any underpants, he's got them. It's his thing, you know. Sniff, sniff, sniff. They say he used to sniff Marlon Brando's behind, for luck, before performances. Brando went on to great acclaim, so I guess it worked. Have some shrimp. It's fresh and very expensive. Did I put out the sauce? Yes, here it is. Brando had himself circumcised when he was about seventy because he liked bald heads."

"Cut or uncut is a matter of taste," Mike gibed while filling their glasses. Then he sat and sampled the shrimp. It was very good, indeed.

Seated at the table, they began to pick, nibble and sip in earnest. "The prosciutto is also excellent," Mike complemented.

"Parma," Wallace boasted. "Only the best when Mike Gavin comes to lunch. So what's Peter's story? That old queen has his nose in everyone's business in more ways than one."

"Ex-hustler refuses to give Bokowski an exclusive interview so the reporter threatens to expose the ex-hustler's former profession and gets a jockstrap around his throat."

"If you believe that you believe Cary Grant was a heterosexual." Wallace dressed the tomato and mozzarella with olive oil and vinegar before passing it on to Mike who filled his salad plate. "What do you know?" he asked.

"Everything I know is in the copy I sent to my paper which they dutifully printed and you, I'm sure, read."

"Okay," Wallace conceded, "what do you suspect?"

Mike wasn't about to tell Wallace what Jack had learned from the doctor interning at Bethesda. That was for Lt. Rocco's ears only, if Mike could devise a way to clue in Rocco without reneging on his promise to keep Travis McBarb out of the frame.

Did Ken Wallace know who Johnny's lover was? He might and it was worth a try. Without showing his hand, Mike said, "I suspect Johnny has a lover, or partner, or whatever polite words are now used to describe a fuck buddy who sometimes shares Johnny's apartment and therefore has a key to Johnny's door. I also suspect Johnny is keeping this affair a deep, dark secret."

Wallace was too sly a fish to go for the bait. Instead he swam around it.

"What makes you think Johnny has a lover?"

"Something Lt. Rocco said. Remember, he searched Johnny's apartment. I take it you've met Lt. Rocco."

Wallace nodded. "He grilled Freddy and me."

"What did you tell him?"

"I told him I wanted to photograph him as the Colossus of Rhodes. The face of Narcissus, the torso of Heracles, legs of steel spanning the harbor and a heroic cock hanging over a mound of gargantuan balls. A piss from that hose could sink a ship."

Mike laughed. "The lieutenant certainly made an impression on you."

"Don't tell me he didn't jiggle your balls."

Mike ignored the comment and hoped the blush he felt didn't show. "If your Colossus wrapped his legs of steel around you he'd snap your ribs like they were macaroni."

"I would die happy," Wallace assured him.

"Not like poor Matt Bokowski who, I'm sure, did not die happy. Who's Johnny's lover?"

There was silence as they made selections from the buffet and replenished their wine glasses. Looking at Wallace's bald pate, Mike wondered if the photographer was also a Baldy down below and refrained from asking, fearing Wallace would show and tell.

"You don't give up easy," Wallace said.

"I don't give up at all. Did Rocco ask you if Johnny had a lover? I'm sure he asked Johnny and I'm sure Johnny said he often entertained overnight guests. Entertained is the operative word. How Rocco must have laughed. The guests would account for the extra toothbrush and razor and even the odd pair of shorts and shirts that didn't fit Johnny and didn't escape Rocco's notice."

Wallace was nodding appreciatively. "That was Johnny's stance. The kid has balls. I'm surprised he didn't put the make on the lieutenant. Rocco and LaBella. How Italian can you get?"

"You still haven't answered my question. Who's Johnny's lover and sometime roommate?"

Wallace surrendered with a shrug. "I know he has a lover but I don't know who it is."

"How do you know?"

"You know where Johnny lives." It was a statement, not a question.

"Grove Street. The Village. Glorified tenement, is how Rocco described it."

"It was a tenement but like so many tenements in the Village it got a face-lift to make it look respectable but it's still a pile of walk-up flats with a fresh coat of paint and a carpet for the minuscule lobby. For Johnny it was a step up and he was thrilled to get it."

Wallace went on to say that as Johnny began raking in more money, thanks to Freddy Fine, he was less and less thrilled with his renovated tenement.

He considered himself a supermodel, which he now was, thanks to Freddy and Ken Wallace, and wanted new digs to go with his new status. Central Park West or the Upper East Side was what he was aiming for. Doorman, concierge, a guy wearing white gloves to press the elevator buttons for him. He began bugging Wallace to help him find what he wanted and would also need Wallace's help to get Johnny accepted as a tenant by the management of such exalted surroundings.

"Then, suddenly last summer, as Tennessee Williams might say, he changed his mind. He wanted to stay with the Grove Street flat. You're a smart reporter, Mike, can you guess why Johnny changed his mind?" Wallace asked. "I'll give you three guesses."

Without hesitating, Mike answered, "Doorman, concierge, elevator operator."

"Bingo."

"Johnny was entertaining a guest who was easily recognizable and didn't want to be recognized by a doorman or concierge or elevator operator," Mike went on.

"The Queen of England could come and go to that apartment and no one would know, or care," Wallace added.

"And you don't know who this recognizable guy is?" Mike asked, certain it wasn't the Queen of England.

Wallace shook his head. "I have no idea. I thought maybe you might know. That's why I'm feeding you this pricy meal."

"You know Johnny better than me or anyone else. Who does he hang with? Who is he fucking or who's fucking him? Who were his customers before he began posing in his underpants? You must have a dozen suspects, at least."

Wallace named a film actor. Very popular and very married. "He picked up Johnny a few years back at the pool table in Destry's. Took him to L.A. a few times and I know he's seen Johnny recently."

Knowing it wasn't a Californian but a Washingtonian who Johnny was seeing, Mike probed further. "Why do you think it's the actor?"

"Because of the play," Wallace said. "Johnny never talked about being an actor. Now he's doing a fucking off-Broadway show for your friend, Bradley Turner. I figure the actor talked Johnny into this and maybe even gives him acting lessons in the bedroom or snuffs a wise guy reporter with a jockstrap."

Taking another track, Mike asked. "Could the actor be the producer of Johnny's play?"

"Who knows? He came to us looking for money."

"The actor?"

'No, the guy who said he was the producer. I forgot his name, if he ever told us."

"Max Berger," Mike told him.

"Whatever," Wallace said. "It costs a fortune to put on one of those shows. Even off-Broadway. This guy, Max Berger, said the play would showcase Johnny and sell more of Freddy's jockey shorts. I told him my pics of Johnny's crotch is all the showcasing Johnny needs to sell come-fuck-me briefs."

"So Freddy is not backing Johnny's show."

Wallace speared a shrimp and waved it at Mike before he answered. "Freddy likes to hedge his bets. He's in for fifty thousand."

"What does he look like?" Mike asked.

"Freddy? You know what he looks like."

"Stop playing the nerd, Ken. If you want to help Johnny just tell me what you know. What does Max Berger look like?"

"He looks like a million other people. He's no beauty. That I would remember." Wallace closed his eyes as if envisioning the elusive Max Berger. "About forty. My height. Maybe a few pounds heavier. Clean shaven. No scars…" Wallace stopped abruptly. "I think he had a little mole over his eyebrow; yeah, he did. A brown mole, smaller than a dime. I notice things like that because my models use makeup to cover moles or zits. In America you have to have a complexion like porcelain to sell the product."

Mike pricked up his ears. A mole? Why did that grab his attention? "Over which eyebrow?" he questioned to keep Wallace focused.

"How the fuck should I know? I saw the guy once for ten minutes. If you're thinking this guy is Johnny's lover forfuckinggetit. Johnny has taste. No class, but taste."

The mole was bugging Mike but with lunch winding down he figured he had gotten all he could out of Ken Wallace. If he wanted to know more he would have to give before he could take. In spite of the facts in Mike's reportage, Wallace had not made the connection between Bokowski and Washington, D.C.

It was typical of Wallace to key in on a married movie star rather than a politico. Mike would have to nudge his lunch host.

"Johnny sang at a party in Washington to make a senator's daughter happy. Did he do that often?" Mike asked.

"Johnny liked to rub shoulders with the rich and famous whenever he could. He thought their sophistication would rub off on him. It didn't."

"Do you know which senator Johnny was rubbing shoulders with last summer? Jack and I were playing a charity gig there at the time."

Wallace was shaking his head, not listening to Mike, his mind on something else. "A daughter?" He asked.

Mike nodded. "Yes. It was a party for the senator's daughter. Sweet sixteen, I suppose."

"I don't know anything about a daughter. I thought it was a VIP's son Johnny was sucking up to."

BINGO.

THIRTY-THREE

Mike had to tread easy. He didn't want to show his hand but he had to know what cards Wallace was holding, even if Wallace was unaware of the game they were playing. "Did you meet him?"

"Fuck, no," Wallace barked. "Johnny's love life is a never ending soap opera. I keep out of it except for the occasional blow job to remind Johnny of his roots."

"Did Johnny talk about him?"

"What's all this about?" Wallace wanted to know. He was a con artist who knew when he was being conned.

"It's about clearing Johnny from a murder rap. He's saying he has the only key to his apartment and he has no idea how Bokowski and his murderer got into his apartment or even why they were there. Johnny is lying. We both know that and so do the police."

"Johnny's a four flusher, like me, but he's no murderer. He's got big balls but he lacks guts. Besides, he was at the theater when the reporter was murdered. We all know that."

"Then he's protecting someone and he could go down for aiding and abetting, not to mention perjury. Johnny knows why Bokowski was in his apartment and who let him in. He's protecting his boyfriend. Who is he?"

"Why do you suspect the D.C. kid?"

"I suspect anyone Johnny was seeing, including your actor. I'm a reporter. An investigative reporter. I gather the facts before I come to a realistic conclusion. Only fools rush in."

Wallace laughed. "Fools rush in and get the best seats. Don't bullshit with me, Gavin. What do you know?"

"I know what was in my column. Bokowski talked about a Watergate-like scandal. Try this on. Suppose it wasn't the actor Bokowski suspected Johnny was fucking but the son of a

Washington VIP."

Looking pensive, Wallace kept his mouth shut, opening it only to sip more wine. Then, reverting to type, he asked, "What's in it for me?"

Mike rolled his eyes toward the ceiling. He knew that sooner or later it would come down to give and take. With Wallace, of course, it was sooner rather than later. He couldn't give much more without exposing Travis McBarb so, as Jack would do, he put the ball in Wallace's court. "What happens if Johnny takes the fall for this?"

Wallace didn't have to ponder over the query. "If you build a thousand bridges and suck one cock you'll be remembered as a cock sucker. If Johnny takes the fall I'll be remembered as the murderer's pimp which, in this town, is tantamount to the kiss of death. I'll be back being a nobody paparazzo who used to be a somebody photographer."

Politics and murder make strange bedfellows, Mike was thinking as he recalled his posthumous promise to avenge Matt Bokowski and crawled into bed with the scum bag Wallace. "Level with me and I'll save Johnny from being prosecuted, thereby saving your career. That's what's in it for you. Now, who's the VIP's son?"

Wallace looked as if he was in physical pain. "I don't fucking know."

"How did you find out he was the son of a Washington VIP?"

"Because of Freddy."

"Freddy Fine?"

"He's the only Freddy I know," Wallace said and explained. "Freddy saw an item in the papers saying Johnny was at a political rally with the boy. Freddy chewed out Johnny. He told him he didn't like the boy's father or his party and advised Johnny not to lend them his support."

"And Johnny told Freddy to go fuck himself."

"I think those were his exact words."

"So who's the boy? Who's his father?"

"I don't know. If I ever heard their names I don't remember them."

"But Freddy knows who they are," Mike said.

Wallace didn't answer. He finished the wine in his glass and picked up the bottle. It was empty. Mike took his mobile from the pocket of the blazer he was wearing and handed it to Wallace. "Call Freddy."

"What will I tell him?"

"Tell him I want to know. Tell him we're trying to save Johnny from destroying himself and maybe taking Freddy Fine and Co. with him. Tell him anything, but get the name of the Washington VIP," Mike harangued, then was immediately sorry for the tirade.

Had he over played his hand? In his euphoria to get the name of McBarb's patient and Johnny's boyfriend had he sounded too eager, too zealous in his need to know? Wallace was aware of Johnny's elusive roommate and the role Johnny's lover probably played in the murder but he thought the guy was a movie star. Mike knew, for a fact, that this wasn't the case. Johnny's lover was a seasoned Washington VIP, not a teenager. Mike had to learn the guy's name without tipping his hand to Ken Wallace.

"Are you going to tell Rocco?"

"Tell him what?"

"Tell him the boy is Johnny's lover."

To deflect Wallace, Mike was quick to point out, "Johnny went to a political rally with this boy. That doesn't make him his lover. I'll tell Rocco about the actor, too, and any other likely suspects that come my way."

Wallace pulled out his own mobile which now took on the appearance of a stiletto he was brandishing at Mike. "Let's make a deal."

Mike knew that Wallace wasn't going to give an inch without taking a yard and Mike was ready to go the yard but with certain limitations – namely S.E.X. He was desperate to learn the name of Johnny's political bedmate but not so desperate that he would rub dicks with a sleaze like Ken Wallace. "What did you have in mind?"

Wallace began to wax elegantly about his pseudo porn collection he called his Art Portfolio. Posing celebrities from the glittering realms of film, fashion, politics, science, including Scientology, as characters from history, works of art, novels, plays and ancient Greek, Roman and Egyptian mythology. "My La Gioconda is fabulous."

Mike imagined an overly endowed, bare breasted film actress in the guise of Mona Lisa and shuddered.

"My *piece de resistance* is Tarzan minus his leather jockeys."

Mike was awed. "Don't tell me you photographed…"

"But of course. Hollywood failed to immortalize him, so I did."

"You cost him his career, which makes you a first class prick."

Wallace laughed. "What else is new? My Art Portfolio will put Warhol's soup cans where they belong – on a kitchen shelf."

The guy had the ego the size of an elephant's behind. Knowing where this was leading, Mike asked, "How do you see me? Little Boy Blue?"

Unable to control himself, Wallace actually rubbed his hands with fervor as he exclaimed, "Dorian Gray."

Mike blinked. "I think Dorian was about twenty, give or take a year, when Wilde created the character. I can see forty, as Jack likes to remind me."

Wallace waved off the criticism. "You were our first male supermodel. The camera loves you. A little makeup, the right lighting and behold, the Picture of Dorian Gray as Oscar Wilde intended the artist to paint it – in the nude."

"Forget it. I wouldn't pose nude for anyone, especially you."

"Michelangelo's boyfriend did and created DAVID, a work of art our Johnny wanted desperately to pose for. Naturally, I had to turn him down."

"Naturally? Why?"

"Johnny is snipped down below and David has a lovely foreskin. Our Johnny threatened to go to Firenza with a chisel and hammer and do guess what."

"You're both nuts. I won't do it. Goodbye, the end, over and out."

Wallace put down his mobile. "And I won't call Freddy. Goodbye, the end, over and fucking out."

"I'll call Freddy," Mike replied.

"Freddy won't tell you dick without getting the okay from me. The murder in Johnny's apartment and Rocco's visit has scared the shit out of him and he was never very ballsy to begin with. He leans on me and I'll tell him to shun you to keep Fine's Finest from getting embroiled in a slimy murder. Your column, as you like to tell us, reaches millions. Freddy will say he doesn't know what you're talking about and bust into tears. Trust me."

Mike was livid. "You're not a bitch, you're a cunt."

"Now that's an insult. Luncheon was fun, now I have to run, for drinks at Twenty-One," Wallace partially quoted the lyrics of a bygone Broadway musical. "Don't slam the door on the way out."

Mike froze. He didn't even blink this time. If he had a weapon he would have used it on Ken Wallace. He needed the information Freddy could give him but to get it he had to join the suckers in Wallace's infamous scrapbook. Now that he knew the much talked about collection existed, he also knew how the poor slobs got roped into posing for him. Like a spider waiting for a fly to land on its net, Wallace preyed upon ambitious people on the way up in need of a boost and on the way down, desperate to avoid the abyss of oblivion. Wallace, thanks to his pop celebrity, was in a position to help those in dire need and did so for a price.

Mike Gavin could perform the same service, even better, but exercised discretion when lending a hand to the hopeful he deemed worthy. He had turned his back on Matt Bokowski and was now trying to make amends for the sake of justice, not revenge. He had mistakenly let Ken Wallace know his desire to get the name of Johnny's current lover and in doing so he had landed smack on the spider's net.

A reporter, Mike had learned to let nothing stand in his way of getting the story. If there was a price to pay he would deal with it after the fact, not before he had got what he wanted. He had come for a story and he wasn't going to leave without getting it.

"Call Freddy," was all Mike said and the spider knew the fly had acquiesced. "But first tell me where Johnny is hiding from his adoring fans."

Wallace closed the deal by picking up his mobile. "He's at Freddy's beach house in East Hampton with instructions to speak to no one but Lt. Rocco."

"Call him and tell him I'm going to pay him a visit and to cooperate with me."

"I will, Dorian Gray."

"Thank you, Alvin Darling."

THIRTY-FOUR

"You spoke to Patient X," Jack shouted for at least the third time.

"I spoke to Tim Samuels, son of senator Sten Samuels," Mike shouted back for the third time.

"He has to be Patient X," Jack said, calmer but no less exuberant. "He fits Travis McBarb's description perfectly. Washington V.I.P. and Johnny's lover. The evidence is overwhelming."

"Overwhelming evidence isn't fact," Mike argued. "The facts are these: Johnny went to a political rally with Tim Samuels. They know each other. That doesn't make them lovers nor does it make him McBarb's patient."

Jack wasn't buying it. "Patient X is a Washington V.I.P. Sten Samuels is a Washington V.I.P. A senator. Tim is the senator's son which makes him a V.I.P. by stint of birth. And I know how we can prove Tim Samuels is Patient X."

Mike cringed, hoping, even praying, Jack wasn't going to say what he knew Jack was thinking. His prayer wasn't answered.

"If Tim Samuels has hepatitis B, he's our man."

"How clever of you," Mike said. "I never thought of that. Will you call him and ask him if he has hepatitis B and while you have him on the phone ask if he bangs Johnny or does Johnny bang him or are they strictly oral soul mates?"

Jack was laughing. "I doubt they only talk to each other," he said.

That got a smile from Mike. They were in their bedroom, preparing to call it a day. Now in their shorts, Mike had washed and brushed; Jack was on his way to do the same when the discussion turned argumentative. Mike cupped Jack's jockey pouch and hefted the family jewels. "Let's talk about this," he said.

"Maybe I'll brush later," Jack suggested.

Mike turned him around and patted his ass. "Brush now, you'll taste better."

Mike had been doing a lot of thinking and a bit of research since leaving Ken Wallace's apartment after consuming a rather tasty lunch and a generous amount of his favorite Ruffino white wine which came from the medieval town of Orvieto, Italy. Mike scored big when Wallace's call to Freddy Fine had revealed that Johnny was a friend of Tim Samuels, son of the Washington senator. Mike fled the west side townhouse agog over the name Freddy had dropped and its implications.

In the cab ride home he went over the facts, again and again, scrutinizing an evening that at the time was innocuous, but now took on all the elements of a Hitchcock thriller.

The cast: Mike Gavin, Jack Montgomery, Amanda Richards, Tim Samuels, Oprah Winfrey and the victim himself, Matthew Bokowski.

The set: Blair House, Washington, D.C.

The scene: The Vice President's dinner party last July. A party Mike didn't want to attend, thanks to the thrashing he had received from Jack on the tennis court that afternoon. A gathering that contained all the elements of a murder to be played out four months later.

The action: Mike is watching Jack Montgomery chatting with Oprah Winfrey when Amanda Richards approaches him. Mike and Amanda have a drink. Tim Samuels enters the scene, approaching Amanda. We learn Tim had escorted Amanda to the charity tennis competition that afternoon, taking the place of his father who was unable to attend.

Note: Senator Sten Samuels is a diehard conservative. Amanda Richards is a diehard liberal. Their relationship is a new one, prompted by Samuels' inviting Amanda to lunch to discuss national funding for the arts.

Amanda introduces Mike to Tim. Amanda and Tim depart. No sooner do they leave than Matthew Bokowski, the reporter whose byline is Matt Burke, approaches Mike and questions him about the ethics of reportage that could create a stir, a la the Watergate scandal. Bikowski refuses to be specific so Mike gives him the brush off and goes to break in on Jack and Oprah.

Finally, Matthew Bokowski approaches Amanda and almost immediately the security people move in on the reporter and escort him out. Why? He's a staff reporter for a Baltimore newspaper and he's wearing his official I.D. tag. Did Tim Samuels finger Bokowski because he was talking to Amanda Richards, an actress? Not very likely. Because he had been talking to Mike Gavin, popular syndicated columnist read by millions? Most likely.

Four months later, in November, Bokowski is strangled with a jockstrap in the New York apartment of supermodel Johnny Jones who claims he doesn't know Bokowski, what Bokowski was doing in his apartment or how he got in the apartment.

Today Mike learned Johnny was a friend, possibly the lover, of Tim Samuels. Since then he had been thinking…

"You spoke to the victim and the murderer at the Veep's shindig," Jack announced coming out of the bathroom, flashing his sparkling white teeth.

Not willing to admit that's what he was thinking, Mike said, "We know the victim, but we don't know who did him in." Removing his shorts to briefly display a dick and balls which, even at rest, could be called prestigious, Mike got into bed. "I believe you have a date with your photographer tomorrow morning."

Dropping his shorts, Jack joined Mike in their very comfortable, king size bed. "Dress rehearsal," Jack said. "I'll be trying on jeans with Freddy's logo on my ass to make sure they look like they were made just for me which, of course, they were."

"Tell Wallace to keep his hands where they belong. On his cameras and not on Freddy's logo."

Jack rolled over to press himself against Mike, his fingers nesting in Mike's pubic bush. "This needs a trimming," he observed.

"I love it when you give me a trim. Tomorrow night?"

"If I'm not too exhausted after posing for my photographer all day."

"No problem. I'll have my barber do it."

Instantly alert, Jack asked, "Has you barber ever trimmed it? The truth."

"In fact he has," Mike admitted.

Aroused, Jack pressed his pecker against Mike's hip. "And what happened?"

Playing dumb, Mike said, "He gave me a crew cut down there."

"And…"

Obviously not the first time their pillow talk took on the distinct aura of foreplay, Mike whispered. "You're a closet voyeur, Montgomery.“

Masturbating his cock against Mike, Jack said once more, "And…"

"He docked me," Mike told him.

"No…"

"Yes. He had the equipment for docking."

"How did it feel?"

"Deliciously warm."

"Shit. I can't do it."

"Don't I know it, baby."

"Did you cum?"

"No. He did."

"All over your dickhead?"

"Where else?"

"How did it feel?"

"Deliciously warm."

"I'm going to cream," Jack pleaded.

They had happily discovered early in their relationship that masturbation wasn't just a substitute for sex but often the main event. Solo or together, the end more than justified the means. It was a boy's first sexual experience and would probably be his last. It was exotic, erotic and SAFE.

"Not in our clean bed, baby. Out. Out," Mike ordered.

Jack jumped out of the bed and ran to the bathroom. Standing over the sink, one arm akimbo, the other in motion, Jack galloped to his climax as Mike entered, rolling a lubed Trojan rubber over his cock. He was behind Jack, aiming for the tennis star's firm ass until he found the masculine opening and began probing its depths. Mike went in slow, inch by inch, as Jack rotated his ass around the invader, insatiable in his need. Now beyond the point of no return and besotted with bliss Jack exploded with a cry, spewing squirt after squirt of thick cream into the gaping sink. Mike rammed into the honey pot, expelling a joyous moan as he dropped his load into the Trojan.

Engulfed in rapture and each other's arms, still panting, they descended from the heights, spent and content.

"Nice," Mike sighed.

"Nice? That was a fucking Grand Slam."

Back in the warmth of their bed, legs entwined, eyes closed, Jack asked, "Are you going to pose for Wallace's art portfolio?"

"Not if I can help it," Mike answered, still irked by the promise he had made to Wallace but not so irked as to regret what he got in return for the promise. Albeit, that knowledge was now keeping him awake. He had spent hours researching the career of Senator Sten Samuels who he now knew was a widower with one son, Tim. No rumors of romance in the senator's very public life, and Mike was certain the senator's lunch date with Amanda Richards was strictly business. What that business was, Mike suspected from his poking into Samuels' life on and off *The Hill*, was a run for his party's choice for president in the next national election.

This, no doubt, was why Samuels was buttering up to Amanda Richards, pretending interest in funding for the arts. The ploy was to soften his rigid conservative stance to appeal to a more general electorate. Mr. America was aiming high. Did he know he had a gay son who was chummy, if not intimate, with an underwear model who used to be a hustler? Did he know that an intern at Bethesda Medical knew, firsthand, about the affair? Did he know a foolish cub reporter had innocently stuck his nose into the family secret? If the answer to all of the above is YES, would he do anything to keep Tim's personal life out of the tabloids? And did anything include murder?

Mike began to mentally compose a list of ASAP *must dos*.

He had to confer with Rocco and tell him what he now knew.

He had to talk to Brad Turner to see if he could learn more about the producer, Max Berger. This was vital. Tim Samuels was interested in the theater. He had talked to Brad, his former classmate, about that interest. Was Max Berger the beard for would-be producer Tim Samuels?

He must call Amanda to learn what she could tell him about Tim Samuels, her escort at the tennis matches and the Veep's party last July. Mike was aware that Amanda's memory could be tinged with drama more in keeping with theatrics than reality but he had learned to separate chaff from wheat when chatting with the actress.

Finally, he had to speak to the cause of all the fuss, Johnny Jones himself, even if it meant a trip to East Hampton in November. Would Johnny bare his soul to Mike? It was doubtful but Johnny might be more cooperative with Mike than he had been with Lt. Rocco, especially when he told Johnny everything he had learned from Travis McBarb. It was more than worth a try. It was absolutely necessary.

Mumbling as he dozed off, Jack said, "Can I ask you something?"

"You may."

"Who's Dorian Gray?"

"Go to sleep, Jack."

THIRTY-FIVE

The Lincoln Town Car was waiting for Mike the following morning, its door held open by the doorman who tipped his hat to Mike as the passenger slipped in next to the driver, Frank Evans. The day was frigid but the sun shined brilliantly in an icy blue sky.

Mike looked especially handsome in his flannel lined chinos, camel hair top coat, belted in back with raglan sleeves and a muffler showcasing the colors of Columbia University.

"Did they arrest the pretty white boy?" Frank wanted to know.

"Good morning to you, too, Frank."

"It's not a good morning. I took a big hit last night playing the number of movies Hattie McDaniel starred in."

"You deserved to take the hit," Mike said. "The wonderful Hattie McDaniel played the maid in dozens of films but starred in none of them, and how do you know the number of films Hattie didn't star in?"

The Lincoln shot down Lexington Avenue, gunning passed amber lights on almost every intersection. "I read it in a magazine left in the car by a movie star who never played a maid."

"You need to read more carefully and a pair of reading glasses might help." Mike stopped short of suggesting Frank get specs for driving as it might help him to occasionally respond to red and green as well as the seemingly perpetual amber. Hoping to get to the Village in one piece, he offered his driver a chance to minimize his losses for the week. .

"Johnny Jones says he has nothing to do with the Jockstrap Murder. I now know he's up to his eyeballs in it but he didn't physically tie the jock around Bokowski's neck. You said he did."

"You egged me on," Frank complained.

In the interest of surviving the ride to the Village, Mike didn't refute the charge. Gramercy Park was now visible just beyond the next amber light. If they swung around the park heading west and turned down Seventh Avenue they would be in front of the Sixth precinct, Lt. Rocco's place of business, in five minutes.

"If Johnny didn't do it himself, I win. But if Johnny was instrumental in causing the murder he would be legally guilty – and you win. Thus, what we have here is a draw," Mike concluded.

"What we have here is a welcher," Frank whined, racing past an amber light to a cacophony of car horns.

The uniformed cop manning the desk greeted Mike with a welcoming smile. "He's expecting you, Mr. Gavin."

Never able to look at a good looking policeman without thinking of his late partner, Mike couldn't resist flirting with the officer. "If they bench Johnny Jones, officer, do you think you could replace him in the Freddy Fine ads?"

With a blush and a grin, he answered, "I'm a Hanes man. They're a few bucks cheaper and do the job."

"Do you own a jockstrap, officer?"

The cop touched the butt of the revolver at his hip. "This is the only lethal weapon I carry."

"Except for your smile," Mike said and turned to move on. "I know the way."

"I'm sure you do," the cop called after him.

Lt. Rocco was at his desk and his room as austere as when Mike first visited, but there was one rather startling change. Rocco's suit jacket hung not on his broad shoulders but on the back of his chair. His white shirt (button down collar) showed not a wrinkle and his rep tie (Brooks Bros. no doubt) was more collegiate than NYPD. "Have you solved the Jockstrap Murder, Mr. Gavin?"

"Mike," Mike reminded him.

"Of course. Have you solved our murder, Mike?"

"What do they call you? James, Jimmy, Jim?"

"It depends on who's doing the calling."

That left the field wide open to conjecture of every stripe and Mike played it as it lay. "Sobriquets aren't for you, James, so James it will be."

"Sobriquet is a ten dollar word."

"You're a ten dollar guy, James."

"How much did Johnny Jones charge for services rendered?"

"It depends on who's doing the calling."

That got a smile from Rocco and smiling was something Lt. Rocco should do more often, Mike thought, and silently resolved to help the lieutenant achieve that goal. This second meeting between reporter and policeman appeared to be more relaxed and congenial than their first encounter. The reason for this could be because Rocco was spinning his wheels and needed Mike's assistance to pull him out of the rut; or was this wishful thinking? Probably, but it didn't stop Mike from going with the flow.

"You called me," Rocco said, "so I assume you have something to tell me. What is it?"

Feeling more confident, Mike responded, "You show me yours, I'll show you mine."

Rocco hesitated a brief moment, then rose, pulled down the fly zipper of his gray flannels and said, "Your move."

If the gesture was meant to fluster Mike, it worked admirably. Not knowing what to do, Mike unbuttoned his top coat which drew another smile from Rocco. Mike was achieving his goal without even trying.

Rocco resumed his seat but didn't zip up his fly which left a gap just large enough to reveal a hint of Rocco's shirt tails and no more. He gestured to the visitor's chair.

Mike sat, grateful for something to do other than stare at Rocco's fly or pull out his own cock and wave it in Rocco's smug face. The guy was indeed a prick tease wearing a badge. How many gay men had the lieutenant opened his fly for to get what he wanted, giving nothing in return but a glimpse of his shirt tail? Rocco was a pompous ass, begging to be forced to put up or shut up and Mike Gavin was the man who could take the starch out of the officer's pressed boxers.

Give and take had transcended into brinkmanship. Now, he who blinks, loses.

Before Mike recovered from the unexpected blow below the belt, as it were, Rocco trumped his own ace with the words, "Travis McBarb."

Mike blinked.

The unmentionable had been mentioned. The name Mike had sworn to keep out of Rocco's grasp was being broadcast by the cop who wasn't supposed to know Travis McBarb even existed. On his way to the station house this morning, Mike had mentally created and deleted a number of lies he might use to tell Rocco about McBarb and his role in the Jockstrap Murder without outing the navy intern. Now, if Mike told any fibs it would be to save himself from being chastised by Rocco for not sharing everything he learned about the murder as he had agreed to do.

In fiction, the shamus is always smarter than the police. Obviously, Sam Spade, Nero Wolfe, Charlie Chan, Ellery Queen, Miss Marple, Hercule Poirot, Sherlock Holmes and Philip Marlow never locked horns with Lt. James Rocco. A chance meeting with the victim, Matthew Bokowski, had led Mike to the intern at Bethesda Medical and luck had placed Travis McBarb into the waiting arms of Jack Armstrong. Mike's success was based on a little work and a lot of luck. Still awed, Mike asked, "How did you connect the murder to Travis McBarb?"

"So the name is familiar to you," Rocco stated.

Mike nodded. "I came here to tell you about McBarb."

"Bullshit. Tell me how you made the connection?"

"After you," Mike said. "You opened your fly so you might

as well let it all hang out." And it's still open, Mike added silently.

"You intend to keep yours zipped up, Mr. Gavin?"

"Mike. Remember?"

"You intend to keep yours zipped up, Mike?"

"Not at all. I'm just waiting to see how far you'll go."

The verbal banter had Mike aroused and Rocco ignoring, or pretending to ignore, the blatant subtext of the conversation. The police officer really got Mike in the balls which just now were telling him that sex with Lt. James Rocco was more than a possibility. Or was Mike's swelling cock clouding his perception?

Mike had had his share of 'trade' and given his luck would certainly have more. Mike had a taste for trade (literally and figuratively) and enjoyed it, especially when it came in the form of Lt. James Rocco. The guy was sitting there with his fly open. Was he waiting for Mike to help himself to the goodies or was he playing his signature role, prick tease? Did the teaser secretly jack-off to the memory of his last performance? The thought had Mike surreptitiously draw his coat closed, covering his crotch to hide the bulge.

Mike had never been so perturbed or distracted while working on a story. This would not do. He had a murder and a partner to contend with. Both required concentrating on his goal which was not taking the starch out of Rocco's boxers but out of himself.

"I suspected Johnny had a roommate from what we found in his apartment." Rocco was talking. "A few articles of clothing that were neither Johnny's size nor his style. A bit too austere for the flamboyant underwear model. But, as Johnny himself never got tired of telling us, he has a lot of guests who spend the night and often leave things behind like he's running a fucking hotel. However, one guest left a train schedule for the run from Penn Station to Union Station and several schedules for the Dallas shuttle from La Guardia to Reagan, Dulles and Baltimore/Washington. The only thing he didn't leave was his calling card."

"I think his card would read Tim Samuels, the senator's son. He and Johnny are buddies."

"Why didn't you tell me this sooner?"

"I just learned it from Ken Wallace, Johnny's photographer."

"You also know the name Travis McBarb. You could only have come by that via Bokowski, so he must have told you something before he was killed that connected him to Travis McBarb and which you didn't tell me."

Lt. Rocco was as sharp as a diamond and twice as brilliant. Mike made a silent vow to never try outwitting the pro. This instant respect seemed to ease the tension Mike felt whenever he went one-on-one with the cop. "It's a long story."

"I have all day," Rocco answered.

Mike recounted, verbatim, his meeting with Bokowski, whose ID tag at that time read Matt Burke, and ended with what he had learned from Jack's meeting with McBarb himself. Rocco listened and nodded appreciatively as the story unfolded. The cop was now as impressed with the reporter's acumen as the reporter had been with the cop's. This mutual admiration had them working in tandem, more receptive than competitive. Mike was thinking that perhaps they could become friends or something more. Rocco didn't wear his feelings on his sleeve so Mike opted to put any idea of friendship in abeyance. Too much, too soon, could kill any chance of camaraderie. Too little, too late, could kill any chance of something more.

"Do you live with the tennis pro?" Rocco asked.

"Jack travels a lot with the pro tennis circuit. When he's in New York he stays with me. He has a house in Aspen." It wasn't a blatant lie but it wasn't the truth, either, which evoked a twinge of guilt in Mike who didn't like passing off Jack as an occasional fuck partner. The partial truth was not typical of Mike Gavin but then Lt. Rocco wasn't a typical guy. Where all this was heading, Mike had no idea, but he wasn't about to jump ship before it put into port – or sank.

"When you learned the victim, Bokowski, was from the Washington area you assumed he was Johnny's lover and part-time roommate." Mike finished Rocco's story.

"But Johnny swore he didn't know Bokowski or how the reporter got into the apartment and I believed him," Rocco said. "I've questioned more punks than I care to remember and can spot a phony after talking to him for five minutes. I talked to Johnny for hours and I'll wager my badge that he doesn't know Bokowski, which brings us to Travis McBarb.

"Since nine eleven, airport ticket agents have become virtual bloodhounds. I had Bokowski's return ticket and went down to Washington to question the agent at Reagan. She remembered him very well. He arrived minutes before the plane was scheduled to take off for New York and the flight was completely booked. He asked her if there were any cancellations. There weren't. Bokoswski, at the ticket desk, pulled out his cell, dialed and talked to someone. Minutes later the agent got a call to say a passenger, Travis McBarb, had cancelled. Bokowski got his seat. How lucky can you ger? Bokowski purchased a round trip ticket. Unfortunately, he'll get a free ride home as soon as we release the body."

Before Rocco could finish his story, Mike cut in, "I can't wait to hear what line of crap McBarb gave you for the cancellation and the switch."

"So would I," Rocco said. "Travis McBarb is beyond our reach."

Mike looked incredulous. "What do you mean?"

"In Navy speak, Travis McBarb has been relieved of his assignment and reassigned to duty on an unspecified base in the Far East. Need I say it's all top secret so don't even try to establish contact."

The news triggered a terrifying chill up Mike's spine. The power of the guy protecting Patient X was awesome. The servants of the people, like Double O Seven, were licensed to kill, maim or mutilate at their discretion. Mike was too savvy to think he could change the system but he could throw a bomb into the drawers of the bastard who tied a jockstrap around Matthew Bokowski's neck – or die trying, which was very likely to be the case. And what about poor Travis McBarb? His plight gave new and terrifying meaning to the label *innocent victim.*

"You once asked if this could be a case for the Attorney General," Mike said.

"And it will be, if it involves a Washington V.I.P.," Rocco answered.

Mike waved a hand at the officer. "Easy. Easy. All I told you was that Tim Samuels, the senator's son, was a friend of Johnny's. This I learned from Ken Wallace, via his boss, Freddy Fine. This doesn't make Tim Patient X, or Johnny's lover, or the guy who has a key to Johnny's apartment. It's a lead, no more than that."

"But it's the only lead we have," Rocco answered.

Did he say WE? As in US? Were they now officially a team? This, too, sent a chill up Mike's spine but it was more salacious than terrifying. Lieutenant Rocco made Mike feel like a tart and the feeling wasn't totally unwelcome.

"I'm going to talk to Johnny," Mike offered, "and see if I can get him to level with me. He may not know who Matthew Bokowski was but he sure as hell knows who has access to his apartment and what they were doing there. The fact that this Mr. Martin set up the meeting in New York at a time when Johnny was at the theater has me thinking that Johnny didn't know anything about the proposed meeting. It was a scam and right now I bet Johnny is shitting in his Freddy Fine's finest."

"Johnny won't tell me anything relevant. I agree, he's afraid, but he's more afraid of the boys he's playing with than of me. Tim Samuels is our only lead so I'm going straight for his balls," Rocco said.

"Proceed with caution. These boys play hard ball. You might end up somewhere you don't want to be. I'm going to see Johnny and try to get him to talk sense. He clams up with you because you're one of the guys who've been harassing him since he was old enough to sell his charms for ready cash. If you offered him a deal to save his ass he wouldn't trust you to keep your word; quite frankly, neither would I. I can give Johnny what he most craves – publicity. Johnny Jones, naive victim of unscrupulous politicians.

For headlines like that he would take a vow of chastity," Mike warned.

Rocco responded with, "At our first meeting I said this might be a case for the Attorney General. With a senator's son as a possible suspect, that's just where we're heading."

"I think the senator is aiming for the big prize, priming his party for a presidential run. If so, the Jockstrap Murder might just be as big a brouhaha as Watergate with Lt. James Rocco playing the instigator. I may ask you for an exclusive interview."

"Fuck off, Mr. Gavin."

"Mike. Remember."

"Fuck off, Mike."

Mike rose. "I know Johnny is hiding out in East Hampton. You don't mind if I intrude on his privacy, Lt. Rocco?"

"James. Remember."

"Of course. James. You don't mind?"

"Be my guest, Mike."

"One more thing, James.

"What's that, Mike?"

"Your fly is open."

THIRTY-SIX

Mike had instructed Milly to book him a flight to East Hampton and Frank Evans got him to the heliport at the southernmost tip of Manhattan, just off Water Street, where the helicopter awaited his arrival. The copter rose above the city's towers, always a thrilling sight now tinged with sadness due to the gap, like missing teeth, where the World Trade Center used to be, but the bird's eye view of Miss Liberty turned the obscene disaster to hope for the future of the unbeatable U.S. of A.

Mike literally descended upon East Hampton an hour after leaving Rocco's precinct. He was met at the airport by John Bennett in, appropriately enough, a pick-up truck. Bennett was a born and bred East Hamptonite who performed services, often reluctantly, for the rich and famous who hired them, often begrudgingly. Both having a need for what the other offered kept them all in a perpetual state of détente.

Bennett knew Mike Gavin by sight and reputation but greeted him with a cursory nod. Bennett was Freddy Fine's house sitter, handy man, lawn mower, plumber, carpenter, gofer and chief liaison between Fine's posh beach house and the town dump. Bennett took Mike's carryall, reluctantly, and opened the truck's passenger door but didn't stay long enough to close it once Mike got in. On his way to the driver's door he tossed the leather carryall on the truck's flat bed, causing Mike to wince as it hit the floor.

Bennett turned on the ignition and spoke for the first time. "Is the pretty boy the Jockstrap Murderer?"

Mike feigned surprise and quipped, "Pretty boy? I didn't think you would notice."

"I ain't no unique," Bennett said.

"Unique?" Mike questioned.

"Yeah, unique. A guy without balls," Bennett explained.

Of course he meant eunuch, but Mike thought it prudent to let sleeping dogs and eunuchs lie. "If you read my paper you know Johnny was at the theater, rehearsing, when the crime was committed."

"We get your paper out here but I don't read it."

Again, Mike thought it wise to keep his mouth shut. They made their way, silently, out of the airport and began the long trek to the highway. Mike, hatless in his Burberry and Bennett in his baseball cap and zip-up red and black checkerboard wool jacket, looked a most incongruous of mates.

When they turned on to Route 27, the main drag known locally as Montauk highway, it was devoid of traffic. Were it summer it would have taken them a good five minutes to weave into the cars heading to town. The nurseries they drove past were adorned for Christmas. A dusting of snow the previous evening clung to the pines and bare trees. Mike, a summer visitor, was impressed with a beach town transformed into a winter wonderland and thought about booking himself and Jack into a posh B&B for Christmas. Then he remembered that Jack now owned a house in another winter wonderland, Aspen. If they were not going to spend the holiday in New York, they would head west, not east.

But perhaps Lt. Rocco might enjoy East Hampton in December. "Can it," Mike thought, "I'm here on business."

Bennett grunted. "Did you say something?" Mike asked.

Silence. Mike returned to his truck tour of the winter landscape when Bennett suddenly pounced. "Do you know Mr. Fine's photographer?"

That certainly was unexpected. "You mean Ken Wallace? Yes, I know him."

"He took my picture and I want it back. Can you help me, Mr. Gavin?"

Mike was nonplussed, to say the least. Before recovering from the shock he turned to look at the craggy face of the septuagenarian and compared it to the beautiful men and boys Wallace had always focused on. "Ken Wallace took your picture?

In your undershorts? For a Freddy Fine ad?"

Bennett kept his eyes on the road, unhindered by traffic in any direction. "I wasn't wearing underpants. I wasn't wearing pants. I was a sea captain with a phony peg leg."

Another look at the driver's weather beaten complexion and perpetual scowl had Mike thinking "Ahab?" and, like a glowing light bulb in a comic strip panel, he knew what John Bennett was talking about. Wallace had photographed Fine's retainer as Melville's Captain Ahab. As much as Mike hated to admit it, Wallace had chosen the perfect model for Ahab. The lined face, the skin the color and texture of well-worn leather and the piercing blue eyes that could intimidate the bejesus out of anyone who came between him and Moby Dick, the whale who had nipped off Ahab's leg.

Mike envisioned the pose Wallace had struck for the portrait. One fisted hand raised in protest, the peg leg pounding the deck, Bennett's dick hanging down (or standing up – one never knew) mocking the world.

"I want my picture back," Bennett was saying, like a man trying to renege on a deal he no longer found to his advantage. "Mr. Fine asked me to do it and he pays me good, summer and winter. But now the photographer and the pretty boy are mixed up in a murder and I want my picture back. If the police see it, they'll ask questions. Even arrest me for flashing my dick. I want it back, Mr. Gavin. Can you help me?"

Another victim of Ken Wallace, Mike thought, feeling more empathy than pity for the man. If he couldn't finagle his way out of his deal with Wallace he would be one of Wallace's pin-up boys, flashing his dick in the guise of Dorian Gray. "You have nothing to worry about," Mike told him. "The police will never see the picture."

"I still want it back," Bennett insisted.

"Did Wallace pay you?" Mike asked, knowing damn well he didn't.

Bennett kept his eyes on the road and his mouth shut.

"Did he give you a blow job?" Mike asked, knowing damn will he did.

Bennett kept his eyes on the road and his mouth shut.

"I'll see what I can do," Mike said, knowing he could do nothing.

Thirty-Seven

Freddy's driveway was a half mile stretch from Further Lane to the Atlantic ocean. The grounds, always meticulously groomed in summer, were even more impressive with trees, bushes and lawns blanketed with snow. Mike spotted a cardinal perched on a holly bush; a favorite coupling for Christmas card art.

He had been there the previous summer to cover a charity event hosted by Freddy. It was the height of the season and had brought out a few hundred people at a thousand bucks a pop. One could go broke attending charity parties in the Hamptons but it gave the rich folks an excuse to see and be seen altruistically.

The house was clapboard with three chimneys. The lawn they had traversed was actually the backyard the front yard being the ocean. Bennett pulled up to a porte-cochere where Johnny Jones stood beside an open door.

As he brought the truck to a halt, Bennett pleaded. "You ain't gonna forget about me, Mr. Gavin."

"I could never forget you, Mr. Bennett. Trust me."

Johnny, looking gorgeous because that's the only way he knew how to look, greeted Mike with a coy grin and extended his hand. Taking Mike's carryall Bennett walked past them and said, "I'll put this in number one."

Before Mike could ask, Johnny said, "We have five guest bedrooms. Number one is the biggest and the only one with a private bath. If it could talk, what stories it could tell."

"I'm not spending the night. I'm flying back to the city in a few hours."

Johnny shrugged. "I thought we might be the topic of a number one saga."

Remarkable, Mike thought. The guy was ready to sell his tail for a Mike Gavin column extolling his innocence. But this was Johnny's forte. Trading his body for cash or favors. Was Mike tempted? Honestly, no. The ploy was too obvious and Johnny Jones, approaching his mid-twenties, was beginning to look a little shop-worn. His modeling career and perhaps acting would save him from a fate worse than death; hustling old men for pocket money. Johnny had to grab the brass ring, RIGHT NOW, and he knew it. Would he kill to secure his old age? Mike Gavin was here to find out.

Mike followed Johnny through the entrance hall. Johnny's on-the-lam outfit was jeans, a white cashmere crew neck sweater and white wool socks minus shoes. They entered the great room, which was worthy of its name. It ran the length of the house and was divided into a dozen sitting areas. One grouped around the fireplace looked perfect for a winter evening; another obviously devoted to games with chess, checkers, backgammon and, of course, Monopoly, all atop a bridge table that also held a caddy of chips for card players. The south wall was a series of French doors that led to a broad terrace overlooking beach and ocean. Mike guessed the room could accommodate fifty people without anyone getting in anyone's way.

"Isn't it cozy?" Johnny commented, taking a chair before the fireplace that was ablaze with a stack of aromatic birch logs.

Mike removed his coat and put it on the back of a chair before taking the one opposite Johnny, then went straight for the jugular. "You've come a long way, Giancarlo Labella."

"And I never want to go back," Johnny answered.

"Going back might be preferable to going to jail," Mike told him.

"Ken said you wanted to interview me, not scare the shit out of me."

"Ken was mistaken. I didn't fly here to interview you but to question you."

"I answered all the questions I'm ever going to answer."

Mike shook his head. "Lt. Rocco is not happy with your answers."

"Lt. Rocco is a scum bag."

"He's a cop doing his job."

"You could have fooled me," Johnny said. "The cocksucker came on to me like a guy looking for a free blow job. He sucks up to gay guys to get what he wants from them. He's a horny prick teaser, Mr. Gavin."

Strange, Mike had the same feeling about Lt. Rocco or was that just wishful thinking? And whenever Rocco's name popped up, why was Mike diverted from his appointed rounds? Back to the business at hand, which was getting the truth out of Johnny Jones and passing it on to Lt. Rocco. (There was that name again.)

"Let's talk about Matt Burke who was born Matthew Bokowski, like you were née Giancarlo Labella. Do you know what née means, Johnny?"

"It means born, Mr. Gavin. Like you said, I've come a long way."

"And you don't want to go back, so tell me what you know about the Jockstrap Murder."

"I don't know dick about it. I never met Matt Burke, or Matthew Bokowski. I don't know what he was doing in my apartment or how he got in or who tied the jock round his neck." The wise guy who had greeted Mike ten minutes ago was fast losing his composure. As he pleaded his ignorance, Johnny's flawless complexion became flushed with anger, his eyes watery and his celebrated body on the verge of collapsing.

"I believe you," Mike said.

"Thanks, Mr. Gavin."

"Reserve your thanks for after you've heard me out. I don't believe you're lying but I don't believe you're telling the truth. What you're guilty of, Johnny, is the sin of omission. You're telling the truth but leaving out what you suspect to have happened in your apartment when you were rehearsing at the theater because you know who has the other key."

"I told Rocco all I know."

"Do you know what hepatitis is, Johnny?" Mike blurted loud and clear.

Johnny started, then quickly resumed his vacant gaze. Too late. Mike, a trained interviewer and observer, was a mind reader who often accurately predicted the outcome of a jury trial by studying the faces and body language of the jurors. The word he had just tossed out had hit Johnny Jones like a pin prick to his eyes. What Mike read in those eyes was fear; of the disease? of the person who carried it?

"It's a sickness. Makes you turn yellow."

"It's a sexually transmitted disease, Johnny."

"Like AIDS?"

"Yes. Like AIDS. Now do you want to talk?"

"About what? Hepatitis or AIDS?"

"Don't fuck with me, Johnny."

"Then stop fucking with me, Mr. Gavin."

"Okay. I'll tell you what I know, then you fill in the blanks."

Johnny crossed, then uncrossed his legs. He started to stand, changed his mind, and sat. Mike noted every move. Johnny wanted to run. From what? From whom?

"You have a roommate," Mike stated. "He left enough telltale items in the apartment to tell Lt. Rocco he's from Washington, D.C. You've been seen, socially as they say, with Tim Samuels who, I believe, lives in Washington. How am I doing?"

"Luke warm," Johnny answered.

"Last July you performed at a party for a senator's daughter in Washington. Your roommate walked you to the parking area. It was a hot night and you and your companion parted in a passionate embrace. You were seen. By a doctor. I repeat, by a doctor. Do you see where I'm going?"

Was Mike imagining it or did Johnny's lips curve, ever so slightly, into a smile before he again checked himself, turning the aborted smile into a frown. "Go on," Johnny said. "This is interesting."

"The doctor got a visit from a goon, a shill, who told the doctor to forget what he saw. He set up an appointment with the doctor to meet with you and your roommate in your apartment. The doctor's schedule got fucked up. He couldn't make it to New York and sent Matthew Bokowski in his place. Now fill in the blanks."

One didn't have to be a mind reader to see that the expression on Johnny's face was screaming, '*so that's what he was doing in the apartment.*' Mike realized he had told Johnny more than Johnny could tell him. Mike's visit to East Hampton was turning the fog that engulfed the Jockstrap Murder into pea soup.

"Why was I supposed to meet with this doctor?" Johnny wanted to know.

"I came here to ask the questions," Mike, clearly exasperated, reminded Johnny.

"Why? You seem to know more than I do," Johnny said.

To Mike's everlasting chagrin, Johnny spoke the truth. All Mike could do now was continue passing on to Johnny what he and Lt. Rocco knew on the chance that Johnny would, unwittingly to be sure, fill in those blanks Mike had come to East Hampton to get. "First tell me if Tim Samuels is your roommate."

Johnny shrugged, uncaring. He seemed more composed now; more the wise guy he had been when Mike arrived less than an hour before. Mike didn't like it. "I wouldn't call him my roommate but he does, on occasion, stay with me when he's in New York."

"Does he have a key to your apartment?"

With another shrug of indifference Johnny said, "I may have given him a key."

"Is he your lover?"

"Lover? Why do relationships have to be defined? All they need to be is felt."

Nice sentiment, Mike thought. Maybe Johnny Jones who used to be Giancarlo Labella was more than just a pretty face with a body and dick to match. Mike repeated his questlion.

"Is Jack Montgomery your lover?" Johnny asked.

"That's none of your business."

"Then my relationship with Tim Samuels is none of your business."

"Sorry, that won't wash. Tim Samuels has a key to your apartment and he opened your door to a murderer or is the murderer himself. Now give me a straight answer because Lt. Rocco is going to ask Tim the same question. I hope you guys have your stories in perfect sync."

Johnny gave this some thought before answering. "Tim and I fool around in bed." Then he added, "Are you getting off on this, Mr. Gavin? Need help?" Johnny rubbed the enticing bulge in his perfect fitting jeans. Jeans by Ken Wallace? The jeans Jack would be modeling before the world? How would Lt. Rocco look in a pair of Ken Wallace jeans? Can it, Mike, can it.

"You haven't told me why I was to meet with this doctor."

"I think you know why, Johnny."

'If I knew I wouldn't ask. Trust me, I'm not asking anything I don't already know. I want to terminate this conversation, Mr. Gavin, not prolong it."

"He wanted to talk to you about hepatitis."

"I don't have hepatitis," Johnny assured him.

"You don't, but your occasional roommate does."

The statement didn't elicit a clever, if evasive, response from Johnny. He was silent. His jaw was rigid as a poker player's trying to pull off a bluff. But his eyes were bright and alert. He was thinking. Pondering. Perhaps conjuring up a scenario with a happy ending for Johnny Jones. Mike got the impression he had come in on the middle of a film. Johnny shook his head, slowly, and sighed, audibly. "Poor Tim. I didn't know that. He never told me."

Brad Turner had told Mike that Johnny Jones was a lousy

actor. The lie Johnny just told, replete with exaggerated gestures, proved the incipient director correct. Mike didn't pursue the point. He might learn more from Johnny's lies than he had gotten from the truth. "The doctor is treating Tim."

"You said this doctor was a friend of Bokowski."

"He is. He sent Bokowski because he couldn't get in touch with the goon who made the appointment to tell him he couldn't be in New York. I believe the doctor was to discuss safe sex with you and Tim."

Johnny gave this some thought before answering. "It doesn't make sense. I wasn't told about the meeting. The goon, as you call him, would be meeting with the doctor and Tim who he was already seeing as his patient."

"What about the man the goon is working for?" Mike said. "Any idea who that might be?"

Ignoring the question, Johnny asked, "What does the doctor have to say about all this?"

"We'll never know. He's a naval intern and was suddenly reassigned from Bethesda Medical to the Far East."

Johnny beamed and almost jumped out of his chair. "Doesn't that prove something, Mr. Gavin?"

"Clue me in."

"You're dealing with someone with a lot of clout. Someone who can move people around like pawns on a chess board to get what he wants and what he wants is for you to bug off."

"Are you talking about the senator? Tim's father."

"I'm not talking about anyone because I don't know what the fuck is coming off here. What I do know is I've been used."

"Don't you want to know who used you, Johnny?"

"And end up on a submarine? Or a rocket to the moon? Or fucking dead? No, thanks, Mr. Gavin. Let Lt. Rocco sniff asses and see where it gets him. He got all from me he's gonna get. Ditto to you."

Mike didn't say that he got very little from Johnny except the fact that Johnny didn't know a bloody thing about the Jockstrap Murder. Or did he? Johnny was a hustler. A guy who lived by his wits and his dick. Slippery as an eel and just as lethal when trapped. And, perhaps, he was a better actor than anyone suspected. His life, remember, was an act starring himself and a supporting cast of anyone he could use to make him look good.

"If you think a United States senator zapped someone with a jockstrap you're off your rocker." Johnny was still waxing his resentment at being used. "I'm a victim, Mr. Gavin. A victim of what could be a terrorist plot. They brought down the World Trade Center, now they want to bring down Johnny Jones."

Mike almost laughed in Johnny's face. This was precious. The victim of a terrorist plot? Would the onset of World War III be the attempted downfall of a guy modeling a pair of Freddy Fine jockeys? Albeit, Mike mused, wars had been started for far less trivial reasons.

"The senator could be protecting his son," Mike broke in on Johnny's reverie.

"From what? Spreading hepatitis?"

"From a scandal. I doubt the senator would be happy with you as an in-law."

"You can't believe he would kill to break us up," Johnny said. "This is the twenty-first century, not the dark ages."

"Samuels is a very far right wing conservative, but no, I don't believe he would kill to avert a scandal, especially a gay scandal. With everyone coming out of the closet, being gay is more a yawn than a news item."

"Then why is a guy dead?"

Mike shook his head. "I don't know. We're missing a crucial piece of this puzzle and without it the Jockstrap Murder looks to be an exercise in futility."

"Would the doctor have been killed if he was the one who kept the appointment?"

"I doubt it. I think Bokowski identified himself as a reporter and the murderer went ballistic. Be that as it may, it doesn't look good for Tim."

"Why?"

"Why? He has the other key to your apartment. If he doesn't have an airtight alibi for the day of the murder I think Rocco can arrest him based on your evidence."

"Me? What evidence?"

"The key. You admit you gave him a key."

"I told you. Not Rocco."

"I'll tell Rocco. We're a team."

"No shit. Did he wave his dick at you, Mr. Gavin?"

The barb was too close for comfort so Mike shifted gears and changed his course. "Is Tim your angel? I mean one with money, not wings. Brad Turner told me Tim was interested in the theater. He talked to Brad about it."

"Tim doesn't have that kind of money. I think the producer sold shares and Freddy got in on the action for a few bucks."

"Who is the producer?"

"I met him once and forgot his name. Check the playbill when we open, if we ever open. We've been dark for almost a week. I haven't even talked to Brad."

Mike was amused at how quickly Johnny had picked up theater lingo. 'Dark for almost a week.' Johnny was indeed a quick study. "The Jockstrap Murder is off the front pages. You can come back to the city in a few days and resume rehearsing."

"I'm no longer under suspicion?"

"Tell Rocco everything you told me and he may let you off the hook."

"What about Tim?"

"Like I said. Tim may be held for questioning."

"This is not good," Johnny said.

"Do you know anything that could make it better?"

Johnny didn't answer.

THIRTY-EIGHT

Using his cell phone, Mike called Milly Perz, his secretary at the News.

"Reception is lousy," Milly shouted. "Where are you?"

"A couple of hundred feet over Long Island."

Having been Mike's secretary, confidante and friend since he took over the column Milly knew better than to ask what he was doing up there. "Anything for me?" Mike asked.

"The usual fan mail and two dozen calls. You want them all or just the ones that matter?"

Trusting Milly implicitly, he opted for the ones she thought mattered. "Amanda called. She wants you to call her. She has something important to tell you. I imagine she also left a message on your phone at home but that, of course, is not enough for Amanda Richards. I'm surprised she didn't call your cell phone, too."

"It's turned off," Mike said.

"I suspected as much because Brad Turner called. He wants you to call him when you get a chance. He also called you at home, too, but Jack answered and Brad hung up on him."

Mike moaned.

"I'm saving the best for last," Milly reported.

"I'm hoping for nothing less than our president, Queen Elizabeth and/or her grandson, Harry."

"No cigar, but not bad. Not a grandson but a senator's son. Tim Samuels. Call him ASAP, he left a number."

"When did he call?" Mike asked.

"Funny you should ask. He called about ten minutes ago."

Mike checked his watch. The marvels of modern communication. Johnny had called Tim, mobile to mobile, before

Mike was off the property. Tim would be on notice to expect a call from Lt. Rocco; he would know what Rocco would ask and compare notes with Johnny. What were those guys up to? This was not Mike's day. You win some and you lose some. Today he had lost and, adding insult to injury, he had given more than he got.

"I didn't know you knew the senator's son," Milly said.

"I don't. Met him once, briefly. Amanda introduced us at the vice president's party last July."

"He seemed very eager to talk to you but why did he wait four months to ring you up?"

"If I knew the answer to that, Milly, I could solve the Jockstrap Murder. See you around the hangar."

"Happy landings, boss."

Manhattan's skyline loomed before him as the copter descended, raced across the East River and alighted on the same spot from which Mike had taken off a few hours ago. The marvels of modern communication.

THIRTY-NINE

"Michael, love, where have you been all day?"

"Working, Amanda. It's what I do for a living."

"And what do you think I do on the stage?"

"Act," he said, "in a prescribed area. I cover the world." Mike had arrived home, hung up his pea coat, surveyed the bedroom to see what Jack had not hung up, which was most of what Jack owned, mixed himself a much needed martini and decided to make Amanda Richards the first of the three calls on his agenda. Hearing her emote into the phone he decided he had prioritized incorrectly. "You had something you wanted to tell me."

"Indeed I do. I had a visit today from a most extraordinary man."

In Amanda's lexicon, describing a man as extraordinary meant she was hot for him. Mike had the feeling he knew of whom she spoke.

"Lt. Rocco of the police," she exclaimed, pronouncing the name as if it were sacrosanct, like Jesus or Ethel Barrymore.

"Hands off, Amanda, I saw him first."

"Really, Michael. I hope you don't think I would interfere with a police officer."

"It depends on what you mean by interfere. If it means chasing his blues away by getting him out of his blues, the answer is yes, I do think you would."

"He didn't wear a uniform. He wore a suit, Gray flannel. Very fine quality. Custom made, I believe. Reminded me of you when you were young and virile, before you took up with pretty boy tennis players."

Mike took a deep breath. It had been a long and disappointing day. He wanted to wash, change and enjoy his martini, not exchange barbs with Amanda Richards. "Why did you call,

Amanda? What do you want to tell me?"

"That I had a visit from the police."

"Was it a social call, Amanda?"

"No. Thanks to you he grilled me."

Mike thought, correctly, that this was going to be about the Jockstrap Murder. "Me?" He pretended surprise.

"You told him I spoke to that poor Burke or Bokowski boy eons ago."

"Well, you did. What did you tell the cop in the gray flannel suit?"

"Nothing, because I know nothing. The man introduced himself to me and before I could answer a polite greeting the security people approached him and, I think, tossed him out. Then the cop asked me about my lunch date with Senator Samuels last July which you reported in your column, calling us the odd couple. The senator invited me to the tennis matches last summer in Palm Beach as his guest. I'm sure you remember that because you made a fool of yourself at the matches for a good cause. I've always admired you for that, Michael."

Bitch, Mike thought.

"Then he asked me if I knew Tim Samuels. I told him the senator stood me up for the tennis matches and sent his son in his place. What's this about, Michael? Are the senator and his son involved in the murder of that reporter?"

There was no reason for Rocco to question Amanda. He knew she had nothing to tell him. He would say he was crossing all his T's and dotting all his I's like a good cop should do but Mike suspected that Lt. Rocco wanted to meet the famous actress and strut his stuff to impress her. Mission accomplished.

"It's too complicated to go into on the phone, Amanda."

"Don't patronize me, Michael."

She was right. Mike had involved her in Rocco's case and he owed her an explanation. "Tim is a friend and maybe a roommate of Johnny Jones, the popular model whose apartment is the scene of the crime. That's as much as I know."

"How thrilling," she said. "I've never been involved in a murder, not even on the stage."

"You're not involved," Mike told her.

"Lt. Rocco left me his card. He said I should call him if I remember anything I may have forgotten to tell him."

"I'm sure you told him everything you know which isn't much."

"We'll see. We'll see. I won't keep you any longer, Michael."

"Amanda, don't…" She hung up.

This day was going from bad to worse. Mike downed his martini and began mixing a second. The tray of ice he had brought in from the kitchen fridge to the dry bar had not yet melted. He thought of not calling Brad Turner until the morning but a few sips of his vodka laced with vermouth (no olive, no twist, no mini onion, no nothing) gave him the impetus to punch out Brad's number. As soon as he heard Brad's voice he was glad he did.

"Milly told me you called. What's happening?"

"Nothing, absolutely nothing," Brad complained. "The theater is dark, the actors don't know if we'll ever open and I haven't heard from Johnny since the murder. The play is jinxed, Mike, and I'm the director."

"Calm down. I talked to Johnny today. He's been hiding out at Freddy's place in East Hampton. He'll probably be back in town and at the theater tomorrow or the next day."

"Is he in the clear?"

"The police know he didn't tie the jock around Bokowski's neck but it did happen in his apartment so he's not completely in the clear. He can't leave town but he can get back to work. What about your producer? I forgot his name."

"Max Berger," Brad reminded him.

"Have you seen him? What's his take on all of this?"

"Haven't seen him but he does call. He says to keep the show on the road, or in rehearsal, until this all blows over. Blows over? How about that to describe a murder? But as long as he pays the bills, and he's paying them, that's what I'll do which, right now, is doing nothing."

"We just learned that Tim Samuels, your prep school chum, stays at Johnny's apartment when he's in New York and probably is Johnny's lover."

"Not surprising. I told you he came to see me not too long ago. He's interested in the theater but in what capacity, he didn't say. I wonder if he put money into the show."

"I'm wondering the same thing. Brad, let's talk more, but not over the phone. Can you come to dinner tonight?"

"Where?" Brad asked.

"Here, of course. Pot luck but we can put something together that resembles a meal."

"What about Jack?"

"What about him?"

"He hates me. Will he be home?"

"I love you, Brad, and it's my apartment. Jack's a brat who's got to learn that the sun doesn't shine upon him alone. It's time to knock off the chip he's been carrying on his shoulder, for no reason, and now's the time to do it."

"He might break his tennis racket over my head."

"If he does, I'll toss him out the window. See you in an hour."

"Can I bring anything?"

"Only your charming self."

Mike put down the phone just as Jack opened the apartment door and entered wearing his work clothes, i.e. Ken Wallace's designer jeans. Mike greeted him with, "I just left Johnny Jones at his seaside hideout. He was wearing similar jeans." Mike took a step back for a better view. "I must say they bulge in the right place."

Jack hefted his crotch. "This bulge is the real thing. No padding."

"So is Johnny's."

"How do you know?"

"I've seen it."

"Up close?"

Jack's jealous streak, even in jest, was appalling. "It wasn't under my nose if that's what you mean. I appraised it from afar. Like viewing La Giaconda when visiting the Louvre."

Jack went into the kitchen for a beer. "Bullshit," Jack called.

"A thing of beauty is a joy forever," Mike answered.

"Are you drinking a dirty martini?" Jack asked, returning with his beer.

"No," Mike said, "we were fresh out of dirt."

Jack raised his bottle of Bass. "Cheers. What a day I had."

Mike returned the toast. "Did Ken behave himself?"

"All business, as promised. In fact, too much business. He took a million snaps under lights so hot my makeup ran. How was your day?"

"My makeup didn't run but I went one-on-one with Johnny Jones."

"Up close?"

"Arm's length but I refused his offer of a bed for the night."

"Bed. That's what I need." Jack headed for the bedroom. "A snooze before dinner. Then I'll tell you about my first day as a model."

"Stop," Mike ordered. "Before you snooze and discuss your favorite topic, yourself, pick up everything in the bedroom, my bedoom, that belongs in the closet on a hanger or in the hamper."

"You're anal," Jack said.

"And you're a slob. Just do it. I want to change and wash. What's for dinner?"

"We'll go out."

"No we won't. Brad is coming here for dinner."

"Brad? Why?"

"Because I invited him," Mike said. "That's why. This grudge you have for Brad, for no reason, has got to stop. You don't have to like all my friends but you sure as hell have to respect them and tolerate them while you're living in my home."

In lieu of an answer, Jack did as he was told, pouting like a ten-year-old whose mother had read him the riot act. Mike was pleased. He hoped he had finally found the solution to Jack's insufferable behavior. When he acted like a ten-year-old treat him like a ten-year-old. But Mike Gavin liked men, not boys. This conjured up an image of Lt. Rocco. Would Amanda score before him? It was a challenge and the race was on. What advantage did Mike have that Amanda didn't? That advantage made itself known. "I think I'll take a quick shower," Mike said. "Want to share?"

Actually straightening up the closet, Jack answered, "I showered at the studio before I left."

"The studio has a shower?"

"And a Jacuzzi." Jack told him.

"Did Ken have a peek, up close?"

"But of course. He asked me to pose as Alexander the Great."

Mike knew that Jack was making this up to get back at him for the lecture he had just received. Would he ever grow up? "I don't believe you. Ken Wallace likes to be very authentic with his private portraits. He refused to photograph Johnny Jones as the statue of David because Johnny is circumcised. He wouldn't want you as Alexander for the same reason."

"You could do it," Jack said.

"I've already been spoken for as Dorian Gray." Mike headed

for his shower. "Now give some thought to dinner."

"I already have. Japanese take-out."

Mike closed the bathroom door.

FORTY

Not knowing if he should bring a bottle of red or white wine, Brad opted for a rosé.

"Sake would have been more appropriate," Jack said, taking the wine.

"Japanese take-out." Brad guessed. "It's a perfect night for miso."

It was a good beginning and went no place but uphill from there. Jack was welcoming without being obvious. He shook Brad's hand and Mike kissed his guest on the cheek without drawing a comment of any sort from Jack. So far, so good. In fact, so far – very good.

Brad was wise enough to comment on Jack's jeans which gave Jack the chance to moan about hot lights and running makeup. "Makeup?" Brad exclaimed. "Why cover that perfect complexion?"

Jack's perfect complexion glowed at the compliment. Mike was thinking that perhaps these two would one day connect sexually. An interesting thought Mike put on a back burner – but not too far back. Who knows where the evening would take them?

Jack filled the ice bucket and brought it to the dry bar as Mike took the drink orders. He continued with the martinis, remembering that this was his third and Brad went for a gin and tonic. "No twist," Mike told him. "We're out of lemons and limes."

"And dirt," Jack quipped, sticking to his beer. He sure was feeling his oats. Mike now saw the man, not the boy, who was the most popular, and successful, tennis pro on the circuit.

When they settled down with their drinks in the comfortable living room; Mike in his favorite club chair and Brad and Jack side by side on the couch; Mike continued the conversation he had begun with Brad on the phone. "You think Tim Samuels may be backing your show."

"Not entirely," Brad told him. "The producer, Max Berger, put together a consortium of interested angels. He sold shares and I think Freddy Fine put in some dough. I know Tim's interested in the theater and when you told me he and Johnny were lovers I made the connection, which is pure speculation."

"Were you and Tim close at prep school?" Jack asked.

"We knew each other but not in the biblical sense." Brad thought a moment, then said, "He may have been part of those nightly circle jerks but it was usually too dark to see who I was spilling my seed with."

"I never went to prep school," Jack said, "so I spilled my seed all by myself."

"Let me know if you ever want to make up for lost time," Brad offered.

Jack's perfect complexion glowed red. Mike was delighted.

"Johnny told me that Tim shared his apartment," Mike went on, "and that he and Tim had played together but that's as far as he would go."

"If he shared Johnny's place he must have the other key to Johnny's apartment." This from the astute Brad Turner.

"He has it," Mike said, "and Lt. Rocco is going to question Tim ASAP. The senator's son is in deep shit."

"What do you think of Rocco?" Brad asked.

"A pro and a prick tease," was Mike's assessment of the officer.

Jack, who had not been part of the conversation since admitting to jacking off solo, suddenly pricked up his ears. "You never told me that," he said.

"You never asked."

"How did he tease you?" Jack wouldn't let go.

"He opened his fly in his office."

"Stop kidding and tell me the truth."

Mike smiled like a man who knows a secret he's not sharing. Always tell the truth if you don't want people to believe you. "Did he open his fly for you, Brad?"

"No, but he asked me if I was blowing Johnny Jones. I told him to fuck off."

Jack looked as if he were about to burst so before he began harping on Lt. Rocco, Mike suggested they tell Brad all they knew about the Jockstrap Murder, fact and guesswork, and perhaps see what Brad could add to their store of knowledge. Here, Jack stood up. "Before you begin I'll call in our dinner orders. We're all having the miso, right? What about the seafood casserole to share as an appetizer? Prawns, scallops, crabs and mushroom over onion rice."

"You sure do know your Japanese vittles," Brad said..

"Chinese and Japanese take-out are staples of the pro tennis circuit. I'm going for the salmon teriyaki."

"Chicken teriyaki for me," was Brad's choice.

Mike wanted the black pepper filet mignon. "That's the most expensive dish on the menu," Jack told him.

"Who's paying for this?" Mike asked.

"You get the steak. Any rolls? Mike's paying."

No one spoke up for the rolls so Jack moved to the bedroom to call the restaurant. Mike noted that this cold winter night was the perfect setting to discuss murder while they were snug, warm and fortified with booze. The consummate reporter filled Brad in on everything he knew, beginning with his chance meeting with Matthew Bokowski last July and up to the time they learned about Travis McBarb and his relationship with Bokowski. Here, Mike wisely allowed Jack to take over and relate what he had learned from his meeting with McBarb. Mike picked up with his meeting with Lt. Rocco and how Rocco had connected with McBarb.

"As I told you I saw Johnny today. He admits to giving a key to his boyfriend and I'm sure he called Tim to tell him that Rocco is going to question him and maybe already has. Tim called me but I didn't return the call because I don't want to confront Tim before Rocco sees him. And that's where we stand," Mike concluded. "What can you add?"

"Not much," Brad said. "Everything you've told me has me awed. Tim has hepatitis? I don't think he had it when we were at school. This McBarb switched with Bokowski and got his friend killed. Why? I don't believe Senator Samuels would hire a professional killer to keep his son's sex life a secret."

"Neither do I," Mike said. "We're missing something that could be staring us smack in the face. Brad, you told me a man in a cab once came for Johnny after rehearsal. You said he kept his face hidden but he was wearing an Oriole baseball cap. Could it have been the producer, Max Berger, having a clandestine meeting with his star?"

Brad shook his head. "I would have recognized him even with his hat pulled down over half his face. The man I saw was someone I had never seen before, I'm sure of that."

"Ken Wallace met Berger," Mike said. "All he remembered was that he had a mole over one of his eyebrows."

"He did. I remember that," Brad said.

Jack jumped out of his seat. "A mole? A mole over his left eyebrow?"

"Right or left, I'm not sure," Brad told him.

Jack, still standing, shouted at Mike. "Don't you remember? McBarb described Mr. Martin as having a mole over his left eyebrow. Mike, Mr. Martin is the producer."

"Easy," Mike advised. "Moles are not unique."

"Bull. How many men do you know have a mole over their left eyebrow?"

"I don't recall if it's the right or left brow," Brad said again.

Jack was reluctant to give up his investigative coup. "He's Mr. Martin."

"Does this make my producer a killer?" Brad moaned. "The play is jinxed, the producer is a murderer and I'm the director." He handed his glass to Mike. "What do you have in the way of arsenic?"

"Jack, sit down and Brad calm down. I'll admit that Martin could be Berger but we have to be certain before we act on it." Mike believed Jack was right but he would proceed with caution. Like many journalists he feared jumping the gun for a scoop only to discover the scoop is a fraud. A prime example is The New York *Daily News* headlining Thomas E. Dewey as the winner and president when, in fact, Truman had won that election in 1948. Mike would, of course, pass this on to Lt. Rocco who would now have a link to the mysterious Mr. Martin via the producer, Max Berger.

"They are the same person," Jack insisted. "It all fits. Martin, Tim Samuels, Johnny Jones, the play. Tim is doing the play for his lover. He got Martin to act as producer and raise the cash. Tim saw McBarb in the parking lot that night."

"Did Tim hire Martin to kill McBarb?" Mike asked Jack.

"I think I'm going to kill myself," Brad told them but they weren't listening.

Mike raised his hands, "I think we should all ----"The doorbell rang.. "Dinner is served. Amen."

The boys carried in many cardboard containers and began to set up the table. Mike excused himself and went to the bedroom, presumably to use the bathroom. When he returned he was wearing a man's kimono. It was blue, genuine silk with a white obi. "I dressed for dinner," he announced. "A gift from friends when I visited Japan." Bare feet and ankles told them he was naked beneath the robe.

Jack and Brad applauded. "Maybe we should take our shoes off," Jack said, "like they do in restaurants."

"I think you should take everything off," Mike suggested.

"Eat in the nude?" This from Brad.

"No. In costume. I have a terry robe and so does Jack. I laid them out on the bed. Go in and change."

The boys looked at each other, gave a shrug, and headed for the bedroom. Mike followed. They kicked off their loafers and in a few minutes were down to T's and jockeys. "Come on," Mike urged. "Dinner awaits." To prompt them he undid the obi. The kimono parted to reveal Mike's semi-boner and generous masculine sack. Off came T's and jockeys. The boys appraised each other, as men do and now the room boasted three semi-boners. They got into their robes and marched out with Mike leading.

They sat at the table and began with the miso everyone declared delicious and just right for a winter night. Mike filled their glasses with the rosé and Jack got up to pass around the tray of seafood casserole. As he bent to offer the tray Brad ran his hand under Jack's robe and hefted his balls. Then he helped himself to a little of this and a little of that. "Thanks," Brad said.

"More?" Jack offered.

"Why not?" Brad again ran his hand under Jack's robe and this time fisted a very hard cock.

"Had enough?" Jack asked.

"Yes. For now."

Mike watched the proceedings which gave him an appetite as well as a hard on. Never had he so enjoyed Japanese cuisine. Mike used chop sticks, Jack and Brad went with conventional knives and forks. The conversation covered a variety of topics with the exception of the Jockstrap Murder and sex. When the rose' ran out Mike went to the fridge and came back with a bottle of chilled Pino.

"We seem to have eaten all our supper like good boys," Mike observed, eying the empty cardboard boxes and trays.

"We forgot dessert," Jack said.

"You can be my dessert, if you're willing," Brad told him.

Jack hesitated. "Go on." Mike egged him on. "You know you

want it."

Jack stood up, went to stand beside Brad and undid his robe's sash. The athlete was as rampant as a stag in rut. Brad got to his knees and went for the king size cannoli.

Mike, always a bit of a voyeur, had his kimono open, slowly masturbating his proud seven plus inches as he fingered Jack's firm behind. Brad serviced Jack and himself. The three men headed for their ecstasy, self-absorbed and sharing at the same time. Eros, orchestrating the bacchanal, let his arrows loose at just the right moment so that the three men exploded as one, spilling their seed with sighs and moans of an almost unbearable pleasure which is a man's thing that cannot be explained, only experienced.

In bed that night, Mike asked Jack how he liked his introduction to prep school.

"I can't wait to go to college," he answered, then fell into a sound asleep.

FORTY-ONE

Ken Wallace called in the morning to tell Jack to pack for a shoot in Canada. The photographer needed snow and Mother Nature had just dumped two feet of it in picturesque Quebec. "We have snow in Aspen," Jack told him. "We can use my new house."

"Quebec is closer," Ken answered. "LaGuardia in one hour. Air Canada. My love to your roommate."

Jack could organize for an overnight trip in minutes, which he did, complaining all the time. "It'll be freezing in Quebec."

"True," Mike said, "but your makeup won't run. Did you enjoy last night?"

"You know I did," Jack said, not sounding pleased with the fact.

"You might call Brad and thank him."

"I was dessert. He should thank me." With that he was out the door with all he needed in his backpack.

The *enfant terrible* of the pro tennis circuit was once again acting like an enfant. Encouraged by last night's three-way, or two and a half if you count Mike's solo, Mike thought Jack had seen the joy of sharing and maybe even caring. The art of give and take. Jack, alas, only took and what he took he declared his exclusively. Mike didn't want Jack, or anyone, to be obsessed with sex, nor did he want him to be strictly a one-man guy before he had a chance to explore and experiment.

Sex is a many splendored thing. One should bask in the splendor, avoid over exposure, hope for the best and be prepared for the worst. This being the tenet of Michael Gavin; investigative reporter, facilitator and masturbator.

Brad called to say he had heard from Johnny who was on his way back to the city so let the rehearsals begin, yet again. He also thanked Mike for a most delectable dinner, especially the rather unique dessert.

"Quite a mouth full, isn't it?" Mike commented.

"Don't be crude," Brad scolded.

"Crude? I was being honest."

"You should know," Brad said.

"Now who's being crude?"

"Crude? I was being honest."

"Brad, we could pussyfoot around your blow job all day but I haven't got time for it. Do you know if Johnny is going to see Tim?"

"He didn't say but he is going directly to his apartment. He may be meeting Tim there. Is Jack available for a quick hello?"

"He's gone to Quebec for a shoot."

"Who's he shooting?"

"Goodbye, Brad. Keep in touch."

Mike had all day and all night to himself. He could fill the day and knew what he would like to do that night. Explore and experiment with James Rocco, lieutenant, NYPD. Hoping for the best and expecting the worst, he dialed the officer. Rocco picked up on the first ring. "Did you speak to Tim Samuels?' was Mike's opening line.

"I did," Rocco said.

"Any joy?"

"A total bust."

"Did he give you a hard time?" Mike asked.

"On the contrary. He couldn't have been more cooperative. Flew here from D.C. and came to my office. He has an air-tight alibi for the time of the murder. I'll tell you more when I see you."

"When will that be?" Mike wanted to know.

"Whenever."

"Whenever is a long time. How about lunch this afternoon? My treat."

"What did you have in mind?" Rocco asked.

What I have in mind would make a sailor blush, Mike thought as he said, "Do you like French?"

"I never had frog legs."

"There's more to French cuisine than frog legs and I'll prove it at Chez Louis. Have you ever eaten there?"

"Only vicariously, thanks to your column."

"I'm honored. Shall we say high noon? One?"

"Let's compromise and make it twelve-thirty."

Knowing Rocco would be dressed like an earl having lunch with the Queen, Mike obsessed over what to wear for his date. For lunch at Louie's (as it was called by the cognoscente) he would usually don flannels, a blazer and maybe an ascot in place of a tie if he felt gallant. Not for this lunch. He got himself up in a navy blue suit, single breasted, three buttons, school tie (would you believe Groton?) and wing tip brogues. And, yes, one of his custom tailored dress shirts that required cuff links. Not wanting to gild the lily he eschewed the black onyx for plain silver links. He topped it off with a chesterfield, boasting a black velvet collar.

Satisfied, he buzzed his doorman three times which said he required a cab and found one waiting when he got to the lobby.

"You look like a million bucks," the doorman complimented as he opened the taxi door for Mike who felt like a million bucks. Euphoric expectation is an apt description of a guy who dresses to get laid.

It was a gray and cold December day but this did nothing to inhibit New Yorkers from gearing up for the approaching Christmas holiday. Everything and everyone moved at a quicker pace; stores stayed open later to accommodate shoppers, Santas jingled bells to solicit coins, people smiled more to say they were not an Ebenezer Scrooge and, finally, carols filled the air. New York's traditional landmarks; the giant tree fronting Rockefeller

Center and the mini trees running the length of affluent Park Avenue were aglow with twinkling lights. This exuberance would climax New Year's Eve.

When Mike alighted from his cab he found Lt. Rocco in a belted top coat and fedora waiting for him. The men exchanged handshakes before Mike led his guest into the restaurant. Alain, the maitre D', greeted them at the door saying, "Have you solved the Jockstrap Murder, Mr. Gavin?"

"Ask him," Mike answered. "Meet Lt. Rocco of the NYPD."

"A pleasure," Alain said with a slight bow. "Let me have your coats." He snapped his fingers at a passing waiter. "Show Mr. Gavin and his guest to their table."

Rocco, looking meticulously splendid in his gray suit, rep tie and black loafers, entered the dining area with Mike at his side. The table reserved for Mike seemed to be the only empty table in the room The diners here were too sophisticated to stare but none of them missed the fact that Mike Gavin had entered Louie's with an impeccably dressed hunk. "Before they leave they'll all know your name, rank and what you had for lunch," Mike commented as they sat.

"I don't see any crystal balls or do they read their tea leaves?"

"Alain, who greeted us, will drop your name and occupation at every table he bends over to see if all is well with the people who lunch."

The waiter interrupted. "Beverage?"

"Campari for me," Rocco responded.

"Good choice, the same for me. In a wine glass not a water tankard," Mike instructed.

"I see faces I usually see peering back at me from the front page of a newspaper," Rocco said. "Do you know who's at the table behind you?"

Mike nodded. "Anderson Cooper, Gloria Vanderbilt's son. He'll call me tonight, wanting to know all about you."

"But he won't drop by the table to be introduced?"

"Heaven forbid," Mike exclaimed. "If you table hop at Louie's you'll be ostracized by those who lunch."

"Do those who lunch ever have dinner?"

"No. That's an entirely different crowd and the two seldom meet. Besides, those who lunch are usually too bombed to make it to dinner."

Their drinks arrived, served in wine glasses with both a lemon and lime twist affixed to the rims.

Mike raised his glass. "Here's to good news."

"You won't get any from me today," was Rocco's toast.

Alain arrived and proffered menus. "The saddle of lamb is on the board today, gentlemen."

"*Grenouille provençal?*" Rocco asked, grinning.

"Always," Alain told him.

"I thought so," Rocco said with a nod. "Is the vichyssoise hot or cold?"

"However you prefer it, Lieutenant."

Realizing he had been bamboozled by the officer Mike was enjoying the repartee and looking at his lunch date with admiration.

Rocco shook his head. "No, I think I'll go for the *Coquilles St. Jacques* and the *Bourguignonne avec* a salad."

"Excellent," Alain said, turning to Mike.

"I seem to be with a connoisseur so I'll have the same and a white burgundy with the beef."

"No grenouille?" Alain questioned.

"God forbid," Mike answered.

Alain thought this too, was excellent.

"You're a sly one," Mike accused when they were once again alone.

"I'm an amateur gourmet," Rocco admitted.

"Julia Child?"

"My bible."

They were both completely at ease now, bantering like old friends. Rocco was thrilled being at Louie's, rubbing shoulders, exhibiting his knowledge of French fare and not a bit reluctant to show his enthusiasm. His white boxers weren't starched today. In fact he may even have gone commando.

Commando? Mike was aroused. His jockeys weren't starched but something else seemed to be. Go easy, he was thinking. Don't jump the gun. Don't draw conclusions based on nothing more than an interest in Julia Child which Mike didn't have. This was a business lunch, not a prelude to sex. But why not? Why the fuck not? Because he was obligated to confess it to Jack. That's why not. But he would confess it to the pope if there was something to confess. He knew the pope would understand. He knew Jack wouldn't.

Rocco put the twist of lime in his drink and raised his glass. "Do you want the bad news now or with dessert?"

With last night's dessert menu in mind Mike said, "Let's have it now."

"Do you know Capital Prep?"

Mike recalled hearing the name. It was a charter school. Tim Samuels was on the staff. He taught drama to the less than privileged students. The day of the Jockstrap Murder, Tim Samuels was at his job, rehearsing his class for their coming Christmas pageant. "Need I tell you how many witnesses he can produce to vouch for this?" Rocco asked.

"No, you need not," Mike assured him.

Tim did not know a Mister Martin. His doctor at Bethesda treating him for hepatitis B was young and good looking but Tim did not recall his name. The doctor had discussed safe sex but never mentioned meeting with Tim's lover whose name Tim had not disclosed to the doctor.

Their *coquilles* were served. They looked like a work of art.

After a taste, Rocco sighed with joy and said to Mike, "The scallops are pure heaven and the cheese is genuine gruyere. Swiss. Don't ever use a substitute."

Mike promised he wouldn't.

Tim admitted being close to Johnny Jones but did not use the word lover or partner to describe their relationship. Yes, he had a key to Johnny's apartment and that key was on his key ring and in his pocket as he was teaching his students to act.

"I talked to Johnny and Johnny talked to Tim. They coordinated their stories. In fact, I advised Johnny to do just that. Did I fuck up?"

"I doubt if Tim Samuels would have told a different tale had he not talked to Johnny Jones. I've saved the best for last. On the night McBarb said he spotted Johnny and his lover in that parking lot, Tim stated he was on Cape Cod staying with the Kennedy clan. The date is verifiable thanks to that senator's daughter's birthday gala."

"And we can't produce McBarb to counter Tim's version of that fateful night. I guess you can't detain Tim, either," Mike said, hopefully.

"His lawyer would spring him in a nanosecond and the D.A. would have my balls on a platter."

Mike tried again. "He can't prove the key was in his pocket."

"And I can't prove it wasn't."

"If we can get McBarb…"

"It would be his word against a platoon of Kennedys. Look, everything we have, or think we have, depends on the word of Travis McBarb, a guy neither of us has ever talked to."

"Jack talked to him," Mike quickly said.

"And got a lot of info on which we're basing this case. How do we know McBarb is telling the truth? What was his relationship with Bokowski? Was he transferred to the Far East or did he volunteer to go when Bokowski was murdered and he was looking to get away. Why was McBarb going to New York?

Why did he send Bokowski in his place? Who met Bokowski at Johnny's apartment? McBarb says he has all the answers but he never named Patient X."

"Why would he lie?" Mike countered.

"Why would Tim Samuels lie? He's not in the closet."

"Maybe his father doesn't like having a gay son," Mike pointed out.

"Tough titty on dear old dad."

"I don't like losing," Mike said, but there was more to it than just that.

Was Mike more interested in getting Rocco in bed than in solving the Jockstrap Murder? He admitted to himself, more than once, that his attraction to the lieutenant was getting in his way of getting the true story; a heinous lapse for an investigative reporter.

To add to his guilt there was Jack, freezing his ass off in Quebec. If Rocco suddenly came on to Mike would Mike refuse the offer to save his integrity and his ersatz marriage? Fuck, NO.

The *bourguignonne* was presented and not a moment too soon.

Alain showed Mike the wine he had selected and poured a tad for the host to sample. Mike sipped and nodded. "A fine chardonnay burgundy," Alain announced as he poured.

The men savored the meal in silence until Mike noted, "We're skunked, aren't we?"

Rocco shrugged and continued to feast on his beef stew and chardonnay burgundy. "Remember, both Tim Samuels and Bokowski were at the vice president's party the night I talked to Bokowski. Why did Bokowski get the boot?"

Rocco answered, "Security that night was provided by the FBI. I should have known that. I've made inquiries but I have to be cleared before they'll tell me anything. All I can do is wait but right now it's the only chance of getting a new lead on a case that's fast growing cold."

"I'll check on Johnny's producer, Max Berger," Mike said. "Jack thinks he's Mr. Martin based on McBarb's description of Martin. They both have a mole over their eyebrow."

Rocco shook his head. "More McBarb hearsay." Looking past Mike he exclaimed, "Look who just came in."

Mike turned in time to see Amanda entering the room with, of all people, Commissioner Andrew Brandt. "Is that who I think it is?" Rocco said in awe.

"Your boss," Mike told him. "I introduced them years ago. He's an old flame and Amanda likes to fan the ashes now and then."

"And I talked to her only yesterday. What a coincidence."

"Yes, isn't it?" Mike said.

Three in the afternoon and it was already beginning to grow dark as December approached the shortest day of the year. "Looks like it might snow," Mike predicted as they came out of Chez Louis.

Rocco offered to share a cab.

"I live a few blocks from here. Care to stop by for a beer, or wine or whatever makes you happy?"

"Lunch made me happy," Rocco said. "What makes you happy, Mike?"

"Your accepting an invitation to my place."

"Is that all?"

"No, that's not all and you know it."

Rocco laughed. A cab pulled up at the curb and two women got out. Rocco held the door open and gestured to Mike. "Jump in and I'll take you home."

"Drop me off or come for a whatever?"

"I'll decide that when we get to your place."

Mike gave the driver his address. "Smart digs," Rocco said.

"Upper East Side."

Mike wondered where Rocco lived but refrained from asking. The provinces, no doubt. Queens or one of the better sections of Brooklyn. "Where's Jack?" Rocco asked on the short ride.

"In Quebec being photographed in the snow."

"You guys lead a charmed life," Rocco said.

So, Rocco wanted to know if Jack would be home. Mike was thrilled. He felt like a boy on his first date. He pressed his leg against Rocco's in the back seat of the taxi. Rocco returned the pressure then quickly withdrew it. Tease. Mike loved it.

If Rocco was impressed with Mike's living arrangements he didn't say so but the officer was loath to say anything that might give away what he was thinking or feeling. Mike would play it as it lay and right now it lay hot and heavy in Mike's jockeys. He took their coats to the bedroom and put them on the bed. Thanks to Jack, the two closets were filled. When he returned Rocco was gazing out the window. "Nice view of the affluent Upper East Side. It's beginning to snow. Jack could have saved himself the trip."

"Ken Wallace wanted Quebec snow and what Ken wants he gets."

"He made Johnny Jones famous, didn't he," Rocco stated.

"And now he's going to make Jack famous."

"Jack's already famous," Rocco noted.

"What's your pleasure?" the host asked.

"What's yours?"

Mike had pressed his leg against Rocco's and didn't get a punch in the mouth so why not carry it one step further? "It would give me pleasure to kiss you. Right here. Now."

"Are you asking me to pay for my lunch?"

"Christ, no. Lunch was on me."

Rocco rubbed his crotch and answered, "And this might be on me if you please me."

Mike's prick went from a semi to a full blown boner. "I aim to please. What would you like?"

"Would a Remy be possible?"

Mike went to the dry bar. "Take off your jacket and sit."

Rocco took off his suit jacket and laid it on the club chair. He sat on the couch. Mike would have to sit on the couch or on Rocco's jacket. He poured two generous shots of the Cognac into snifters .and handed one to Rocco, then took his place next to his guest. "Cheers."

Rocco raised his glass to his nose, not his lips, and inhaled deeply. The guy knew as much about booze as he did about French cuisine. Mike wet his lips with the brandy but didn't drink. Brandy after the wine would put him to sleep and he wanted to be wide awake and prepared for what he hoped Rocco might do next. Hope for the best. Be prepared for the worst. What he got was a combination of both.

Mike turned to Rocco and went for a kiss on the clean shaven cheek. Rocco blocked the move with his hand and Mike kissed Rocco's wedding ring. Holy shit.

"Too much too soon," Rocco scolded.

"Tell me when."

Rocco put his hand on Mike's neck, rubbing the nape none too gently. The touch sent Mike into an orgiastic spasm. His jockey pouch was moist with anticipation. He was going to pay for being the guy Rocco's wife dreamed about fucking when Rocco dreamed about fucking her. Mike would be used. Mike knew it and didn't care. Pleasing the cop was all that mattered. Mike might regret it after the fact, but it would most certainly be *after the fact*.

With a minimum amount of pressure the hand pushed Mike's head down till his lips were pressed against the bulge that ran down Rocco's trouser leg. Lt. Rocco dressed to the left. Mike nibbled on the flannel bulge. "You love to tease," Mike mumbled.

"It's like waiting for a fine dinner," Rocco explained. "The aroma of garlic sautéing in olive oil. It's half the joy of the meal."

Mike bit the stiff cock under the flannels. "When do we eat?"

"Horny bastard, aren't you?" Rocco pushed Mike's head off his crotch. "Undress me," he ordered.

"With pleasure." Mike got up and bent to undo Rocco's tie. Rocco pressed his lips against Mike's, filling Mike's mouth with his tongue. Mike sucked the invading tongue and felt his man juice oozing out of his cock. He got the tie off and began work on the dress shirt. Rocco helped him take it off. Mike pulled the Tee over Rocco's head. A fine line of dark hair ran down the center of Rocco's torso, the nipples hard and beckoning. Mike took one in his mouth, lapping gently.

"Nice," Rocco said.

Mike began giving Rocco a tongue bath from throat to belly button and when Rocco raised an inviting arm Mike buried his nose in the pit and got a taste of a popular deodorant and man sweat. Moving down, Mike opened Rocco's belt and began working on his fly zipper. "Get my shoes off," Rocco said.

On his knees Mike undid the laces of the regulation black oxfords. He got them off then tugged off the black socks. Rocco stuck his foot in Mike's face. Taking the hint, Mike sucked the neatly trimmed toe nails. As he did, Rocco parted his fly zipper and pushed his pants down to his knees. White boxers. As Mike watched from below the boxers joined the pants.

Rocco's prick lay flat against his belly, reaching for his navel atop the curly bush. His generous ball sack hugged the base of the cock. No low hangers here. His erection had pulled the foreskin half off the inflamed rosy head. "You like?"

Mike could only nod.

"Skin it back with your lips."

Mike went for it, putting his mouth on Rocco's pride and teased the prepuce back until the unadorned head filled his eager mouth.

"The mighty Mike Gavin," Rocco observed.

The mighty Mike Gavin went at it with such gusto Rocco had to push him off, ranting, "Christ, I'll cum."

"I want you to cream," Mike told him.

"I will, but not like this. I want your tail, Gavin."

"I'm a top."

"No problem. I'll let you sit on top and ride me. Get out of your clothes."

Mike, reluctantly, left his post and stood up, opening his shirt and dropping his pants. Rocco kicked off his pants and shorts.

"You have a good body," Rocco said when Mike was nude. "Big cock." He reached for it and began to masturbate Mike's foreskin.

It was Mike's turn to beg off, fearing he would ejaculate too soon. "Feels like you already dropped a load," Rocco said, wiping his hand on Mike's balls.

"I've been leaking since we got here," Mike said.

"You've been leaking since the day you met me." Mike couldn't protest because it was true.

They now stood, face to face, dick to dick. Rocco put his arms around Mike and kissed him as he would a lover. Mike was in ecstasy. He would do what Rocco wanted because now it was all that mattered. Rocco's hand went down Mike's back and came to rest on Mike's ass. A finger traced the crack.

"You've been fucked?" Rocco asked.

"Never."

"Really? Two virgins on their wedding night. How does that grab you, Mr. Gavin? Lead the way to the boudoir."

Rocco stopped to pick up his jacket. From the pocket he pulled out a pack of Trojans. "Lubed," he said, displaying an exaggerated wink. Mike was anxious but judging from his lover's banter, so was Rocco; perhaps even more so. All Mike had to do was lay back and take it. The officer had to give it. So, even sex came down to give and take but didn't it always?

Mike pushed the coats off the bed. The gesture, rough and uncaring, seemed to be a harbinger of what was to come.

"Kneel by the bed."

On his way to his knees, Mike kissed the piston that would deflower him. It responded by oozing a drop of warm, salty, nectar. Mike knelt by the bed as one might do when saying a prayer before retiring and raised his firm ass for inspection. Rocco probed the puckered hole with a finger. "You like?"

Mike wiggled his ass in response.

"No," Rocco suddenly shouted. "Not like this. I want to see your face when I nail you." He raised Mike and positioned him on the bed, face up.

Rocco looked down at his eager virgin, heaved a sigh and lay down beside Mike. "I can't rape you."

"It wouldn't be rape."

"I wanted to humiliate you. Wipe the condescending smile off your face. Take you down a peg."

"You're doing a pretty good job of it," Mike told him.

"Now I want to…I don't know what I want."

Mike kissed Rocco's cheek. The cop turned and grazed his lips against Mike's. They embraced. Hesitantly at first, then passionately. "I'm not good at this," Rocco said.

"You're doing fine."

Then came the unmistakable sound of a door being opened and closed with a loud bang. Both men froze. Mike, sitting up, thought of Peter Grimes. No, he had come yesterday. The only other person who could get past the doorman without a courtesy call to Mike was Jack.

Rocco: "I thought your friend was in Canada."

Mike: "So did I."

"MY LIFE IS A SHAMBLES." Mike Gavin.

Brad summarized the situation. "Caught *in flagrante delicto.*"

"Not exactly," Mike corrected. "The act had not yet occurred. We were in bed, smooching."

"Naked?"

"As the day we were born."

"That Rocco is some hot number. Did you go down on him?"

"Youi're getting off on this, Bradley."

"I'm here in answer to your call. You sounded distressed."

"Distressed? Would you say Christ on the cross was distressed? Would you say Napoleon at Waterloo was distressed? Would you say…"

"I get the picture," Brad interrupted. "Did Jack recognize Rocco?"

"He walked into the bedroom, took one look at us on the bed and shouted, 'You must be the cop.' Rocco turned on his belly and buried his face in the pillow in a vain attempt to disappear. Then Jack said he would send for his things and marched out."

"What did Rocco say?"

"Not a word. He was livid. He got dressed and followed Jack out the door. All he left behind was the unused Trojan. Lubed. I thought about killing myself but got plastered instead. I'll spare you the rest."

"I don't want to be spared. I'm here as a caregiver. You got plastered and started to think about the man that got away."

"Which one?" Mike asked.

"The one who left the Trojan behind. What did you do with it?"

"I flushed it down the loo."

"After you jacked off in it, I'm sure."

"You're not being sympathetic to my plight."

"I don't know if you deserve sympathy," Brad said. "You were hot as a pistol for the cop. You thought Jack was up north. You invited the cop for a drink and put the make on him. You went down on him. Jack came home. The cop left. Jack left. You got drunk and jacked-off in a lubed condom; a perfect climax to a day filled with surprises. There are those who would envy you."

"As a caregiver you don't show me dick." Mike complained. "Any suggestions?"

"You can begin by making a few phone calls and eat humble pie."

"I called Lt. Rocco twice this morning. He's not answering his phone and the sergeant who picks up for him says the lieutenant is not available. Not available to me, I'm sure. I called Jack's mobile a dozen times but he doesn't pick up because he sees my number and knows it's me. *I am persona non grata.*"

"Now tell me why Jack didn't go to Quebec."

"He didn't take his passport with him. Ken told me this when I called, trying to reach Jack. You now need a passport to go to Canada. They missed their plane and went to the studio for more snaps of Jack's basket. While there Jack talked Ken into shooting the snow scenes in Aspen where we were going to spend Christmas. I imagine Jack is on his way there."

"With no clothes?"

"Jack called Peter Grimes and asked him to pick up his gear and ship it to Aspen. Peter called me and I await his nibs who'll have much to say about love affairs and shit like that. Grimes I don't need this day."

"I bet Jack will be minus a pair of jockeys and Peter plus a pair," Brad predicted.

"I believe he already helped himself to one," Mike said.

"Better than jacking off in a lubed condom."

"I wish you wouldn't harp on that, Brad, and tell me how to put Humpty Dumpty back together again."

"There's nothing you can do until one of them responds to your plea. Jack will, I'm sure but I don't know about the cop. He's a tough egg; excuse the analogy. In the meantime take two aspirins and think about something else. Don't you have to grind out a column in a few days?"

"I'm too distraught. I'll tell Milly to pull one from my reserve file and run it this week."

"Reserve file?"

"All columnists keep a spare for times like this." Mike explained. "They're usually columns that were usurped by breaking news or beaten to the press room by a competitor. They're our reserves. I think I'll tell Milly to pull the one I did on same sex marriage. That seems to be a hot topic right now."

"I think you should avoid same sex marriage at this moment in your life," Brad advised. "Divorce would be more your forte."

"I think you've overstayed your welcome, caregiver. Don't you have a play to direct?"

"I do and it's now going splendidly. Johnny is back emoting as best he can and his lover, Tim Samuels, visits the theater to aid and abet the budding thespian. The affair is out of the closet thanks to you."

"It did nothing to solve the Jockstrap Murder. Tim denies knowing anything about Bokowski's fatal visit to Johnny's apartment and no one can prove that he does. Ditto Johnny Jones."

"Case closed?" Brad asked.

"A murder case is never closed, it's put on a back burner till something comes along to stir the pot. I'm supposed to be checking on your producer, Max Berger. Have you heard from him?"

"Not a word, which is fine. The money is still forthcoming which is all I care about. You don't really think he's the mysterious

Mr. Martin."

"Matching moles is all I have," Mike told him. "The kingpin of our investigation is in the Far East."

"Johnny is thinking of moving. He says the apartment gives him the willies."

"Fear does nothing to jog his memory."

"You think he's lying?" Brad asked.

"I think they're all lying."

"Including the guy in the Far East?"

Mike sighed despairingly. "I don't know, Brad. I just don't know."

FORTY-FOUR

Mike called Milly and told her to resurrect the gay marriage column. The Supreme Court was finally going to decide on the legality of same sex unions so it dovetailed perfectly with a most current topic. In fact, if Mike were writing a new column this day he would select the same theme to tell his readers that our United States was woefully lagging behind the world because it had not already endorsed same sex unions. That he would be striking a blow for justice perked him up on this ghastly day after the night before. But not much.

He got himself a hair of the dog in the form of a cold Bass and sat to await the arrival of Peter Grimes who would chastise him for the fool he was. Mike did not doubt for a moment that Jack would have told Peter why he was moving out. Peter would be thrilled, wanting to know all the details, mostly about the cop and that evening jack off in the jockeys he had pilfered from Jack. Well, it was better than jacking off in a lubed condom. Or was it?

Mike refused to weigh the pros and cons of that dilemma.

Instead he purposely blocked any thoughts of his love life, or what was left of his love life, and the stupidity of going ballistic over trade. Mike always had a weakness for trade but usually controlled the urge. Hell, Rocco was asking for it and just before Jack arrived the lieutenant was acting less like trade and more like competition. No, he mustn't think of that. It's what got him into this mess. Besides, he didn't have a condom, lubed or otherwise, to take his load and Jack's jockeys were packed to go.

He turned to the Jockstrap Murder which, like his love life, was in a state of flux. He knew all the facts but those facts had come second hand from Travis McBarb who had conveniently disappeared. Convenient to whom? The murderer or McBarb?

He got himself another Bass, it helped, and sitting at his desk opened a pad to a clean white page and began jotting the facts of the case as he knew them.

McBarb sees Johnny Jones in a passionate embrace with his lover. McBarb recognizes the lover as one of his patients being treated for hepatitis. McBarb calls him Patient X. The patient sees McBarb observing him and Johnny.

McBarb tells Matt Bokowski about the sighting but does not name Patient X.

Bokowski tells McBarb that Washington gossip has it that a senator's son is about to come out of the closet and announce he's gay.

Four months later, McBarb gets a visit from a Mr. Martin who tells him to forget he saw Johnny and Patient X. Martin sets up a date for McBarb to meet with Patient X in New York, at Johnny's apartment. It's obvious that Patient X is a Washington VIP with clout he's ready to use against McBarb if McBarb does not comply with orders from Mr. Martin.

McBarb's schedule gets fucked up and he can't make it to New York. He sends Bokowski in his place.

Bokowski is strangled with a jockstrap in Johnny's apartment.

Johnny, who was in the theater rehearsing at the time of the murder, denies knowing Bokowski and how he got into Johnny's apartment.

From Brad we learn that one Max Berger is the producer of the show Brad is directing with Johnny as the star.

Rocco knows Johnny has a roommate who's from Washington D.C. He passes this on to Mike.

Mike pressures Ken Wallace into saying he's seen Johnny out with Tim Samuels, Senator Sten Samuels' son.

Mike goes to East Hampton to see Johnny. Johnny admits Tim is his roommate and lover but says he didn't know Tim had hepatitis.

Rocco questions Tim Samuels with the same results. Tim admits being Johnny's roommate and lover but knows nothing of Matt Bokowski or Mr. Martin. Tim says he is being treated for hepatitis but does not know his doctor's name; only that he is young and good looking, which could describe Travis McBarb.

From McBarb we know that Mr. Martin has a mole over his left eyebrow.

From Ken Wallace and Brad Turner we learn that the producer, Max Berger, has a mole over his eyebrow but neither remembers which eyebrow.

And that's the case for the defense or for the prosecution. Take your pick. Given what Mike and Rocco know it could work either way. Thinking about and discussing the Jockstrap Murder as the story unfolded, focusing on segments rather than the entire mosaic, Mike was not aware of the glaring fallacies in his analysis of the case. Reading it, point after point, Mike saw that there was not one fact in the whole kit and caboodle known as the Jockstrap Murder case.

It was all supposition based on hearsay. Mike was reminded of an old adage a professor at Columbia preached to his budding journalists. "As you go through life brother, let this be your goal, keep your eye upon the donut and NOT upon the hole." Mike and Rocco were chin deep in that hole.

Back to square one: the vice president's party. Matthew Bokowski, the fledging reporter calling himself Matt Burke, hears about a senator's son about to come out as gay. His pal, McBarb, tells him about Patient X and Bokowski immediately thinks Patient X is that senator's son. His evidence? A rumor. Tim Samuels, a senator's son who is cute and possibly gay, is at the party. Bokowski, or Burke, hell bent on uncovering a scandal talks to Mike who gives him short shrift. Did Bokowski trail after Tim that night, possibly try to talk to him? Did Tim signal the FBI who moved in on the scandal seeking reporter? Probably, but like everything else in this case, not factually.

McBarb never named Patient X. He didn't even say if he was young, old, blonde or bald. We assume he's young because Johnny is young. Because of Bokowski we assume he's Tim Samuels. Pure assumption. No facts.

We now believe Mr. Martin, the hit man, was hired by the senator to keep the relationship between his son, Tim, and Johnny Jones, in the closet. Why? The senator, an arch conservative, took Amanda Richards, an arch liberal, to lunch. From this we think the senator is thinking of running for the big prize and is seeking to get a broader voter base. Is he? And would he kill to keep his son closeted? We don't know and most likely will never know.

Our director, Brad Turner, has never seen his star, Johnny Jones, with a lover or even a friend except once when a man in a baseball hat picked up Johnny at the theater. The man kept his face hidden but the hat was labeled Orioles. From this we assume the man was from Baltimore (Baltimore Orioles) and a close neighbor of Washington, D.C. In fact, such a hat could be purchased by anyone, anywhere including China where it was probably made.

Mike now cringed when he recalled his interview with Johnny in East Hampton. He had called the meeting a disappointment. In fact, it was a travesty.

Mike had told Johnny that he and Lt. Rocco knew Johnny had a roommate they believed was a Washingtonian. Mike told Johnny that he knew Johnny and Tim were friends and implied that Tim and Johnny were lovers. Here, Johnny said that Tim was his roommate and occasional lover. HELL, Johnny had volunteered nothing. He simply verified Mike's guesses.

Mike told Johnny that Tim had hepatitis. Johnny, for once being candid, said he didn't know this. We know Johnny called Tim to compare notes and keep their stories in sync. Did Johnny tell Tim that he (Tim) had hepatitis?

Mike felt depleted and ashamed. He had kept his eyes upon Lt. Rocco and not the donut. True, Lt. Rocco was an eyeful but so was Michelangelo's DAVID. One could look and admire but one must not touch.

Did Johnny tell Tim that he (Tim) had hepatitis? The line kept repeating itself in Mike's hung-over brain like a religious mantra when suddenly, as if in answer to a prayer, an idea popped into his head and began to grow with alarming speed. Mike's recently bruised heart let itself be heard, then he shoved back his chair, stood and began pacing the room. This panic attack (what else to call it?) to an archetype as yet unfulfilled was most familiar to Mike Gavin, investigative reporter, columnist. and masturbator.

He was blessed with the ability to ferret out a news breaking story before it broke out, like an itch before the rash appears. He could sniff an item on page six and predict it would be a headline in a week with Mike Gavin's byline heading the story.

Mike was on to something and he knew it. He was on to solving the Jockstrap Murder and he knew it. He was on to redeeming himself for the fool he had become under the hypnotic gaze of Lt. Rocco, and he knew it.

Out of respect for the office he held, Mike placed a call to Lt. Rocco to tell him what he was about to do and why he was going to do it. He identified himself as the caller (error?) and asked to speak to the lieutenant. The polite sergeant who picked up Rocco's phone put Mike on hold. He came back on a moment later and said, "Lt. Rocco is not available. Would you like to leave a message?"

Fuck you was the message Mike would have liked to leave. Instead he hung up with nary a word. He had tried, but the team of Gavin and Rocco was kaput. Good. Who needed a partner who unzipped his fly in the middle of a business meeting? Mike worked better alone. He didn't need James Rocco. He didn't need Jack Montgomery. Two's company. Three is a catastrophe.

Mike called Milly and got his scheme off the drawing board and in operation. He got dressed. Chinos, blazer, penny loafers, navy pea with university muffler. He was too preoccupied to note which university he was showcasing. His goal was 'preppy' and a glance in the bedroom mirror said it worked. On the way out he ran into Peter Grimes on the way in.

Grimes: "We must talk."

Mike: "Haven't got the time. Got a plane to catch."

Grimes: "Are you going to Aspen?"

Mike: "No, but Jack's wardrobe is. Make sure it all gets there."

FORTY-FIVE

Ms. Marvel was the prototype of a school administrator. Tall, thin, rimless specs, black dress adorned with only a lapel watch, sensible shoes and a nervous smile that greeted Mike with, "Your secretary called and told us to expect you, Mr. Gavin. We're honored but short of more prestigious personnel to help you."

Mike breathed a sigh of relief. He didn't want anyone more prestigious than Ms. Marvel to delve too deeply into his surprise visit. Nervous Ms. Marvel suited his purpose. He endured a tour of Capital Prep which took a surprisingly short time because this particular charter school was rather small and unimposing in spite of its name. What they lacked in grandeur was compensated by enthusiasm. Ms. Marvel enthused and Mike make all the right sounds to say he was impressed.

Once seated in an office and handed a cup of tea (clearly Lipton, not Earl Grey) Ms. Marvel asked Mike to explain, in more detail, the purpose of his visit. He had prepared for this on the short flight from New York to Washington. The same trip Matthew Bokowski had made in reverse. Mike hoped to discover why Bokowski had never returned to his point of origin and believed Capital Prep could answer the question. It was a long shot but screw the odds. One had to play to win.

Mike enthused about all the famous people he knew on a first name basis. Ms. Marvel made all the right sounds to say she was impressed. Clearly the two were a good match for Mike's purpose in being in school this day.

Mike explained to Ms. Marval that he wanted to encourage his celebrated friends, all masters in their chosen profession be it the arts, science or business to volunteer to visit, even lecture, charter school students to encourage them to emulate these successful notables and perhaps achieve similar success in the future. "In effect," he concluded, "give them teachers who DO rather than SAY."

He thought of adding, "Who ARE rather then HOPE TO BE," but feared that would be gilding the lily or flooring an awestruck Ms. Marvel. The fates would get Mike for this outrageous lie but he was doing a good turn and they would surely take this into account on judgment day. What would the fates say about his aborted affair with Lt. Rocco? Mike didn't want to think about that.

"Of course those accepted by the school would be above reproach. I know many celebrated persons get their names in the tabloids for all the wrong reasons. I would state that those who wish to offer their services must be innocent of scandal."

Like finding a needle in a bale of hay, Mike was thinking.

"Of course," Ms. Marvel agreed. "Of course."

"Also," Mike said, going in for the kill. "those in contact with the children must be in good health and not liable to pass anything on to the children like the flu or measles, or mumps or *worse.*"

"Of course," Ms. Marvel agreed. "Of course. All our staff gets a clean bill before joining us and they are also given semi-annual physicals. We're fully covered by medical insurance."

"I understand Tim Samuels, the senator's son, works with your students."

"Oh, yes, Mr. Gavin. Tim teaches drama. In fact he's directing our Christmas pageant this year."

"This is confidential, Ms. Marvel, but as you know in my business I hear rumors; some true, most unfounded. I believe I once heard that Tim Samuels was under a doctor's care. Is that true?"

Ms. Marvel shook her head vigorously. "I cannot comment on our volunteer instructors, Mr. Gavin, especially when it concerns an intimate aspect of the instructor's life."

Intimate? "I believe you mean personal, not intimate, aspect of the instructor in question," Mike corrected her.

The blush on Ms. Marvel's face rose from her neck to her

eyebrows. "Intimate or personal, Mr. Gavin, it's still a most inappropriate question."

""Reporters ask inappropriate questions, Ms. Marvel, it's why newspaper readers number in the millions. I withdraw the question and assure you I will never allude to Tim Samuels' ill health."

"No need to allude to any such thing, Mr. Gavin. Tim Samuels is a healthy American boy," she blurted before realizing she had answered Mike's question.

BINGO.

Not fils but pere. Or perhaps pere et fils.

Matthew Bokowski had indeed been on to a scandal but he didn't know its full inference. When it stared him in the face, he was murdered.

Pere et fils?

Mike took a window seat on the Delta shuttle back to New York. The stewardess brought him a coffee and asked, with a wily grin, if he had been in Washington in pursuit of a political scandal. If she only knew.

Mike stared down at the clouds which appeared to be an ethereal highway over which his plane was gliding with incredible speed. He was sitting on a time bomb but wasn't sure when or even if he would detonate the fuse. He was trying to digest the plethora of information the unsuspecting Ms. Marvel had fed him in nine words. *The only thing infectious about Tim is his smile*; therein ending a career, solving a murder and hopefully allowing Matthew Bokowski to rest in peace, Amen.

What he should do was hand Lt. Rocco the fuse and a match but Mike, in this, his hour of triumph, was feeling smug or was vindictive more accurate? Hell has no fury like trade caught in the act. Fuck Rocco. Mike had another score to settle before the ship hit the sand.

Mike took out his cell phone, hoping he could get a clear connection at thirty thousand feet. He punched out Brad Turner's number.

FORTY-EIGHT

"Welcome to the scene of the crime," Johnny said as he opened the door to Mike.

Mike stepped into a small entrance foyer. To the right he could see into the living room which had a skylight, making it almost worth the climb to the top floor. Directly in front of him was a closed door which would be the bedroom. He followed Johnny into the main room where Johnny didn't offer to take his coat so Mike kept it on. Clearly, this wasn't a social visit.

"Brad said you wanted to talk about the play."

"I do," Mike said, "not the play Brad is directing but the one you wrote."

Johnny turned to look at Mike but didn't offer him a seat. "I never wrote a play."

"Oh, but you did and I fed you the plot."

Johnny went on the offensive. "What's this about?"

"It's about you and your lover."

"Get the fuck out of here."

"I will when I've had my say. Let's begin at the beginning. Act One, Scene One."

"I don't have to listen to your bullshit." Johnny plopped down on a couch and stuck out his legs in a defiant gesture.

Having no intention of leaving, Mike unbuttoned his pea coat. "Act One, Scene One. Place, a parking lot. Time, night. Action, Senator Sten Samuels is giving his lover, you Johnny, a goodnight kiss. He is caught in the act by, of all people, the senator's doctor whose name is Travis McBarb, in case you don't already know that. The senator, a bastion of family values and other conservative causes, is perturbed at being caught with his tongue in the wrong mouth, but not panic stricken. Doctors, like Catholic priests, are adept at keeping their mouths shut."

Johnny stood up, went into a small galley kitchen and came back with a bottle of beer. He returned to his seat, sat, and drank out of the bottle.

"A few months later, Sten thought he might make a play for the White House. This was serious business. One could no longer hope the doctor would keep his mouth shut. The senator had to be certain his secret was safe. He hires Mr. Martin, if that's his name which I doubt, to pay a call on the doctor and coerce him to keep the senator's secret. To make the cheese more binding, Martin arranges for the doctor to meet the senator in New York, at your apartment, Johnny, to which the senator has a key. However, he forgot to tell you, Johnny, about the engagement on the premise, I believe, that less said, soonest mended. Also, the senator didn't want to give you any ammunition you could one day use against him."

"Are you fucking finished?"

"No, but I'm almost there. Act Two. Using his senatorial pull at which he's an expert, Sten gets the doctor a day off and a ticket on the shuttle to New York. Martin got his wires crossed and the doctor was given the wrong leave day. Not able to go when scheduled, McBarb sends his friend, Matthew Bokowski, in his place. Bokowski is a reporter which freaks out Martin who kills to keep the senator's secret.

"This entire charade had one purpose; to keep the senator's secret. I told you Tim had hepatitis and I told you Tim was your roommate and possibly your lover. I told you who Bokowski was and what he was doing in your apartment. You knew nothing except that the senator had a key to your apartment and that the senator was in deep shit. As I blabbed to you in East Hampton, you took it all in and saw how you could save Sten Samuels. Tim has hepatitis. Tim is your lover. Neither of you know Mr. Martin, how he got into your apartment and what Bokowski was doing there. Using more senatorial pull, the doctor disappears. Case closed, or so you thought. One thing puzzles me," Mike added.

"Really. I thought Mike Gavin knew everything."

Mike started and turned to find himself face to face with the senator. "I was in the bedroom," Samuels said.

Mike had not seen the senator since the previous summer when he lunched with Amanda at Louie's. Then the senator had looked handsome and robust. Now, several months later, he looked pale and haggard. Mike took in this fact but didn't allow it to interfere with getting his story. Unperturbed by the interruption, he asked, "Where does Tim fit into this lethal comedy of errors? Is he Johnny's lover, your lover or do you share the goodies?"

"We are a congenial threesome. I caught Tim in the act a long time ago. It looked like such fun I joined in but I never jeopardized my boys. I practiced safe sex. Are you shocked, Mr. Gavin?"

"The only thing that shocks me is the inability to be shocked."

"Nicely put. You do have a way with words," Samuels said. "A psychiatrist, I don't recall his name, or it may have been a woman, thought fathers should masturbate with their sons as a means of bonding, so perhaps I'm ahead of my time."

"You're ahead of a long line of shits," Mike told him.

"Nasty, Nasty. Remember that line from the play *Tea and Sympathy. 'When you speak of this, be kind.'*"

"I have no intension of speaking of this. I'm going to hand what I know over to Lt. Rocco."

Johnny, clutching his beer, was taking all this in with great delight. A United States senator and a celebrated newsman were going one-on-one in his apartment. Johnny had indeed come a long way from the pool table at Destry's and seemed certain he was even going further.

"Before you go to the police I think you should know that I, not Mr. Martin, put the jockstrap around that poor boy's throat. When he opened the door to see me instead of Johnny, he knew at once that I was McBarb's Patient X and he panicked. I tried to calm him, I truly did, but he was having no part of it. He wanted to run. To the New York *Times*, I imagine. He went ballistic and shoved past me trying for the door. I gave him a karate chop to the neck and brought him down. He was dazed. I used the moment to go into the bedroom and get something to tie him with. The jockstrap was in the first drawer I opened."

"And you just left him there?" Mike shouted. "Like an animal?"

"What was I to do? Call the police? Really! I did what all we senators do when faced with a problem. I ran."

"And you pulled your strings, like a puppeteer, and got rid of Travis McBarb," Mike said.

"You make me out to be the only rotten apple in the barrel. The United States Senate is the most corrupt parliament in the world. We all have one goal. First, to get reelected. Second, to make the other party look bad. Everything we do, say and enact is directed toward that end."

"What about Matthew Bokowski?" Mike accused.

Samuels shrugged. "Consider him collateral. I mean you certainly didn't think all this was going to end happily, with all the bad guys in jail and all the good guys grinning. You're too wise for that, Mr. Gavin. Shit happens."

"And people like you make it happen all the time."

"I am what I am and I do what I do," Samuels said.

"What you do is your own business. What you preach is my business and what you preach is anti everything America stands for. Equality and freedom of choice. You're today's Elmer Gantry." Mike began to button his pea coat, getting ready to leave. "Expect a visit from Lieutenant James Rocco."

Samuels laughed. "Spare Rocco the trouble, the city of the expense and Washington yet another sex scandal. My hepatitis will play judge, jury and executioner. Mine was a case of too little, too late. My liver is dying. So, I fear, am I. But perhaps we can compromise. What little our government does is achieved by give and take."

Unable to resist, Mike asked, "What are you proposing?"

"Keep my secret," Sten said, "and I'll have Travis McBarb

returned to Bethesda, putting him on the road to a brilliant career. Do this in memory of Matthew Bokowski so Bokowski will not have died in vain.

Instantly, Mike saw a way to placate his guilt for ignoring Bokowski's plea and went for it. "You have a deal, Senator."

Johnny, who had not spoken a word, suddenly took an interest in the proceedings. He reared up and asked, "What's gonna happen to my play?"

FORTY-NINE

MIKE GAVIN'S NEW YORK
Mike's Selected Shorts:

Will The Jockstrap Murder one day take its place beside other fascinating unsolved mysteries such as Jack the Ripper, Amelia Earhart and Judge Crater? I posed this question to the man who heads the case, Lt. James Rocco, but as I write he has not returned my call.

Johnny Jones' off-Broadway debut was less than auspicious. The director, Brad Turner, received more praise than the star. However, Johnny was offered a Hollywood contract. Brad Turner was offered zilch.

The untimely death of Senator Sten Samuels has left the conservatives without a leader. The senator's son, Tim, is not interested in filling the vacancy. He prefers the company of actress Amanda Richards. Amanda boasts being old enough to be Tim's mother, perhaps because Tim likes to keep it all in the family.

The Supreme Court wisely booted DOMA and returned gay marriage to California. Did my column on same sex marriage sway the justices to the side of equality? I like to think so.

Last summer I played tennis opposite the pro Jack Montgomery and lost miserably. Since then I've been practicing the game and would like a return match. How about it, Jack, would you give me another chance?

Other Titles by

VINCENT LARDO

CPSIA information can be obtained at www.ICGtesting.com
Printed in the USA
LVOW05s0019170514

386219LV00001B/45/P

9 781608 209170